BOYS WILL BE BOYS

Two black-bearded men, built like NFL nose guards, forced their way into the room. They'd been hammering the door with their sword pommels.

Delendor's weapon had looked serviceable. The swords *this* pair carried would have been two-handers—in hands smaller than theirs.

They didn't even bother to look at Joe. "Where are you, bitch!" one shouted.

"*There* we go!" the other intruder boomed as his eyes lighted on the cedar chest as the only hiding place in the room.

Both men stabbed repeatedly at the fragile wood until it was quite obvious that the chest was empty.

They'd thought she was inside that, Joe realized. His body went cold. He'd already put his briefcase down. Otherwise his nerveless hands would've dropped it.

"We saw 'er come in, so she musta got out the . . . ," one of the men said. He peered through the open casement. There was no ledge, and the walls were a smooth, sheer drop to the flagstone courtyard.

The two men turned toward Joe simultaneously. They held their bare swords with the easy naturalness of accountants keying numbers into adding machines.

"And just who the hell are you, boyo?" asked the one who'd first stabbed the cedar chest.

In what seemed likely to be his last thought, Joe wondered whether the FAA kept statistics on the number of air travelers who were hacked to death by sword-carrying thugs . . .

THE UNDESIRED PRINCESS & THE ENCHANTED BUNNY

L. SPRAGUE DE CAMP
AND DAVID DRAKE

BAEN
FANTASY

THE UNDESIRED PRINCESS AND THE
ENCHANTED BUNNY

This is a work of fiction. All the characters and events
portrayed in this book are fictional, and any resemblance to real people or incidents is purely coincidental.

A Baen Books Original

Baen Publishing Enterprises
260 Fifth Avenue
New York, N.Y. 10001

ISBN: 0-671-69875-3

Cover art by Gary Ruddell

First printing, May 1990

Distributed by
SIMON & SCHUSTER
1230 Avenue of the Americas
New York, N.Y. 10020

Printed in the United States of America

THE UNDESIRED PRINCESS

L. Sprague de Camp

1

Rollin Hobart looked up from his flow charts through the haze of smoke and said: "Come in." When the door opened, he added: "Hello, George." Pause. "Didn't you say something about bringing a friend?"

George Prince answered the hello. He was a young man of no great importance either in the world wherein he lived or in this story, so there is no point in describing him. He added: "He'll be along. My gosh, Rolly, don't you ever do anything in the evenings but work?"

"Sometimes. Who's this friend?"

"His name's Hoimon."

"Hermann?"

"No, Hoimon. H-O-I-M-O-N."

"Hoimon what? Or what Hoimon?"

"Nothing; just Hoimon. H-O-"

Hobart gestured impatiently. "Heard you the first time. *What* is he?"

"He calls himself an ascetic."

Rollin Hobart frowned, or rather the already permanent crease between his eyebrows deepened. He was a rangy, large-boned man, young but not very, with slick blond hair, a narrow straight nose, and narrow straight lips. "Listen, George, I'm sorry but I haven't time to admire your eccentric friends. I've got to figure how to save these guys three-quarters of a cent per ton."

Prince answered: "This one's different. You'll see. Oh, by the way, have you changed your mind about the party tomorrow night yet?"

"Nope. I told you, work."

"Oh my gosh. You don't go anywhere any more." Prince shrugged hopelessly. "I suppose that now the strike-breaking business isn't so hot—"

Hobart straightened angrily. "Higgins and Hobart are *not* strike-breakers. I thought I explained—"

"How about that—"

"It isn't our fault if our investigator exceeded his instructions. It was his idea to hire those—"

"Yeah," interrupted Prince, "but you and Higgins knew Karsen was a hard egg when you took him on. So you're partly responsible for that riot—"

"Not at all. You know the judge decided, when Karsen sued us because the strikers had knocked out all his teeth, that he hadn't been acting as our agent at the time."

Prince laughed. "That was the *funniest* darn thing—"

Hobart grinned wryly. "To you, maybe, but not to those on the inside. The company lost business, the strikers lost their pay, we lost our fee and the legal expenses, and Karsen lost his teeth. My point just was we were legally cleared, so we're not strike-breakers. Q.E.D. We're consulting engineers, and it's only natural that our clients should consult us about their labor-relations problems."

Prince replied: "The trouble with you, Rolly, *is* that you're a black-and-white thinker; everything either is so or it isn't. That's Aristotelian logic, which has been long since exploded. You'd make a good Communist if you hadn't got started in life as a shellback conservative—"

Hobart gave up all effort to concentrate on his engineering figures and pitched into his friend: "You're the black-and-white thinker, my lad. Because I accidentally get associated with a strike-breaker, I hate the poor toiling masses; and from the fact that I think that permanently unbalanced budgets mean trouble either for individuals or government, you infer I'm a hidebound reactionary! The trouble with you guys who dabble in social theories is that you invent a lot of pretty laws and expect the world to conform to them—"

"I only said—" interrupted Prince. But Hobart, once started, was not so easily stopped.

"And you're wrong about Aristotelian logic's being exploded," he continued in an authoritative rasp. "All that's happened is that it's been recognized as a special case of the more general forms of logic, just as plane trigonometry is a special case of spherical. That doesn't mean it's useless; it's just more limited in its application than was once thought. We could hardly conceive a world where Aristotelian two-value logic did apply generally; for instance everything would have to be red or not red, so nothing would be pink or vermillion . . ."

"Speaking of which, my friend—"

"I'm not through, George. Matter of fact Plato did have some glimmering of the concepts of continuity and multiple causation, which Aristotle missed. If Plato hadn't been so full of foggy idealistic mysticism— what's that about your friend?"

George Prince, caught off balance, took a few seconds to get back in his groove. He finally said: "Well—uh—it's kind of hard to explain. I don't know him very well, and I don't really believe in him yet. But if you see him, too, he must be real."

Hobart frowned, "I should think so. But what's the matter—seeing things? Too many hot rums?"

"Yes and no. I see him, but the question is am I seeing something that's really there?"

"That ought to be easy," said Hobart with an impatient gesture. "Either he's there or he isn't—"

"There you go!" cried Prince triumphantly. "Either—or! I knew—uh—come in!"

They stared at the door, which opened to reveal a gaunt old man with unkempt white whiskers. This individual wore an overcoat that Hobart recognized as belonging to his friend Prince. As far as one could tell, that was all the oldster had on; below its hem extended a pair of hairy shanks ending in large calloused bare feet. He carried a rectangular wooden object with hinges and snaps, about the size of a suitcase.

Hobart asked Prince: "Is—this—your—Mr. Hoimon?"

The apparition himself answered in bell-like tones: "It is true, O man, that my temporal name is Hoimon. But kindly do not use the term 'mister.' I am informed that it is derived from 'master.' Such an epithet is most repugnant to my humility; I do not wish to have superiority over any living thing ascribed to me."

"Well," said Rollin Hobart, flustered for the first time in a couple of years. "George, what's—"

"Hoimon will explain, Rolly," answered Prince.

Hoimon smiled a sweet, patient smile. "May I," he tolled, "recline?"

"Uh—oh, sure!"

The old man unsnapped the clasps of his wooden contraption and unfolded it, whereat it was seen to be a collapsable bed of nails or spikes. Hoimon set the thing down with a solid wooden sound, shucked off the overcoat (under which he wore a towel-like piece of textile around his middle) and settled himself at length on the spikes with a luxurious sigh.

For some seconds he sprawled silently. His eyes swept Hobart's room, taking in the shelves of textbooks, the adding machine, the large iron dumbbells, and the photograph of Frederick Winslow Taylor on the wall.

When he spoke, it was to Prince: "O George," he said, "is this man indeed possessed of a keen and logical mind?"

"Keenest and logicalest I know," replied Prince. "One of M.I.T.'s best. Least, when it's something he's interested in. Outside his special fields you'll find him a bit narrow-minded. Frinstance he thinks Thomas Dewey's a wild radical."

Hoimon waved aside the question of Mr. Dewey's radicalism. He asked: "Is he intact physically?"

"If you mean is he healthy, yes. I think he's had his appendix yanked—"

"Look here," snapped the subject of the discourse, "what the hell's the idea—"

Hoimon ignored him, and spoke again to Prince: "And his departure would not wreak grievous harm or sorrow on those near him?"

"Guess not. Some of his friends would say they wished old Rolly was around to lend his crushing ironies to the conversation, but they wouldn't go into a decline on account of him being gone. He's a good, steady sort of guy, but not exactly *gemuetlich*."

Hobart cleared his throat, and interjected: "What

my misguided young friend means, Mr. Hoimon, is that I value my independence."

Hoimon gave him merely a brief glance, and inquired of Prince: "He has, then, no wives or offspring?"

"My gosh no! You ought to hear him on the subject—"

Rollin Hobart, who had been polishing his glasses in a marked manner, now interrupted: "George, I admit you pique my curiosity with this ingenious nonsense. But I've got work to do; this defense boom isn't going to last forever, and Higgins and I have got to make hay. When I want a character analysis I'll go to a psychia—"

"He is also, I see," boomed Hoimon, "a person of strong and determined character. He will do, I think. But one more thing: Is he adept at the solution of paradoxes?"

Prince looked blank; Hobart frowned, then grinned a little. The engineer remarked: "Now how did you know I was a puzzler? Hobby of mine, as a matter of fact." He picked a small white magazine entitled *The Engima* out of a pile and handed it to Hoimon. "I was president of the National Puzzler's League, last year. Haven't time for that sort of stuff now, though. What is it I'll 'do' for? Solving a paradox?"

"Precisely," responded Hoimon. "It is without doubt by the providence of Nois that I was led to the one man in the three-answer world who can best assist us. Arise, O Rollin, and come with me to Logaia. There is not a minute of your finite time to be lost!"

"What the hell?" scowled Hobart. "What sort of gag—"

"I have no intention of gagging you," said Hoimon, folding his bed of spikes. He turned piercing blue eyes on Hobart. "Do not haver and quibble, O Rollin. The life of the fairest, wisest, and best depends on you. Already the androsphinx draws nigh unto the Stump of Sacrifice."

"But!" cried Hobart, "what's Logaia, who's this fairest etcetera, what's—"

"All will become clear," said Hoimon calmly. Though he was standing a good ten feet away, his free arm shot across the room like a chameleon's tongue and grabbed Hobart by the coat collar of the latter's conservative brown business suit. The indignant Rollin was hoisted out of his chair and across his desk. He swung a pair of knobby fists, but Hoimon held him dangling just out of reach.

"George!" yelled Hobart. "Stop him! Get a cop! He's a nut!"

Prince registered indecision. He said: "Hey, Hoimon, if he doesn't want to go, you got no right—"

"That will do, O George," rumbled Hoimon. "It is not for you to judge. It is but natural that one of his character should resist. Waste not your breath in shouting, as this room is now part of Logaia. By my spiritual perfection I have caused it to be so, temporarily."

Prince stepped across to the window and looked out. He turned a blankly dismayed face. "Hey, there isn't *anything* outside!"

"Of course not," said the ascetic, dodging an extra-long punch that Hobart threw at him. "Will you open the door, O George, as my hands are occupied?"

"Well—I—"

"Open it!" roared Hoimon.

Prince obeyed, asking hesitantly: "Hey, Hoimon, how can a skinny old guy like you do it?"

Hoimon replied: "My strength is as the strength of ten because my heart is pure. Farewell, O George.

Danger awaits your friend, but also opportunity. We go!"

"Help!" screamed Hobart. "My glasses!"

"You have them on, O Rollin." And the ascetic, with the folding bed of nails dangling from his left hand and a struggling Rollin Hobart at arm's length from his right, marched out the door.

*   *   *

As the darkness closed around him, Rollin Hobart tried to slip out of his coat. But Hoimon had gathered a considerable fold of shirt and vest into his iron grip. Hobart felt for the ascetic's fingers and tried to wrench them apart, but he might as well have tried to twist the tail of one of the New York Public Library's lions.

The environment through which he was being hauled was not the hallway outside his spic three-roomer, but a dark tunnel. The light from the door of his living room picked out sides and roof of rock. Then his feeble illumination went out sharply, as though George had closed the door. Hobart thought of the folly of keeping up with lightweight friends whose sole virtue was that they were fun to argue with.

Hobart continued his struggles long after it was obvious that they were getting him nowhere. When he finally stopped kicking and clawing it was from exhaustion. His relaxation allowed his mind to take in the implication of the tunnel.

He gasped: "What the hell—is—this, the fourth dimension?"

Hoimon spoke softly behind him: "Talk not, O Rollin, lest you draw the cave-folk nigh."

"Oh, is that so? Well, you answer my questions or I'll raise a hell of a holler!" Hobart filled his lungs to shout.

Hoimon conceded: "In that case I must speak, lest you ignorantly bring disaster upon yourself. Not that the cave-folk would harm me, but you—"

"All right, get to the point! What's the idea of this kidnapping?"

Hoimon sighed. "I fear you resent the high-handed tactics I was forced to use—"

"You're damn tootin' I resent 'em! The F.B.I.'s going to hear about this! Now what—"

"I had to use force, and therefore, unless you abandon your hostility, I shall be forced to punish myself, oh, most grievously, for having laid constraint upon a living creature. I should not have considered a course so out of keeping with my humility, had it not been necessary in order to avert a greater evil. Know, O Rollin, that by the ancient curse laid on the Kings of Logaia—hark!"

Hoimon broke off, and Hobart kept his silence for the nonce. Through the darkness came a shrill sound, like the highest note of a violin; a spine-tickling cry.

"The cave-folk!" breathed Hoimon. "Now we must hasten. If I put you down, will you accompany me in orderly fashion? You cannot return to you own world in any case."

"I'll walk," grumbled Hobart. "What d'you do, unscramble the dimensions?"

"As I am no scholar, I cannot fathom your talk of dimensions. All I know is that by purity of heart I have acquired powers, said to have been possessed by certain philosophers of yore, of visiting strange universes like yours, where the laws of reason hold not and nought is what it seems."

"What d'you mean, the laws of reason don't hold?"

"In your world the earth appears to stand still while the sun goes around it, but I was assured on good authority that the reverse is the case. In Logaia, when the sun seems to go around the earth, it really does so. Let there be more progress and less talk."

The shrill wail came again, lending more speed to Hobart's legs than exhortations from his abductor would have done. A spot of daylight appeared ahead. Soon they arrived at the exit, and stood on the crest of the fan of detritus that spread out from the mouth of the tunnel. Hobart swiveled his head, blinking. The sun was high in the brilliantly blue heavens. All about were mountains, steep and conical, and somehow not quite right. After a few seconds Hobart saw what was wrong with them; they were too regular and too much alike. They reminded him of a lot of ice-cream cones—that is, the cone part without the ice cream—placed upside down in regular rows on a flat table.

"Come," said Hoimon. The ascetic bounded down a steep trail, swinging his folded bed of nails, his long white hair flapping behind him. Now that Hobart got a look at his kidnapper in daylight, he saw that the saintly slave-raider was not at all a clean person. But for a man of his apparent years he was uncommonly agile. Probably, thought Hobart, the result of some screwy diet of nuts and lettuce. The engineer followed, fascinated by the way the towel about Hoimon's equator stayed in place by the most precarious of frictional holds.

They reached the bottom of the steep slope. The mountains were a phony-looking golden yellow; so was the scanty grass. An occasional shrub had leaves of a bright blue. Yes, *blue*, thought Hobart after a pause to peer. Well, if they were blue they were blue. He contemptuously dismissed the idea that he might be dreaming; fear of being insane never entered his mind. If he saw blue foliage with his own eyes, blue foliage there was, period.

There was a little flat space between the bottom of one cone and the next. Hoimon marched briskly along this, skirting mountain after mountain. Hobart, following, got his breath back after that run down the trail. He used it to demand to know, in slightly petulant tones, what was meant by all this nonsense about androsphinxes, Stumps of Sacrifice, and the rest.

Hoimon the ascetic dropped his folding bed beside a gnarly little tree with an unrealistic geometrical appearance; it reminded Hobart of somebody's attempt to build an imitation tree out of lengths of pipe. They would call it a functionalistic or surrealistic tree, he thought, but nobody had ever persuaded him that a thing that neither looked, felt, nor acted like a tree could be made a tree by calling it such.

Hoimon took a grip on the pseudo-tree and broke it off close to the ground. Then he snapped the trunk across his knee to make a massive four-foot walking stick. He spoke: "We must hasten, O Rollin, leaving the full account for a more propitious time. Briefly, know that King Gordius of Logaia is bound by the curse to offer his first daughter to the androsphinx upon her coming of age. As His Altitude has been kind to us ascetics, I undertook to find a champion who would rescue the maiden. You, O Rollin, are he." He set off briskly again, twirling his stick.

"Interesting if true," groused Hobart. "But listen, mister, I never rescued a maiden from anything, unless you count the time my secretary got her head stuck in the waste basket."

"So think you," replied Hoimon serenely. "My search carried me through several universes, and nowhere . . ." His voice died and ceased sharply in Hobart's ears as the engineer flattened himself against the side of one of the cones. Hoimon, continuing around the curve, was immediately out of sight. Hobart listened, then began to tiptoe off in the opposite direction.

"Ho!" came the ascetic's deep voice around the curve. Rollin Hobart began to run. A muscular hand from nowhere came down on his back with staggering force, and gripped coat, vest, shirt, and a considerable fold of skin. Hobart yelped as he was jerked off his feet and whisked around the bend by an arm that had stretched out to a length of at least thirty feet to grab him.

The arm contracted to its normal length, and Hobart found himself looking into the ascetic's melancholy eyes. Said Hoimon: "Little know you of Logaia, O Rollin, or you would not try to escape. If you remained in the mountains after sunset, the cavefolk—lest you try such a stupid trick again, you shall precede me. March!"

Hobart walked slowly, scowling. He protested: "Maybe you think this is fun, but I've got a job to get back to!" Hoimon gave him a push that almost sent him headlong.

"Hasten," said the old man. "Now must I punish myself for using force on you."

Hobart continued: "You're impeding the defense program! My firm has some important contracts—"

Another push. "The loss of the State of Unity is the gain— Ah!" The last exclamation announced their exit from the mountains—just like that. There were no foothills. The two men emerged from the last pair of conical peaks, and then the country was as flat in front of them as a skating rink, except for a cluster of hemispherical domes of black rock off to the left.

The black domes rose from a vast expanse of flat pebbly ground, like an indefinite enlarged gravel driveway except that the gravel was a startling red.

Hobart supposed that from this tract's lack of vegetation it should be called a desert, even though it did not look like any desert he had seen. It extended to a sharp, straight horizon, unbroken in front and to the left by any feature except the black hemispheres.

But to the right the landscape was something else. Thirty feet away began a fantastic jungle. Along a line as sharp as if it had been surveyed the red gravel gave way to blue moss, and from the moss rose tall, regularly spaced trees, every one with an implausible even-tapering cylindrical trunk, apparently covered by black patent leather. The leaves were blue; some were circular, some elliptical, some other shapes, but all geometrically precise as though they had been cut out of blue paper to go into a store window display.

In fact, reflected Hobart, this whole garish landscape looked as if it had been laid out with drawing instruments either by a gifted child or by a draftsman who had gone insane on the subject of functional design.

He had hardly begun to absorb his surroundings when his attention was attracted by something else, which riveted his eyesight precisely because it was not built from a blueprint. "It" was a girl tied to a section of glossy black tree-trunk, sawn off at the top and planted in the gravel of the desert a few paces from the edge of the forest. As Hobart crunched unbidden over the pebbles toward the girl, he realized that she was the most beautiful thing he had ever seen.

"That," came Hoimon's voice behind him, "is the Princess Argimanda."

2

THE FIRST FACT THAT ROLLIN Hobart noticed about the Princess Argimanda was that her hair was red. That was the first thing that anybody from the Earth, Solar System, or Newton-Einstein universe would have observed, for this was not a coppery-red or russet, but a real honest-to-gosh red like that of a stop light or a two-cent stamp.

It was also borne upon him as he approached that her skin was very pale, and the contrast between the white skin and the bright red of her cheeks gave her a heavily-made-up look. When he got closer it appeared that the color was natural. She was tall, with delicate features, and wore a loose white knee-length garment of a very flimsy sheer material. She was tied to the stump by what appeared to be a few loops of ordinary package-string.

Nor was she alone. A little way off a young man sat on a chair with an easel in front of him. This youth wore what looked at first sight like a suit of long red underwear, which matched his hair.

The princess' blue eyes took in Rollin Hobart, and

she cried in a strained voice: "Is this your champion, Hoimon?"

"Aye, O Princess," rumbled the ascetic. "How far have the painful proceedings gone?"

The princess tossed her head toward the black rock domes. "The Court's taken to the hills," she said. Hobart, shading his eyes, made out a cluster of tiny figures atop the nearest dome. Some sort of banner rose from their midst. "And," continued Argimanda, "my dear brother has set up his sketching-pad, so everything is ready. I sent Theiax into the forest that he might warn us, but he has not returned. I do hope the androsphinx has not eaten him."

"Might diminish his appetite for you, my girl," said a high male voice. It was the young man of the long underwear, which Hobart saw was really a skin-tight suit of red silk, with a jewelled belt and a little round feathered cap. The resemblance between the youth and the Princess was obvious. He was nervously tossing an octahedral pebble from hand to hand, and inquired: "This the champion, eh? Don't tell me I've set up my kit for nothing!"

Hoimon boomed: "I think Your Dignity might show more concern for the fate of your innocent sister!"

The young man shrugged. "Can't be helped, you know, so we might as well have an artistic record."

Hoimon growled, and finally articulated: "O Prince Alaxius, I present Rollin Ho—"

"Don't bother me with names, old thing," interrupted the artist, "especially as he'll probably be devoured shortly. Greetings, champion. Mustn't mind me; an aesthete puts his art first, you know. By the way, what *is* the color of that thing you're wearing? I've been making color notes; can't be expected to do a complete painting when the whole thing'll be over in a few minutes. I'm a hero if I know what to call your—ah—suit."

Hobart glanced down at his conservative business suit. "Brown," he responded. "But look here, what the devil's this all about? What am I—"

"Brown?" repeated Prince Alaxius wonderingly. "Never heard of it. That suit—I won't comment on its appalling lack of fit—it's something like yellow, yet it isn't—I tell you, sir, it's an *impossible* color! Either a thing's yellow or it isn't! I shall have to omit you from the picture; I haven't—"

Hobart raised his voice: "Damn it, listen! What's all this nonsense about the young lady's needing rescue? Why can't she bust those little strings and walk off?"

"Because," said Alaxius, "then there wouldn't be any sacrifice, and the androsphinx would harry the kingdom instead. Hoimon, is this your idea of a champion? Stupidest ass—"

"Shut up!" howled Hobart. "Why can't one of you birds rescue her then?"

Hoimon tolled: "Neither of us has the means, O Rollin."

"Whaddya mean, means? I haven't got a gun or anything!"

"The androsphinx," explained Hoiman, "is to be defeated, not by guns or swords, but by wit and logical acumen."

"Yeah? I'd be willing to save your young lady if I knew how, if you'd promise to let me go home when it's over. But—"

Hobart stopped as something emerged from the forest. He jumped, and controlled an impulse to flee when he saw that the other two men showed no alarm. The newcomer was a huge bright-yellow lion.

"Is—is this your androsphinx?" asked Hobart, beginning to sweat.

"No," said Hoimon, "this is one of our friends: the social lion. O Theiax, I present Rollin Hob—"

"He comes," said the lion, whereat Hobart jumped again. The lion's voice was a prolonged groan.

Prince Alaxius shrilled: "Oh dear, I must get to work! I wish you luck, dear sister."

"What kind?" asked the lion.

"Good or bad; I don't care." Alaxius trotted back to his easel and began sketching furiously.

"Some day," growled the lion, "that precious brother of yours learns what being eaten feels like—"

"You promised, Theiax!" said the Princess firmly.

Hobart cried: "What am I supposed to do?"

Hoimon explained: "The androsphinx will ask you a question; you shall try to answer it. It is simple."

"Yeah? Suppose I can't?"

"Then I regret to say, you will be eaten. So will the Princess Argimanda. That also is simple."

"Does that happen often?"

"It has always happened up to now. Ah, our enemy approaches!"

Around the corner of the forest where it abutted the conical mountains lumbered another beast. It was superficially much like a lion, but vastly larger, almost elephantine in bulk. Its face was human; four times life size, and a very lowbrowed, Neanderthaloid sort of human, but still anthropomorphous, with a yellow goat-beard wagging from a chin whose recession it failed to conceal. The creature was splay-footed and sway-backed, with scabby patches of disease on its wrinkled yellow skin.

The princess watched its approach with her lips pressed together in a tight red line. The social lion crouched trembling a little way off with his tail between his legs. Prince Alaxius sketched harder than ever. Hoimon folded his arms across his bony chest and stood erect. Neither of these two men showed any fear of the brute, which presumably followed certain rules as to whom it should devour.

On came the androsphinx in dead silence except for the crunch of its paws on the gravel. When it was close enough for its stench to pucker Hobart's nose, it lowered its broad hindquarters heavily to the gravel.

It spoke in a hoarse, foggy whisper: "Do you serve me another champion?"

Rollin Hobart was not eager to identify himself as such, but Hoimon jerked a thumb: "This is he, O androsphinx!"

"Ah," drooled the monster. "Are you ready for the question, champion?"

Hobart tried to say "no," but his vocal organs refused to function.

"Then," said the androsphinx, "is it not true that no cat has nine tails?"

"I—uh—what?" said Hobart, taken off guard. His mind was so full of conflicting urges and inchoate schemes that he had missed all but the last few words.

The androsphinx repeated, and continued: "And is it also true, will you not stipulate, that no cat has eight tails either?"

"I suppose so," muttered Hobart, wondering how far and fast the androsphinx could run.

"But it is also—"

"Hey!" Hobart broke in. "Haven't I answered a couple of questions already? Thought there was only one."

"Those were mere rhetoric," gasped the androsphinx "Addressed to the atmosphere, as it were. You need not have answered—yet. *The* question is yet to come

Now, it is also true that every cat has one tail more than no cat. Hence, if no cat has eight tails, every cat must have nine tails! Explain that, champion!"

"I—uh—you—if—"

"I shall count three," wheezed the androsphinx. "One—"

That "One!" brought Hobart's whirling mind into focus. It shouldn't be too . . .

"*Two*—" the androsphinx rose to all fours.

Hobart threw up a hand. "Hold on! Got it! You're using two different 'no's!' "

"What mean you? 'No' means 'no.' Thr—"

"The hell it does!" crackled Hobart. "When you said no cat had eight tails, you used 'no' in the sense of 'not any'; when you said a cat had one more tail than no cat, you used it in the sense of 'the absence of a.' "

"But—"

"Shut up! In the first sentence you make a statement about the class of cats; in the second you were talking about things of another class, incommensurable with the first: the absences of cats. The absence of a given cat may have any number of tails you like; for instance in place of the cat you might have a dog with one tail. So your last statement is simply not true in general."

"But," protested the androsphinx, "I meant not the absence of a cat; I meant a non-existent cat . . ."

"Even worse! Not only is 'no' meaning 'not any' different from 'no' meaning 'non-existent,' but real cats have real tails whereas unreal cats can have only unreal tails; hence an imaginary cat can't have *any* number of real tails, from zero up! So your statement that a real cat has one more tail than an imaginary one is inherently meaningless, since it uses both 'no' and 'tail' in two quite different and incommensurable senses . . ."

At this point the androsphinx interrupted with a mighty belch which made Hobart stagger and cough. Another followed, and another. The Princess coughed also; Hobart reeled back out of range. Hoimon stood with folded arms and a martyred expression as long as he could; then the ascetic, too, beat a retreat.

He cried: "Observe, O Rollin! Nois be praised!"

The androsphinx had sat down again; its head hung, drooling, with half-closed eyes as belch followed belch. Hobart jerked out his pocket knife and cut the Princess' nominal bonds. When he looked at the monster again—it had shrunk! It was no bigger than a rhinoceros, and with each burp it lost further bulk.

When the Princess without warning threw her arms around Rollin Hobart's neck and pressed her ruby lips to his, he was so busy watching the biological marvel that he practically ignored the girl's embrace; he held her limply and let her plaster his chin with kisses while he stared over her scarlet hair at the androsphinx.

The creature was now down to the size of a mere Alaskan grizzly. There was a flashing blur of yellow past Hobart's right as the social lion charged with a thunderous roar. The androsphinx reared wearily to meet the attack; the two great bodies slammed together, and then were rolling over and over and kicking showers of geometrical red pebbles in all directions. Hobart heard a ripping sound as Theiax's hind claws found the androsphinx's belly; then the monster shuddered and relaxed, the lion standing over it with his teeth fixed in its neck, shaking his foe's anthropoid head and growling through his nose.

The Princess, meeting only the most tepid response from her champion, started to release him, but stopped at a cry of "Hold it, please!" from her brother. The gravel around Prince Alaxius was littered with sheets from his drawing-board, and the young man in the tight costume was working frantically on another: evidently a sketch of the hero embracing his rescuee.

A large sinewy hand fell on Hobart's shoulder. "O Rollin," intoned Hoimon, "you have won where every previous champion has failed. Go and claim your temporal reward: the hand of the Princess, and half of the Kingdom of Logaia!"

"Huh?" said Hobart. "But—I don't *want* the hand of the Princess—excuse me, young lady; nothing personal—and I don't want half the kingdom either!"

3

Hoimon took his hand away with a puzzled frown. "How now? Is not the greatest reward that King Gordius can bestow enough for you?"

"Not that at all," said Hobart. "This infra-dimensional world of yours is very interesting, but I can't stay around to admire it. Want to get back to my work."

"Strange," mused Hoimon. "But I fear I cannot help you. I must return to the Conical Mountains to collect my bed of nails, after which I must punish myself for doing violence to the integrity of living creatures in bringing you here and causing the death of the androsphinx."

"Can't you even tell me how to get back?"

"Nay, that I cannot. Of all the ascetics of Logaia, I alone have achieved sufficient spiritual perfection to pass from universe to universe."

"Well—look here, I didn't ask to be brought; I've got every right to return. If you refuse to take me back you're doing more violence to my integrity; constructively, that is."

Hoimon frowned. "Now that you put it that way—"

"What is this?" groaned the lion, who had left off shaking the androsphinx's corpse and ambled over. "Who makes my mistress cry?" Hobart looked around, startled, to see the princess with her hands pressed to her face and her shoulders shaking.

"My love—" she got out "—wants—to go away!"

"Huh?" cried Hobart in new alarm. "I'm sorry, miss, but I'm not your love! I'm a confirmed bachelor! I—"

He stopped at a low rumble from Theiax: "You talk foolishness, champion. Rescuer *always* falls in love with princess and versy visa. You behave, or—"

"What?"

"Guess," said the lion, showing fangs.

Hoimon the ascetic slapped Hobart on the back. "That settles that, O Rollin," he said cheerfully, "for I should be committing a greater constructive violence if I conducted you hence, thereby causing Theiax to eat you, than by leaving you here. Farewell!" He took a hitch in his towel, and off he strode twirling his stick.

Hobart watched him go with sagging shoulders. The lion sat down in front of him and cocked his head on one side.

"What is matter?" he grumbled. "Man does not look mournful when he marries girl who is clever, good, and beautiful! Look, I do trick!" Here the lion lay down and rolled over. Hobart could not help smiling.

"Better," said Theiax. "Here comes His Altitude." The lion lay down and began licking the scratches inflicted by the late androsphinx.

Hobart turned as a faint tooting, and thumping came to his ears. Across the red gravel advanced a procession: undoubtedly the party that had lately occupied the top of the nearest black dome. In the lead puffed a stout, white-bearded man in a long robe and a crown. The party with him included a standard bearer in a glittering brass cuirass—his standard was a pole on which was a square of stiff black material with the word "RAIT" in white block letters— several men in tight suits like that of Prince Alaxius, and some soldiers in kilts and chain-mail shirts; some of these last carried spears and circular shields, others antique-looking muskets.

Princess Argimanda had already started to run to her father. Prince Alaxius gathered up his art equipment and sauntered after, and the social lion padded after the prince. Hobart, feeling more ill at ease without his peculiar company than with them, followed.

The princess turned from the king as Hobart approached and cried: "Father, this is my peerless champion and future husband! His name is—uh—"

"Rollin something," said Prince Alaxius.

"Well, well," beamed the king. "Where's that eccentric Hoimon? Somebody must make a proper introduction, you know."

"He's gone," said the prince.

"Too bad," wagged the king. "Charion, you'll have to do it." He spoke to a tight-garbed, hatchet-faced man at his right; a bald, sinister-looking person with a large black mustache, the ends of which turned up arrogantly.

Charion shrugged. "It's non-regulation, Your Altitude. Anyhow, I present the puissant prince, Rollin Something. Rollin Something, you stand before that high and mighty autocrat, Gordius the Affable, king of Logaia."

"R-r-r," muttered Theiax nearby. "You kneel."

"Huh? Me?" Hobart looked around.

"Yes, you," persisted the lion. "Court ekkytet."

Rollin Hobart's rugged independence did not take

kindly to kneeling before anybody, but he went to one knee, lowering his face to conceal his scowl.

"Arise, Prince Rollin," said the king. "Welcome to the bosom of the Xerophi family!" He spread his pudgy arms.

Hobart glanced sidewise at the social lion. "What do I do now?" he hissed.

"Embrace His Altitude!" the lion whispered back.

This, thought Hobart, was the damnedest thing yet. He allowed the king to subject him to the double hug used by Latin-Americans.

When Rollin disentangled himself from the king, he protested: "There must be some mistake, Your Altitude. I'm not a prince; just an ordinary practical engineer . . ."

The king waved him to silence. "You needn't be modest with me, my boy. A prince is a king-to-be; you're a king-to-be; therefore you're a prince, heh, heh."

"You mean half your kingdom?"

"Of course, of course; you can pick either half, too."

"But, Your Altitude, I don't know anything about running kingdoms . . ."

"You'll learn quickly enough. Anyway my daughter can only marry a person of the rank of prince or better; hence you must by definition be of the rank of prince or better."

"That's another thing!" cried Hobart. "I don't know where the young lady got the idea I was her—"

"R-r-r-r," went Theiax. Hobart subsided. Come da revolution you eat strawberries and like 'em, he reflected.

Charion was plucking at the king's sleeve. "Sire, is it not about enough amenities . . ."

"Eh? Yes, yes, I suppose so. Time to return, of

course; the queen must be told and must meet her new son-in-law. You, Charion, take charge of Prince Rollin Something. Laus!"

He spoke to a thin, elderly man in a dark-blue robe and a conical hat. As the word was pronounced to rhyme with "house," Hobart half expected to see the oldster display resentment; but he learned eventually that "Laus" was a name, not an epithet.

The king continued: "Get out the wings of the wind!"

The old man shucked a bag off his back, loosened the drawstring, and began to take out small umbrellas and hand them around. Hobart took one and looked at it in puzzlement. There was no cloud in the sky. Everybody was taking an umbrella except the lion Theiax. Prince Alaxius was standing close to the king and talking quickly in low tones; Hobart caught: ". . . a simply impossible fellow, I tell you; look at that suit he's wearing; it's of a color that doesn't exist. And he argues all the time . . ."

"Later, later," muttered the king. "If he couldn't argue he wouldn't have overcome the androsphinx."

The princess was bending over the lion, who had resumed licking his wounds. She asked:

"Dear Theiax, can you return to Oroloia afoot all right?"

"Sure," grumbled the lion. "Mere scratches."

"Why didn't you wait till the androsphinx had shrunk down smaller?"

"That is not sporting," said the lion.

"Silly males," said the princess, giving the beast a pat.

Since Charion had been detailed to take care of Hobart, Rollin Hobart attached himself to the sinister-looking courtier. He held out his umbrella and asked: "What's this thing?"

"The wings of the wind," replied Charion.

"I know; but what does it *do*?"

"We're traveling on the wings of the wind, Your Dignity. How do you expect us to do that without any wings of the wind to travel on?"

"Yes, but how does it work?"

"Oh. You grip the handle tight, and when the king opens his, you open yours and it takes you. We used to travel as the crow flies, but Laus's crow-wings were dangerous to use, so last year he invented this."

"Who's Laus?"

Charion looked annoyed. "The Wizard of Wall Street, of course."

"Huh? I don't get it."

Charion concealed his exasperation with visible effort. "Laus is the royal wizard; Wall Street is a street built on the city wall, on which is the royal wizard's official residence. Now do you understand?"

"Ready, everybody?" cried King Gordius. Everybody raised his umbrella.

"Go!" shouted the king, and snapped his wing of the wind open. Hobart did likewise with his. At once a terrific wind smote him from behind and almost wrenched the umbrella out of his hand. His feet left the ground, and he was trailing through the atmosphere behind the device. It swooped this way and that. When he got a glimpse of the rest of the party, now quite a distance off, he observed that they were all sailing along serenely in a sort of formation. The trick apparently was to grip the handle in both fists just in front of one's solar plexus. Hobart did, and soon found that he could manage the contrivance easily.

He caught up with the convoy, his hair and clothes blown stiffly forward by the gale. A soldier—the commander to judge by his plumed helmet and gold-plated mail-shirt—shouted:

"You could use some practice, couldn't you, youngst —I mean Your Dignity?"

The princess threw him a tender smile that made him shudder. He thought of making a break for freedom, but the sight of the disciplined ease with which the soldiers managed their umbrellas with their left hands and their spears and muskets with their right dampened the idea.

They swept over the string-straight boundary at which the red desert and the blue jungle left off and yellow crop-land began. A city came into view and expanded to a mass of prisms, spires, and domes, every last structure either black, white, red, yellow, or blue. The most remarkable feature was a tall screen or lattice arising from each of the four walls, which formed a square. The streets inside were laid out on a strict gridiron plan. In the center of the square was a cluster of extra-large buildings which Hobart took to be the local Kremlin.

The wind dropped as they approached the walls, and the wind-borne fliers dropped, too. They came to a running landing on a broad stretch of lawn that ran around the walls. Hobart almost pitched forward on his nose; the officer caught his arm.

"Thanks," said Hobart. "What's your name?"

"General Valangas," grinned the soldier. "Chancellor Charion should have introduced us, but he wouldn't of course. Here he comes looking for his ward."

The man with the Wilhelm II mustache came up closing his umbrella. "You made the trip, I see," he said inanely, staring down his nose. Laus was collecting the umbrellas and putting them back in his bag.

Hobart asked: "Why didn't we land inside the walls?"

"Laus's work," answered Charion. "He doesn't allow the wind inside the walls, for fear they might bring in an army of barbarians. That lattice—" he pointed "—keeps out the west wind; the others keep out the east, south, and north winds."

"Are those the only winds you have here?"

"Obviously! A wind is either a north wind or it isn't!"

The bugler blew, and the drummer drummed, and the king and his company walked briskly up to the huge gate. There were more tootings from inside, and the gate creaked open. An explosion made Hobart start; as his eye caught a puff of thick white smoke drifting from a gate tower there was another report, and so on. By the time the salute had ended they were under the archway.

An arm was slipped through his; it was the red-haired princess, gazing fondly up at him. "Dear Rollin," she murmured, "let us not start our life together with such cool formality!"

Hobart fumbled for an answer; life together my foot, he thought. He should have taken a firm stand sooner. He should have made a break for freedom while they were flying on the wings of the wind; he certainly shouldn't have let them get him into this crowded city. Not that Rollin Hobart was so completely hostile to the institution of marriage as he sometimes professed. He had considered favorably the possibility of waiting till he was forty and then marrying some squab half his age; with that advantage of years and experience, he could bring the girl up in the way *he* thought she should go. A romantic marriage would be bad, and an insane union with an incredible female from a delirium-world in which he did not fully believe would be out of the question.

But Hobart said nothing for the present, as he seldom hurt people's feelings—deliberately, that is—and, more practically, though Gordius might be called the Affable Monarch, he might use an ax on those who presumed on his affability too far.

Besides, to walk down the avenue arm-in-arm with an intoxicatingly beautiful woman was a self-justified act. The people lined the sidewalks and bowed and waved in most entertaining fashion. And the city itself was worth seeing. It reminded Hobart of a world's fair wherein the exhibits constituted the crowds. Besides the uncompromisingly brilliant colors of the geometrically severe buildings, the people presented an incredibly heterogeneous aspect. The clothes included robes, togas, shawls, gowns, saris, turbans, burnooses, and the hardly-decently tight coveralls such as worn by Prince Alaxius and Chancellor Charion. A man in a spiked helmet and white cloak pulled his mount over to one side; the man's skin was black; not any mere negroid chocolate-brown, but the black of india ink. The mount was a camel-like beast, yellow with black rings all over, like a leopard.

"Good God, what are those?" said Hobart, pointing.

"Those?" said the princess. "Oh, just Ikthepeli savages, in Oroloia to sell their fish." The savages were a family of tall, flat-faced, butter-yellow people with soup-bowl haircuts. Papa Ikthepeli came first with a spear and a bone through his negligible nose; then came mama Ikthepeli with a baby slung on her back, and then five children, diminuendo. All were quite naked.

"Who is God?" added Argimanda.

"Huh?" Hobart frowned. "Let's see—the creator

and ruler of the universe, or so most of us are taught in my world. Personally I'm willing to concede that He probably exists, but I doubt if He pays any attention to anything so insignificant as the human species."

"That sounds like our Nois," said Argimanda. "But Nois is not indifferent to the human inhabitants of this world—quite the reverse. Anybody can see him any time he wants."

"Is he a god or a man?" asked Hobart.

"Both," said the princess. "Here—we turn." The procession filed into a narrow street, and almost immediately came to a shuffling halt.

General Valangas shouted: "What's the matter up there?" and pushed forward to see.

Hobart pulled the princess along in the bulky soldier's wake, and presently saw over and between heads the cause of the delay. It was an immense tortoise, like those of the Galapagos but three or four times as big. An unpleasantly distorted dwarf with a tomato-red skin sat in a chair bracketed to the reptile's back. The tortoise filled the street from side to side and proceeded down it at an unvarying testudian plod. The dwarf was leaning over the back of his chair and waving his hands and apologizing.

Prince Alaxius was saying to the king: "Told you you should have widened this street before, governor."

"Get along, get along!" shouted Charion. "Laus, *you* do something!"

"Ahem, all right, all right, rush me not," muttered the Wizard of Wall Street. "Where's my wand? My wand?"

"In your hand, you old pantaloon!" snarled Charion.

"My hand? Oh yes, so it is!" Laus waved the wand, and recited:

> "Beilavor gofarseir
> "Nonpato wemoilou,
> "Zishirku zanthureir
> "Durhermgar faboilou!"

The tortoise opened its beak, hissed, shimmered, and began to shrink. The dwarf scrambled down from his seat; just in time, as the shrinkage progressed rapidly and stopped when the tortoise was a mere foot long. The dwarf picked up his pet, crying:

"Oh, my little Turquoise! What have they done to you?"

The king's procession crowded past; Hobart noticed that the wizard stayed with the dwarf. When they were all past, Hobart heard Laus's old voice reciting another incantation. It ended with a shriek of joy from the dwarf, by which Hobart judged that the reptile had regained its former size; he could not see from where he was.

They came out of the alley onto a vast plaza in which rose another walled inclosure. The domes and cones and prisms of the royal palace appeared over the wall. The gate was open, and another procession was coming out: a procession of women in black. Some of them held lyres which they mournfully twanged.

"That, my love," said the Princess Argimanda, "is your future mother-in-law, Queen Vasalina!"

4

ROLLIN HOBART ENDURED THE second joyful family reunion and presentation with a fixed, slightly ghastly smile. He had just observed that Queen Vasalina under her funeral garb was a comfortable-looking middle-aged woman when Charion pulled at his sleeve.

"I'll show Your Dignity your apartments," said the Chancellor. And in they went between a pair of black cylindrical pylons the size of sequoia trunks and through an entrance big enough to admit a battleship. After the first three turns inside Hobart was quite lost; his attention was less on direction than on the architecture, which carried out the same style as the exterior. His memory clicked, and he remembered where he had seen structures of this kind before: made of a set of stone building-blocks, of simple, elementary shapes, which he had received in a big wooden box on his eighth birthday. Those blocks, too, had all been red, yellow, or blue.

"Apartments" turned out to be something of a euphemism. Chancellor Charion conducted him to a single room of modest size. As the chancellor held the door open for Hobart to enter, there was a sharp click, and something hit the engineer's shin an agonizing thump.

"Yeow!" shrieked Hobart, hopping on one leg. The missile rolled a little way along the floor; it was a steel ball the size of a marble. Inside the room, a crimson-haired boy crouched over a toy canon.

"Your Dignity!" snapped Charion; Hobart saw that the chancellor was addressing, not him, but the boy. "I thought you were to have vacated your room by now!"

"Don't want to vacate," squealed the boy, rising. Hobart's scalp prickled a little at the sight. There was something wrong about the boy: he was big enough for a thirteen-year-older, but he had the proportions, including the large head and smooth, characterless features, of a child of six.

"This is my room," he continued, stamping his foot.

"Now, now," said Charion, his voice full of obviously synthetic honey, "you don't want your new brother-in-law to sleep outdoors, do you?"

The boy's eyes widened, and he put his finger in his mouth: "That my new brother? What you mean? Got brother, Alaxius," he mumbled past the finger.

"I know, but Prince Rollin Something will marry your sister soon. Then he'll be your brother-in-law."

"Don't want such a funny-looking brother-in-law," said the boy. "Let him sleep outdoors; I don't care."

"Will you go," gritted the chancellor, "or must I call your father?"

The boy went, slowly, turning his head to stare at Hobart as he did so. Charion closed the door after him.

"Who's that?" asked Hobart.

"Didn't I introduce you? Prince Aites."

"Is he normal?"

"Normal? Why—what do you mean?"

"Well—how old is he?"

"He'll be thirteen day after tomorrow."

"He—uh—looks like such a child, in a way."

"What do you expect? You f—I mean, of course he's a child! Being normal, he'll become an adolescent when he's thirteen, and not a minute sooner."

"Where I come from," said Hobart, "you change from a child to an adolescent gradually."

Charion scowled. "I don't understand you—either he's a child or he isn't. But then, I dare say you barbarians have peculiar customs."

"What do you mean, barbarian?" asked Hobart sharply.

"You have yellow hair, haven't you?" Charion dropped that subject and opened a chest full of clothes. "I suppose I should apologize for not having your room ready. In theory we always have a chamber prepared for the champion in case he defeats the androsphinx, but that has never happened hitherto, and the preparations have become lax in consequence. What color do you want?"

The chancellor held up one of the skin-tight Logaian suits; red: others of yellow, blue, black, and white lay in the chest.

"What? Oh—I'll keep my own clothes, if you don't mind."

"Those things? My dear man, they're literally impossible: neither tight nor loose, and a color I can't even name! Would you prefer a robe?"

Hobart looked down at the cuffs of his shirt, the inside rims of which were showing the irregular dark stains that shirts acquire after a few hot hours of wear. But between a dirty shirt and a Logaian garment . . .

"I'll wear what I have on," he said firmly.

Charion shrugged. Hobart left the chancellor to his own devices while he washed up; he was agreeably surprised to find almost-modern plumbing. When he returned, Charion was seated in the best chair smoking a cigarette.

Hobart looked at this with more surprise. Evidently the chancellor thought Hobart's stare a hint, for he rasped: "Will you have one?"

Hobart had two cigars in his pocket, which he would have much preferred. But he'd better save those for times when he could relax and enjoy them properly. "Thanks, I will," he said.

The cigarette was vile. Hobart coughed, and asked: "What's the program?"

"Don't you know? There will be a grand state banquet to celebrate your betrothed's rescue and approaching nuptials. Tomorrow there will be a royal hunt, and the day after comes Prince Aites' birthday party."

"Hm." Hobart wanted to ask how to get out of this predicament, but did not trust Charion that far. He inquired: "What's the condition of this kingdom I'm supposed to get half of?"

Charion opened his mouth halfway; it stuck silently for a few seconds before he said: "It is improving under my new policy."

"What policy's that?"

"Retrenchment."

"Good." The word had an encouraging sound to Hobart. "But I'd like some more information—area, population, funded debt, and so on?"

Charion stared coldly, muttered something about having to get ready for the banquet, and left.

A queer bird and far from ingratiating, thought Hobart, staring after him as he finished the cigarette.

Maybe Logaia was a gift horse whose mouth deserved scrutiny.

Not that it would make any difference to Rollin Hobart's determination. This half-world was interesting enough; a fine place to spend a vacation, if Hobart had been in the mood for vacations. And if his firm had not been snowed under with work, and if Hoimon had come with a sensible, contractual business proposal—a job as public works overseer, for instance—and if . . . But if anybody thought they could kidnap him and high-pressure him into the silly fairy-tale king's-daughter-and-half-the-kingdom business—well, they didn't know their Rollin.

He was still masticating his plans when a gong boomed through the palace. Almost immediately Charion stuck his head in without knocking. "Dinner, Your Dignity," said the chancellor, who had changed from his black skin-suit to a loose blue robe which struck Hobart as a sissy garment for a grown man.

* * *

The banquet hall was as big as a railroad terminal. People made way for them in most courtly fashion. As they approached the royal end of the table—or rather, the interminable meandering line of tables placed end to end and end to side—they passed a trough-shaped thing on one of the tables. It was too big for any reasonable platter, and had too low a freeboard for a coffin. Hobart asked what it was.

"That," said Charion with a wry smile, "is the dining trough of Valturus, the gunsmith. He has the table manners of a pig."

Prince Alaxius appeared before Hobart, with another exquisite in tow. "Look, Rhadas," exclaimed Alaxius, "didn't I tell you?"

Rhadas shook his head wonderingly. He reached

out and fingered Hobart's dark-green necktie, whereat
Hobart stiffened with ruffled dignity. Rhadas said:
" 'Tis true that in days of yore, certain philosophers
proclaimed that in theory at least it was possible to
have colors other than those we have. But since they
could not produce examples of the same, their claims
were held to be but the loose-tongued license of the
learned."

"See?" said Alaxius. "Oh, before I forget, this is
my brother-in-law to be, so they tell me, the mighty
Prince Rollin. Actually it was the social lion who
finished off the androsphinx. This is my friend Rhadas,
Rollin; mustn't mind him; he's an aesthete, too."

Hobart found a place-card reading:

PRINS RɑLIN SƎMΘIꓷ

which he supposed to be "Prince Rollin Something"
—he was apparently going to be saddled with that
spurious surname from now on—spelled in Logaian
characters. Come to think of it, the Logaian alphabet
seemed to be made of letters from the Latin, Greek,
and Cyrillic alphabets. And had he been speaking
English all the while? Or had he just thought he
was? If he had, how come English was the language
of Logaia? . . .

"Greetings, my love," said the princess' clear voice.
She was going to sit beside him, naturally, he thought
with some pleasure and more panic.

While he fumbled for a reply, a trumpet tooted,
and the king and queen came through the door behind the royal chairs. Everybody bowed toward them;
they sat; everybody sat.

One thing about the Logaians, reflected Hobart,

was that when they ate they ate, with a minimum of chatter. The food startled him: instead of the ultra-fancy super-sauced Byzantine concoctions he had braced himself for, he was given generous helpings of roast beef, baked potato, and peas, with a large sector of apple pie for dessert.

Another curious thing was the behavior of Valturus the gunsmith. This fat, smiling individual, a few places away, waited until several helpings had been put in his trough. Then he climbed into the trough and wallowed.

Hobart murmured to Argimanda: "I see Charion didn't exaggerate when he said Valturus had pig's manners."

"Not that time," smiled the princess. "But beware of believing Charion when he answers any question of importance. Now that I observe our friend Valturus, I must say that he seems uncommonly cheerful for a man facing ruin."

"Who's going to ruin him?"

"We—the government, that is." She indicated the royal family, conspicuous by their red polls in the black-haired assemblage, and the ministers sitting in a row on the far side of the king.

"What for?"

"Oh, we're not doing it deliberately, but his business will not survive the disbandment of the army."

"The disbandment—what's this?" frowned Hobart.

"Charion's idea; he says that expenditures must be reduced, and that besides we should set a good example for other peoples."

"Is this such a peaceful world you can afford unilateral disarmament?"

"On the contrary, the barbarians . . ."

At that moment Queen Vasalina, on the other side of the princess, touched the girl's arm, Hobart heard the queen's stage-whisper: "Argimanda dear, Gordius wants to know whether your young man has his speech ready."

Speech! Hobart had not thought of that. He had no idea of what he was expected to say. To be more accurate, he supposed he was intended to give them some conventional guff, when he would have preferred to tell them to go plum to hell . . . but that wouldn't do for a number of obvious reasons . . .

King Gordius took a last gulp of wine and rose as the trumpets went off. Oh, lord, thought Hobart; it would have to be something, and quick . . .

". . . and so, ladies and gentlemen of Logaia, the puissant champion, the successful suitor, will tell you in his own words how he, the unknown barbarian, by unflagging resource and unremitting effort, gained that insight which enabled him to save our darling princess, and which has made him worthy and more than worthy to be enrolled in that line of heroes, the Xerophi family, of which we are—ahem—a modest representative; wherefore, ladies and gentlemen, we give you, with high hopes and fatherly affection: PRINCE ROLLIN!"

The applause was tremendous. The king smiled all over and sat down. Hobart pulled himself angularly to his feet.

"I—" he began. A thunderous burst of applause stopped him.

"I—" Again the roar of handclapping.

"I—" He paused deliberately, but this time there was no applause. He glanced over at the king and saw why: Gordius had his finger to his lips. The king winked at Hobart. The engineer drew breath and began:

"Thank you, ladies and gentlemen of Logaia. Perhaps I should have warned somebody that I had used up most of my words on the androsphinx today. In any case I am more adept with a pencil and a slide-rule than with my tongue, so I—uh—trust you won't take it amiss if I—uh—

"Concerning the means whereby I acquired the knowledge necessary to answer the monster's riddle, I can do no better than to refer you to the works of Ogden, Richards, Brouwer, Tarski, and other leaders of modern logic. I could I suppose give you an epitome of their doctrines, except for the facts that, first, it would take all night, and second, I haven't read any of their books myself. But if you wish to—uh—

"To conclude this mercifully brief address, I ask you, how did it happen? Again, how? Ah, ladies and gentlemen, that's the question! And what's the answer? I'll tell you; I admit—nay more, I assert, frankly and unequivocally, that, not being able to state with any reasonable degree of accuracy, and fearing lest I should deviate from those paths of rectitude and veracity in which it has been my unwavering custom to perambulate, I experience a certain natural hesitancy in giving oral expression to an opinion, the correctness of which might be interpreted somewhat erroneously! I thank you." Rollin Hobart sat down.

There was a short interval of silence, then a patter of applause, then a mighty surge of it. Hobart grinned a little; either they were glad of the brevity of the speech, or it was a case of "If this young man expresses himself in terms too deep for me, why what a very singularly deep young man this deep young man must be!"

There were no more speeches. A pair of public performers appeared; one girl in a noticeable lack of filmy clothing, who plucked a lyre; her partner a man, gorgeous in plumed helmet, who went through calisthenic motions with his spear while he sang. The song was a slow repetitive thing with about as much tune as a set of church-bell changes.

Hobart was grateful when the banquet broke up. His gratitude at once gave place to apprehension when the princess caught his hand and towed him after the king and queen.

She led him through a maze of halls and rooms until they came to a moderate-sized one with sub-dued lighting and a large sofa. The king and queen were standing; Gordius laid a pudgy hand on Ho-bart's shoulder, saying: "I thought you'd like it better if I didn't order a full-dress state banquet, my boy. Some kingdoms do for their champions and wear the poor fellows out. When a man's fought a dragon all day, he's not apt to feel like reveling all night."

"Fine," said Hobart.

"You'll be up early for the behemoth hunt tomor-row, won't you?"

"Huh? I suppose so."

"Splendid! If there's anything you want, or any information— "

"Gordius!" interrupted Queen Vasalina. "Don't talk the poor boy to death. Can't you see they want to be alone?"

"Heh, heh, I guess you're right. So, good-night, Rollin. *You* know what to do." King Gordius poked Hobart's ribs with his thumb, grinning. Hobart de-spairingly watched the royal pair depart; they beamed back at him from the door, and his soul sickened.

Princess Argimanda leaned back against one end of the couch, with one leg doubled under her and one arm along the back. She was a dazzling creature, but Hobart repeated to himself: I won't propose, I won't propose . . .

"Rollin," she said at last, "won't you sit down?"

That seemed like a harmless request. He complied, then remembered some girls were repelled by cigars. He got out one. "Mind?"

"Not at all, dear."

Hobart bit off the end and lit up. When it was going comfortably, he asked: "What's become of your friend the lion?"

"Oh, Theiax will be along some time; I don't know when. He has no sense of time, which is why he always speaks in the present tense."

Silence. Then Argimanda said: "You made a remarkable speech, Rollin."

"Thanks. Didn't think it was much good, myself."

"I did not say it was good, dear."

"Oh. You mean remarkably bad?"

"No. It was remarkable in that I could not understand it." Hobart looked at her sharply, and she explained: "You see, my fairy godmother gave me intelligence as her foremost gift. Yet, as nearly as I could make out, the last paragraph was simply a complex way of saying 'I don't know.'"

"That's all it was," grinned Hobart. "What about this fairy godmother? Is it a metaphor?"

"A—what? Your language must differ from pure Logaian, which has no such word."

"Sure of that?"

"I should be; I edited the new standard dictionary," said the princess calmly.

"I meant," said Hobart, "do you really have fairy godmothers and all that?"

"Of course! The word exists, so the thing the word refers to must exist. I know mine well; her name is Kyzikeia, and she visits me every year on my birthday to see how I'm doing."

"And if a fairy godmother gives you a quality, such as intelligence, you have to have that quality all your life?"

"But naturally! For example, Alaxius received the qualities of selfishness and superficiality along with his virtues, so selfish and superficial he must be. Poor Charion had the worst luck; he got neurosis, irritability, and mendacity."

"That what you meant when you warned me against believing him?"

"Yes. Not that he lies all the time; so much mendacity in one soul would be impractical. But in important matters you can generally count on him to lie."

"Then why does your father employ him?" asked Hobart.

"Because Father has affability, and no matter what anybody says about Charion, Charion can always talk his way back into Father's good graces."

Hobart mused: "When I tried to pump him—"

"Excuse me?"

"To get information out of him about the kingdom, he shut up like a clam."

Argimanda thought a while, and explained: "He has some plan afoot; I don't know what, but connected with his disarmament project, and I think he fears you and would like to frighten you away. The most logical way to do this would be to tell you that the kingdom is nearly bankrupt and is threatened by the barbarians. But this unfortunately is the truth, and Charion could never tell the truth in such a crucial matter. So his only remaining course was to say nothing."

Some reward for the champion, thought Hobart. He puffed silently.

Argimanda's voice came softly through the smoke: "Rollin, are we not going to discuss—dates and things?"

"Nope," said Hobart. "I don't want to be brutal,

but I'm not going to ask you to marry me." He threw a glance at her widening blue eyes, then looked quickly away. "Sorry as hell if it hurts your feelings, but I've got my own plans, and they don't include a wife."

The blue eyes brimmed with tears, but she did not break down or sniffle. The tears rolled slowly and hesitantly, with a decent interval between each.

"Now, now," said Hobart, "it's not as bad as that. Look. I don't belong in this world. I've got my own world and my own life."

She said very softly: "I'm sure I could make you happy in any world."

"But—good lord, I couldn't be in love with you: I've only known you a few hours!"

"I love you," she whispered.

"For Pete's sake why? How?"

"A princess *always* falls in love with her rescuer. When I knew you were he, I could not help it." She gave a sigh with a little catch in it. "But, strange man, if you do not want me, I could not force myself upon you, since I love you and would not do anything to make you unhappy. What is it that you wish?"

Hobart hesitated, then said: "Tell you one reason I couldn't marry you, Argimanda. You're beautiful, intelligent, kind, and so on; practically perfect. That's the trouble; you're too perfect. You'd give me an inferiority complex a yard wide."

"You need not labor the explanations, my love that was to be. What do you wish?"

"Well, mainly I want to get back to my own world. That means locating Hoimon and arranging an escape from Oroloia for me, and it would have to be fixed so Theiax wouldn't catch me at it."

"Why Theiax?"

"He practically promised to eat me if I tried it."

"Very well, my prince. I will do what I can."

"Okay; I'll appreciate that. And better not say anything to the king about it. Tell him we're in no hurry, will you?"

"I will."

"Swell. I'll go, now. Good-night."

"Farewell." The tears were coming faster. Hobart hurried out of the room and almost ran to his own quarters.

5

A<small>T</small> 6:00 A.M. BY H<small>OBART'S</small> watch, his bedroom door
flew open; the business end of a trumpet was thrust
into the room and began a maddening *tah-taa-teh-tah-taa-teh-tah-taa-teh*. The impact of the sound almost made Hobart bounce out of bed with shock.
When his racing heart slowed and his vision cleared
enough to become aware of surroundings, he shouted:
"Stop that racket!"

The racket stopped and the trumpeter's face, red
with blowing, appeared. "Your Dignity—"

"Get out!" yelled Hobart, reaching for a shoe to
throw.

"The hunt, Your Dignity!"

"Oh," yawned Hobart. "Excuse me."

A phalanx of servants trooped in with breakfast.
He was rushed through the meal, shaved, and dressed
before he knew it, though he tried fuzzily to do as
much for himself as possible.

The hunting party congregated at the mammoth
main entrance to the palace. Hobart was just as glad
to see that the sinister chancellor was not among the

49

gaudy crowd of Logaians, though the burly black-bearded General Valangas was. The king slapped Hobart's back, gripped his arm, and hauled him about introducing him to Counts and Sirs and Esquires whose names Hobart promptly forgot. A man on a horse trotted around from one side—Psambides, the Master of the Horse, the king explained—and after him came a swarm of grooms afoot towing horses. The king grinned fondly at his prospective son-in-law, and said: "I ordered Xenthops specially for you, son."

"Who, your Altitude?"

"Call me Dad. Xenthops is my fierce barbarian stallion. It takes a real hero to ride him at all. Heh, heh."

Hobart opened his mouth to protest that he was at best a mediocre rider, but as he did so he noted that all the Logaian gentlemen had swung into their saddles. There was one horse left, a large black creature with staring eyes. It would cause a lot of fuss to make a change now. Anyway, he'd be damned if he'd let a mere horse . . .

As he walked up to Xenthops, the horse bared a set of large white incisors and extended them tentatively toward him. Hobart reached out and cuffed the stallion's muzzle, saying: "Behave yourself!" Xenthop's eyes opened still wider as he jerked his head back and shifted his feet angrily. Hobart mounted without delay and took as firm a knee-grip as his unhardened thigh-muscles would allow. Xenthops fidgeted but did nothing otherwise untoward. Hobart reasoned that he could get away with it as long as he kept an attitude of confident superiority; but if he once showed hesitation or timidity, Xenthops would feel the difference, buck him off, and probably step on him.

The king's mount now appeared: a spotted camel-like beast similar to the one Hobart had seen the day before in the streets of Oroloia. To Hobart's question, Sir Somebody explained: "The king's cameleopard." Hobart had always thought a cameleopard was a giraffe; everything was so remorselessly literal in this world . . .

And more servants appeared carrying lances and muskets, which they handed out to the huntsmen. Hobart, given his choice, took a gun and the power-horn and bullet bag that went with it.

They were all clattering out of the palace lot when a groaning made Hobart turn in his saddle to look back. Bringing up the tail of the procession was a wheeled, horse-drawn cannon manned by a squad of kilted soldiers commanded by General Valangas. Evidently the behemoth was no chipmunk.

Hobart would have liked to ask questions, but talking while trotting is not the easiest combination. Besides, he had to keep his eye peeled for chances to escape, and keep this fiery nag under both physical and psychological control.

After an hour's riding, the agricultural checker-board gave way with the usual abruptness to a rolling, roadless savannah. After another hour Psambides halted the crowd with upraised arm and began assigning them missions, as if this were a full-fledged military operation. Hobart found himself assigned to a squad of four who were to reconnoitre. The horses had to be kicked along a bit, as they wanted to crop the long swishing grass. Presently the troop halved. Hobart's companion, a lean young Logaian named Sphindex, informed him:

"We're to scout along the bed of the Keio, and come back here to rendezvous in an hour."

"Is that a river?" asked Hobart innocently.

"Of course."

"What's a behemoth like?"

Sphindex stared. "Mean to say you've never hunted one?"

"Right."

"What have you hunted then?"

"Nothing, except a few targets."

"But—but my dear Prince, how do you *exist*?"

"I manage." The subject of hunting did not seem promising. "Do you know an ascetic named Hoimon?"

Up went Sphindex's brows. "Me know an ascetic? Great Nois no! They don't hunt."

Hobart persisted: "Know anything about the cave-people?"

"Fellas who live in the Conical Mountains, that's all. Never seen one; Gordius won't let us hunt them. Though I don't know why; they're not really human. Look, there's the Keio ahead."

He pointed with his lance toward a dark streak on the landscape. When they had topped a few more rises they overlooked the nearly-dry bed of a small river, bordered by clumps of trees and brush.

Sphindex at once exhibited signs of excitement; he spurred his horse down the slope and ducked through the screen of blue vegetation for a closer look at the stream bed. Hobart, following at a more cautious pace, met him dashing back. "Come on!" cried the hunting enthusiast.

Xenthops banked for a turn without a signal on Hobart's part and galloped after Sphindex's horse. Hobart called: "Find your behemoth?"

"No," Sphindex flung back, "but there's one drinking upstream."

"How do you know?"

"Don't be absurd; what other game can drink a river dry?"

Hobart saved his breath till they rejoined the main army, which at once set out at a gallop in a direction at a small angle to the one the scouts had taken. The cannon bounded thunderously in the rear behind its team, followed by the ammunition-caisson.

"Your Dignity!" It was the Master of the Horse, speaking to Hobart. "You're to join the troop covering the artillery."

"Yes, but what am I supposed to *do*?"

"Oh, stay with the king and do what he does." And off went Psambides to complete his arrangements.

The party deployed on a wide front, with the gun in the middle. They stopped on the last rise before reaching the Keio; somewhat farther upstream, Hobart judged. The gun and caisson were trotted up to the crest, and the teams unhitched and led back. Hobart got his first good look at the cannon. It had a cylindrical barrel with no taper; Logaia must still lack an Admiral Dahlgren. Instead of an elevation screw it had a crude arrangement with a shiftable cross-bar like that of a morris chair. The gunners were ramming in the powder, followed by the ball. Valangas himself filled the touch hole.

Hobart could not see anything through the trees bordering the river, though the sun flashed on the metal of huntsmen closing in from above and below on the section of stream in front of the cannon.

"Son!" called King Gordius from the back of his cameleopard, "over this way! You're in the line of fire!"

Hobart had no more than started to trot to the group of Logaians, sitting in their saddles with lances and muskets around the king, when his ear caught a sucking, burbling sound from the river. There were loud, plopping reports as of something huge being pulled out of the mud. A slate-black back appeared over the treetops.

A wave of retrograde motion ran through the huntsmen nearest to this portent. The trees whipped; one of them came down crashing, and the behemoth appeared.

Hobart's first reaction was: is *that* all? The behemoth combined an elephantine body, twice the dimensions of an elephant, however, with a long thick tail and a head like that of a magnified hippopotamus. From its nose grew a pair of lateral horns. The beast, which might have been classed with the titanotheres, was big enough to be alarming but too plausible to be very interesting to Rollin Hobart *per se*.

The first members of the party to attract the behemoth's attention were a group of riders picking their way among the bushes on the hither side of the trees. It lumbered toward them. There was a sharp pop-pop-pop of muskets, and the riders whirled and galloped off to the right, upstream, leaving white puffs of smoke hanging in the still air behind them like clouds of ink from a group of retreating squids.

The behemoth crashed after them, apparently unhurt, exposing its right flank to the cannon as it did so. One of the riders fell off his horse, scrambled up, and disappeared into the vegetation. A yell from Valangas made Hobart swing his regard 180 degrees.

"Ho!" roared the general, "you there, Something, get out of the way!"

Hobart got, his horse bounding toward the group around the king. Then, as the gunners hauled the trail still further around, the king and his party streamed clockwise in a big circle around the gun to get out of the line of fire.

"Here it comes," said a voice.

Hobart looked around to see the behemoth head-on, trotting along the ridge on which the gun stood. It moved with deceptive speed, and was growing with panicking rapidity; it looked fifty feet tall though it was less than half that.

The cannon banged somewhere on Hobart's left, and the cloud of smoke leaped into the tail of his eye. He heard the smack of the ball hitting hide, and got a glimpse of a receding black dot against the sky: the shot, high, had glanced from the creature's back. The behemoth kept right on looming.

Then the muskets around Hobart went off, one or two and then all the rest with a crash. Hobart had not had a chance to examine his gun closely. Now he learned to his dismay that it was some sort of match-lock, and that the little tarred string that was led from a spool on the left side of the stock to the swivelled clamp that substituted for a hammer was not even lit. Then the black-powder smoke stung his eyes shut, and he felt Xenthops under him begin to move, first with little nervous steps, then faster. He heard the earth-shaking thumps of the behemoth's tread just about the time he could see again.

His first glance picked up gunners afoot and hunters on horseback, all making tracks, and then King Gordius of Logaia, down near the river, rolling over and over in the yellow grass like one who has fallen from an express train in motion. The riderless came-leopard was doing crazy buck-jumps; as Hobart watched, it disappeared into the trees. A back-glance showed Hobart that the behemoth, too, was looking at the king; was in fact heading in that direction.

Hobart thought that if he could control Xenthops, he could get to his Altitude first. Of course if that fat old fool wanted to provoke a fifty-ton animal into squashing him like a strawberry, it served him right, and it was certainly none of his, Hobart's business . . . but he had already headed the horse toward the king, who had ceased his dizzy roll and was getting up. Gordius put up a hand as Hobart approached; the engineer braced himself and reached out to haul the king up behind him. It did not work that way: Gordius got a good grip on Hobart's wrist, heaved— and Hobart left the saddle and came down on top of the king.

The king yipped as the musket barrel got him over the ear; but with the behemoth towering over them they did not stop to feel for broken bones. They scrambled up and bolted into the timber like frantic rabbits. The monster crashed in after them. It blundered about for a bit, snapping tree trunks; then headed back for the deserted cannon.

Rollin Hobart and King Gordius, lying in a thicket, drew a pair of whews. The king said: "Can you see what he's doing, son?"

Hobart raised his head to peer. "He's trampling the gun." A wooden crackle confirmed this statement, as the gun carriage was flattened. "Good lord, he's eating the barrel!"

"Strange," said the king; "I thought they ate nothing but grass. What now?"

"He seems to have some trouble swallowing it— it's down now." They heard a snort from the behemoth; it thumped off out of sight over the crest of the rise. There were a couple of distant musket shots and some thin shouts, and all was peaceful.

"We had better start looking for our mounts," said the king, getting up with a grunt. As he did so, something went *whtht*.

"What—" said the king. *Whuck!* An arrow stuck quivering in a tree trunk six inches from His Altitude's nose.

Gordius turned to Hobart, mild blue eyes round. "Somebody," he said in an awed voice, "is shooting at me!"

"Duck!" cried Hobart. The king did so, just as a third arrow whistled through the leaves.

"How do you work this thing?" said Hobart in a stage whisper, indicating the musket. "It is loaded?"

"It is unless you've fired it," replied the king. "Let's see—you have to light the match—this thing." Hobart did so with his cigarette lighter. "And the powder was all shaken out of the firing pan when you fell off Xenthops. You put more in, like this, and smooth it down with your thumb. Then you close the pan cover, so. Blow your match now and then so it doesn't go out. Ho, not so hard; you'll blow a spark into the pan."

Hobart extended the barrel cautiously toward the source point of the arrows, meantime moving his head to bring holes in the greenery—or rather bluery—into line. The gun weighed well over twenty pounds, but Hobart could manage it from his prone position. He whispered: "Got a sword or spear? I'm going to shoot and then go after the guy."

"I lost them when I fell off," said Gordius. "Use the musket butt."

The firearm had a front sight—a knob—but no rear sight. Hobart lined the barrel up as best he could. His eye caught a suggestion of motion, and he pulled the trigger.

The gun roared; smoke blotted out the foliage; the butt came back like a mule's kick; and Hobart's right thumb, which he had injudiciously wrapped around the stock; hit his nose an agonizing blow. Though his vision was as full of stars as of woods, he jumped up and bounded over the bushes after his shot, reversing the musket as he did so.

But there was no lurking assassin for him to club. He hunted for some minutes without result; then he saw something dark lying on the blue moss, and picked it up. It was a wig of short black hair.

King Gordius frowned when he saw the object. "I don't know who might wear it," he said. "Good Nois, what happened to your nose?" The member was grotesquely swollen and bleeding.

Hobart explained, and added irritably: "If you want to hunt behemoths, Your Altitude, why go to all this bother, with horse and muskets and things? Why not take one of Laus's magic umbrellas, locate a victim from the air, and have your wizard conjure him down to vest-pocket size?"

"It's against the game laws to hunt with magic," explained the king. "As a just ruler, I couldn't violate my own laws, could I? Besides it doesn't work. Animals are sensitive to magic, and if you practice it in their neighborhood they'll run away before you can get within sight of them." As they set out afoot to try to rejoin the rest of the party, the Affable Monarch continued: "You saved my life, Rollin. I must do something to reward that. You already have my daughter and half my kingdom. How would a coronet do?"

"Fine," grumbled Hobart. At least such a bauble should have cash value back in New York.

6

A DISTRACTED PSAMBIDES PICKED them up after an hour's walk, and by late afternoon had rounded up the rest. General Valangas clucked when he heard the fate of the cannon. "Our latest model, too," he commented, but added with a grin: "It matters not; it would have been melted up in the course of disarmament anyway."

Hobart reflected that Valturus the gunsmith was not the only person to display a peculiar cheerfulness about a policy that threatened his livelihood. He remarked: "I should think a general like you would want to keep your army."

Valangas shrugged. "I would, but our Chancellor convinced me that wars never settle anything, so why fight them? Besides, this new stuff gunpowder will probably put an end to war soon by making it so horrible that none will fight. What happened to your nose, lad?"

Hobart told him. The general guffawed, then asked: "Is it broken?"

"Don't think so," said Hobart, fingering the member tenderly. It had at least stopped bleeding.

"Good," roared Valangas, clapping Hobart on the back. "Then we'll see you in the tournament. I have promised myself to break a lance with you."

"What tournament?" snapped Hobart, feeling like a man caught in quicksand, whose every movement gets him involved more deeply.

"Why, tomorrow, at Prince Aites' party!"

"Not with my nose," said Hobart.

"What? But you just said it was not broken! We'll wear closed helmets, so a mere bump on the nose is no excuse."

"It is to me. I'm not going in any tournament."

"But, my good Prince, surely you're no coward?"

"Not interested, that's all."

The king spoke up: "What's this about my future son-in-law's being a coward? After he saved my life—"

"Your Altitude," said Valangas, "do you admit that a man is either a coward or he is not?"

Rollin Hobart spoke loudly: "I said I wasn't going to enter any damned tournament, and that's that. Make anything of it you like."

The king looked unhappy; General Valangas sniffed contemptuously and began talking to someone else. Hobart asked a few questions about Hoimon, but all he gathered was that the gentlemen of the hunting party knew little and cared less about the activities of members of the brotherhood of ascetics.

They had to hurry to make the city of Oroloia before dark, for, as Hobart knew by now, there was no twilight. When the sun dropped below the horizon, darkness came down with a clank.

"The Onyx Room for cocktails in half an hour, my boy," King Gordius told him before leaving him in the palace. "We're eating privately tonight. Nois, I'm tired!"

Half the half-hour was spent by Hobart's new valet, Zorgon, in a rather futile attempt to sponge out of existence the two beautiful shiners that had appeared around the unwilling prince's eyes. When he entered the Onyx Room to find Princess Argimanda, and the social lion lapping a gallon of tea out of a bucket, the first words were a chorus from the princess and Theiax:

"What happened-to-your-nose?" The princess made a movement toward him, but he had his firm face on and she restrained herself.

Hobart told them the story of the hunt, and asked Theiax where he had been. The social lion looked sheepish, if one can imagine such a thing.

Argimanda spoke up: "There's a lioness in the Pyramidal Mountains, my l—Prince Rollin."

"Some day," rumbled Theiax, "you go hunting with me. You eat plenty of good meat. I kill lots of animals; don't eat any."

"Why not? You mean you kill just for the fun of it?" said Hobart.

"Sure. I am sport. Sport is one who kills for fun, men tell me; one who kills for practical reason is wicked poacher. You come with me; I show you. When you and Argimanda have cubs, you bring them, too."

The princess gave a small sigh, and Hobart was just as glad to see King Gordius come in before the conversation got any more speculative. Following the king came Prince Alaxius and a couple of men carrying two small cannon turned into holders for potted plants.

"Put them—let's see—there and there!" said King Gordius. The men lowered the cannon, plants and all to the floor. Gordius said: "At least it's fairly easy to dispose of those things. You've no idea, Rollin, how awkward swords are to beat into plowshares;

and as for making spears into pruning-hooks, it works all right, but we'll have enough pruning-hooks for ten kingdoms the size of ours. Ah, the drinks!" The butler poured and handed. The king said: "Here's to a long, happy, and fertile married life, my children!"

Hobart sipped to hide his expression, and sat down when the king did.

"*Boom!*" It went off right under Hobart, who jumped a foot straight up, spilling the rest of his drink.

The king started a little, too, as did the others. "Nois bless that boy!" he cried. "Wait till I get my hands on him!"

"Oh, Father," said the princess, "he'll be an adolescent tomorrow!"

"I take it," said Hobart frigidly, "that you refer to my future brother-in-law, Prince Aites?"

"Yes, yes," said the king harrassedly. "He *will* put firecrackers around. It runs to quite a bill. But that'll be all right now, heh, because we'll transfer the gunpowder in the royal arsenal to our privy purse at a forced-sale price. We have to get rid of it somehow now that the army's being disbanded. Here, dear boy, have another drink!"

"Doesn't Argimanda take any?" asked Hobart, accepting.

"Why no, she's *good*. Thought you knew. How's your appetite?"

"Could eat a horse and chase the driver," said Hobart.

The king looked a little taken aback; then he took the butler aside and whispered to him.

Prince Alaxius had just finished his second cocktail. He now stood up and stalked about, swinging his long legs, and said: "Rollin, I've spent all day mixing pigments to try to get those unearthly shades you wear. But the mixtures come out the same old red, yellow, and blue. Now how—hehehehehehe!"

At the end of this inane giggle, Prince Alaxius sank slowly to his knees on the rug, a wide foolish smile on his face, and collapsed to the floor.

Hobart jumped up and tried to raise Alaxius to his feet.

"Dear, dear," said the king. "The fool's intoxicated again. Put him on something, Rollin; it'll wear off."

"Seemed perfectly sober a minute ago," said Hobart.

"Of course, of course; he wasn't intoxicated then; just about to be. Either one's intoxicated or one isn't."

Alaxius stretched on the sofa, suddenly revived. He passed a hand across his face, grimaced, and said: "Did I make a fool of myself again? Sorry, Father; I miscalculated."

Hobart, who happened to be bending over Alaxius, said in a low tone: "Could I see you later?" The aesthetic prince nodded briefly.

Hobart turned to King Gordius: "What's this about the privy purse and so? I ought to know something about the way the finances of the kingdom are handled."

"Well," said the king, "let's see. Suppose Charion decides we need more revenue. He gets the royal treasurer to draw up a tax bill, and brings it to me for signature—"

"Excuse me," said Hobart, "but don't you have any sort of parliament or congress?"

"What? I don't know what you mean."

Hobart started to explain about these institutions. The king seemed intensely interested; pressed Hobart for more and more details, while Argimanda hung fascinated on his words and Alaxius oozed boredom. The lion had begun to snore. After they had sat down to dinner, the Affable Monarch continued to pump the engineer.

"Yes, yes," he said. "That's a most remarkable idea. I see I shall have to take it up with Charion."

Queen Vasalina put in a worried question: "Rollin dear, don't you like your steak?"

"What is it?" asked Hobart with a sickly smile. The meat was not only tough, but had a strange and not very agreeable flavor.

"Horse," said the king. "You just said you'd eat one. And in case you still feel like chasing a driver after dinner, I've ordered one to wait outside. Of course if you catch him you mustn't really eat him, you know . . ."

* * *

"All right, my man," said Prince Alaxius, disposing himself on Hobart's bed with his hands clasped behind his head, "say your little say."

Hobart had begged off any extended visit with the king and queen or their daughter after dinner. He sat in his armchair and lit his remaining cigar before answering: "I need a little advice, Alaxius."

"Ask away."

"How do you react to the last two days' events?"

Alaxius yawned. "If you expect me to say I'm pleased, I shall have to disappoint you."

"Not so disappointed at that. Mean I'm not the brother-in-law you'd have picked?"

"It is not that, Rollin. While I don't know what Argimanda sees in you, I'd ordinarily not care whom she married. But it's this half-the-kingdom business."

"Ah," said Hobart, "now we're getting somewhere. Mean you'd have gotten the whole thing if I hadn't rescued your sister?"

"Uh-huh."

"But what would have happened to Argimanda?"

"She'd have been eaten, stupid."

"Wouldn't that matter to you?" asked Hobart in slight surprise.

"Not particularly. My art comes first."

"Hardly an altruistic point of view."

Alaxius raised his eyebrows. "Of course I'm selfish! Didn't you know? My fairy godmother saw to that."

"Anyway, she seems to have given you veracity along with your other—uh—virtues."

"Candor. I can't help saying what I think, though it gets me into trouble constantly. Look here, this is all very dull. Wouldn't you rather come up to the studio and pose—"

Hobart put up a hand. "Easy, Alaxius. What would happen if I disappeared?"

"Why—that depends. If it happened before you married my sister, I'd be the sole heir again, I suppose. But if Argimanda were your widow, the succession would pass to her, and then to any male children—"

"Okay, okay; it's an immediate disappearance I'm interested in."

Alaxius looked puzzled. "I don't see what you're getting at. *I* am certainly not going to murder you; haven't the necessary qualities. And it would be unprecedented for the champion to disappear voluntarily—"

"This champion," said Rollin Hobart grimly, "is about to establish a new precedent."

Alaxius' mouth dropped open, and he sat bold upright on the bed. When the full implications of Hobart's statement sank in, the young prince's eyes rolled up, and he fell back on the pillow. He had fainted.

7

NEXT MORNING, THE TRUMPETER awoke Hobart again with his cacophonous racket. While Hobart was fumbling over the side of the bed for a shoe to answer this assault on his nerves, the fellow announced:

"His Altitude, King Gordius of Logaia; Her Luminescence, Queen Vasalina; His Dignity, Prince Alaxius; Her Purity, Princess Argimanda . . ."

The whole Xerophi gang trooped in; Hobart pulled the covers up to his chin, thinking that his underwear would not give an impressive aesthetic effect. Speaking of aesthetics, he wondered momentarily whether Alaxius might have blabbed, despite the fact that it was to his selfish advantage not to . . . But a searching look at the prince's face disclosed an expression of no more than usual superciliousness.

A member of the group whom Hobart had not seen was a gangling red-haired youngster. At his inquiring look, the queen said: "Don't you know Aites, Rollin dear?"

"Aites? But he didn't look at all like that when I saw him last!"

"Oh, but now he's an adolescent! I thought you knew. How is your poor dear nose?"

"Better, thanks," said Hobart, feeling it. The swelling was less, but the goose-egg lump on the side of the king's head was still flourishing; His Altitude wore the Crown of Logaia cocked to one side as a consequence.

"Ahem," said the king; "my dear Rollin, as a small token of my—uh—appreciation for your heroic action yesterday, let me present you with a small—uh—token of my appreciation." He extended a package.

"I'm thrilled," said Hobart sadly, not wanting to hurt the old codger's feelings. The package contained the promised coronet: like the king's crown but with a simple scalloped top border instead of the tall spikes with knobs on their ends. It fitted remarkably, and the Xerophi all went oh and ah and how well it becomes you.

He thanked them out. After breakfast he found the king with his feet up, a pipe in his mouth, and his crown askew, reading the *Logaian Ephemerides*. Gordius passed him the first section, which he had finished. It was printed in large hand-set type on obviously hand-made paper; the language appeared to be the same phonetically spelled English that he had seen before in Logaia. He asked the king how this came to be. Gordius merely said:

"The people of this country of yours are civilized, aren't they, son? Then they speak the language of civilized people, don't they? Well, we're civilized, so naturally we do also. As for the spelling, I don't see how it could be otherwise; a letter either stands for a certain sound or it doesn't."

The gangler that Aites now was entered with an armful of boxes, saying: "Father, where shall I put my toys and things?"

"Leave them here and I'll order Charion to distribute them to the poor children, Aites."

Hobart asked: "Giving away all your stuff?"

"Sure," said the boy. "They're child's things. And I'm sorry about the firecrackers, sir. It won't happen again."

"Okay," said Hobart.

Something was bothering the boy; he fidgeted and produced a small pad. He said hesitantly: "Sir—would you mind—I'm starting a collection of the autographs of heroes—"

Hobart signed promptly, whereat the boy said, "Nolly!" in an awed tone. The rest of the day he stuck to Hobart like a burr, asking questions with respectful sirs on them, and in general displaying all the symptoms of hero worship.

The tournament took place in the huge concourse inside the palace walls. Hobart found it long and dull. Two regiments that were being disbanded, one of pikemen and one of musketeers, staged an elaborate parade; the pikemen charged in phalanx formation; the musketeers fired blank charges. As each rank fired the men of the rear rank finished reloading and ran forward to the front and fired in their turn. They solemnly turned over their standards to General Valangas, who made a speech during which some of them wept; they stacked their arms and filed into the stands to watch the rest of the show.

A fence was now set up along the central axis of the arena, and men with huge round shields and bucket-shaped helmets that covered their whole heads rode horses in opposite directions along the opposite sides of the fence, trying to knock each other out of the saddle with padded poles like those used in canoe tilting. Thanks to the fence, and the heavy armor of the jousters, and the blue moss with which the floor of the arena was carpeted, the risk was negligible.

Rollin Hobart peacefully puffed a new pipe and waited for it to end. His expression did not even change when General Valangas, having won several of the tilts, rode by close enough to give him a scornful glance. He could afford to wait for the bee he had put in Prince Alaxius' bonnet to produce some honey. If the prince was selfish he was selfish, period. The people of this screwy world had the simple monochromatic characters of the cast of an old-time melodrama. That was one more reason for not wanting to stay here—imagine being married to that girl on his left, with her magazine-cover beauty and her ultra-modern goodness that allowed not one human vice . . . But this inhuman consistency had the advantage of dependability. Alaxius would not fail him.

Nor did he. When Hobart excused himself and retired, he found the prince waiting for him with a pair of monkish robes with hoods, the sword and musket he had requested, and a map of Logaia.

Alaxius explained: "You take the Great West Road to here where it forks; this way goes to Barbaria and that way to the Conical Mountains, where we first met you. Are you sure you want to go there? The cave-people are not to be fooled with."

"Don't care if they're ten-foot cannibals," said Hobart. "I'll find Hoimon if I spend the rest of my life looking."

Alaxius shrugged. "No concern of mine. I'll accompany you to the fork, though."

"Nice of you."

"Not at all. I want to make sure you're on your way."

When Hobart started to pull the face-shading hood

over his head, he was reminded of the coronet. He hesitated; if it was real gold it ought to fetch—but then he took the thing off and put it on the bed. He would not take advantage of old Gordius by accepting his gold under false pretenses.

In the dim hall they almost ran into the Princess Argimanda. Hobart started, expecting an alarm and the urgent need for explanations. But all she said was: "You are going, Prince?" He nodded.

"May I—just once—"

No harm in that, he thought. She was in his arms as he was still opening them; kissed him passionately; whispered: "Farewell, my dearest darling," and fled silently.

He was grateful for her having neither made a fuss nor tried to dissuade him; if only she weren't so *too* perfect . . . Wait, maybe it was just as well he was getting out; no telling what mere propinquity would do to the best of resolutions . . .

A sentry passed them without a word. Outside, an anonymous groom handed them horses and a big food-bag in the uncertain light of a pair of flambeaux bracketed to the palace wall. They plop-plopped through the deserted streets of Oroloia; the Logaians must keep early hours.

Out of the city, Alaxius led the way briskly, apparently steering by clairvoyance or by the faint stars overhead; the landscape as far as Hobart could see was as black as the inside of a cow. The uncertain feeling of jogging through a black void on an invisible steed oppressed Rollin Hobart, who had been accustomed to the definiteness of this orthogonal world.

Now that he observed them, the stars were peculiar. They were all of the same magnitude, and were arranged in neat patterns: circles, squares, and configurations like diagrams of the molecules of organic compounds. In such a cosmos there was a real reason for naming constellations: that group on their right, for instance, was probably called the Tiller Wheel; at least it looked like a tiller wheel, whereas Taurus had never to Hobart's exact mind borne the slightest resemblance to a real bull.

He waited with some interest for more constellations to appear over the horizon. But after an hour's jogging none came, and it was gradually bore upon Hobart that none were coming: that the vault of heaven here stayed put relative to the earth. Maybe Hoimon had been right: the earth was the center of the solar system here, and the universe was built on Ptolemaic lines . . . Come to think of it, between its black-and-white logic—which got plenty of support from the behavior of people and things—and its geocentric cosmogony, this whole plane of existence looked suspiciously as though it had sprung from the brains of a crew of Hellenistic philosophers . . . The correspondence was too close for coincidence. The question would bear looking into, if somebody cared to hire him under a decent contract to investigate it . . .

"The fork," announced Alaxius. "You turn right; I return to Oroloia. It's up to you to decide whether you want to rest till dawn and then ride hard—for Father will have sent men after you—or continue slowly now."

"Guess I'll wait," said Hobart. "It oughtn't—hello, what's that?"

They fell silent as unmistakable hoof-sounds came down the Great West Road, mixed with the creak of wheels.

"This is no time for honest travelers to be abroad," whispered Alaxius. "Could it be that Father already pursues us?"

"Doesn't seem likely he'd do it in a wagon," replied Hobart. "Let's hide anyway."

They dismounted as quietly as they could, which unfortunately was not very quiet, and pulled their horses off the road. The clink and shuffle of their movements must have carried to the approaching vehicle, for its sounds ceased. For some seconds all concerned froze, listening to their own breathing. From the direction of the unknown came a spark and then a sputter of light: a little yellow flame flickered and went out. But it left behind it a small red spark. This moved about the darkness erratically, then came toward them. It would move a little, halt as though to listen, then move some more.

Hobart guessed it to be the match of a gun. He held his breath as it came right up to the fork, perhaps thirty feet from where he stood with his hand over his horse's muzzle.

The spark halted. Again came the flicker and the little yellow flame, near the spark but not identical with it. The light showed a taper in the hand of a man standing in front of the signpost, peering at it. In his free hand was the grandfather of horse-pistols, and his nag's face was dimly visible behind him. He had an ordinary bearded Logaian face.

The stranger moved the taper back and forth in front of the sign, then stared into the darkness, little wrinkles of intentness around his eyes. He blew the taper out, and the red spark was moving back toward where the wagon should be, when Alaxius sneezed —uh *khyoo!*

The darkness flicked out in one brilliant flash and the pistol roared. Hobart heard the clatter of the man's scramble back into his seat, shouting to his animal, and horse and wagon rattled off down the road to Barbaria.

"Are you hit?" cried Hobart.

"Never came near me," came Alaxius' voice, "but that is a peculiar way to treat strangers in a peaceful country. I do not like being shot at, even by ear. I want to get back to my nice, safe palace."

They pulled their horses back on the road. Hobart stubbed his toe.

"Now what," he murmured, "can that be?" He bent down and fumbled. It was a musket like the one he carried under his arm.

"Did you drop a musket, Alaxius?" he asked.

"Not I. I hate the things."

"Somebody did. Let's have some light."

Alaxius, grumbling at the delay, lit his own taper. Another musket lay in the dust of the road twenty feet down the road the stranger had taken. Beyond, on the rim of the dark, they could see another.

"Who," said Hobart, "would be running a wagonload of guns this way at this time of night?"

"I suppose Valturus," said Alaxius, "and to the barbarians. He's not supposed to, but that is all I can think of."

"No wonder he looked so cheerful the other night! Does that mean trouble for Logaia?"

"It should. The barbarians with guns and us with nothing—you can guess the rest."

Hobart thought. "I suppose you'll go back and warn your father?"

"Now that I think of it, I don't believe I will," said Alaxius. "If Logaia is to be conquered, I prefer to be somewhere else. I'll go to Psythoris, where my cousin rules . . ."

"But then who—"

"I don't know; it's no concern of mine. If you're interested, why do you not go?"

"I will," snapped Hobart, "and you're going with me!"

"But why . . ." bleated Alaxius.

"Corroboration. Think I want your old man to get the idea I murdered you and then cooked up a yarn to hide it? Come on!"

Alaxius looked startled, glanced about wildly, and suddenly blew out his taper. But while he was still turning to run, Hobart pounced on him and caught his robe. They scuffled; Alaxius kicked Hobart in the shin, and Hobart cuffed the prince's face. Alaxius suddenly gave in, crying:

"Don't hit me! Don't hit me!"

"Shut up," growled Hobart. He tied the trembling aesthete's hands behind his back, and heaved him aboard his horse. Then the engineer picked up his musket, mounted his own horse, and lit the match with his lighter.

"Now," he said, "one break and you'll learn some more about being shot at by ear. March!"

Alaxius got under way, complaining: "I do not see why you must concern yourself in the fate of Logaia. But a few minutes ago you were trying to escape from it!"

"No good reason," agreed Hobart. "It's just that I'm not as consistent a heel as you are. Hmm, guess we'd better have a story for Gordius, about how we suspected this gun runner and followed him out of town."

"Why should I agree to your lies? Suppose I tell Father about your real plans?"

"Okay, then I'll tell him how you helped me." Alaxius got the point.

8

HOBART WAS WARNED BY Prince Alaxius that it would take more than the threat of a barbarian invasion to divert the easy-going king from his after-breakfast pipe and paper. So the young men waited, Hobart impatiently and Alaxius in resignation, until the coast was clear. Then they descended on His Altitude in the royal study.

At Hobart's somewhat elliptical account of the night's experiences, the king said worriedly: "Dear, dear, mercy me! You are no doubt right about there being a plot. But who would want to plot against me? I've been the mildest of monarchs—"

"Looks like your gunsmith, Valturus, ought to be in on it," said Hobart.

"Yes, yes, I suppose so. But who else? I'll call Charion at once . . ."

"I wouldn't, yet," said Hobart sharply.

"Why not, pray?"

"How do you know he's not in on it?"

"My chancellor? Absurd, my boy, absurd!"

"Not so sure. What's the financial history of his administration?"

"I don't see that it matters . . . But when he came in, five years ago, we had a surplus of forty-three thousand talents. Charion convinced me the the kingdom needed a big public-works program, to occupy the people and give us prestige abroad. His arguments were entirely logical, I assure you. Then when the surplus was all spent, the kingdom in fact had acquired a large funded debt—a perfectly normal, healthy condition, Charion explained to me—he said we should have to cut our rate of expenditure before it became too difficult to borrow more money. So Charion made it clear that if we disbanded the army, our neighbors would be so ingratiated by our noble example that they would do likewise, and war would be banished from the earth."

"How far has your disarmament program gone?"

"Those regiments you saw disbanded yesterday were the last; there remain only the palace sentries and the town watch. Dear, dear, so, I hope this action was not premature . . ."

Hobart rasped: "If I wanted to steal your kingdom, and knew I could persuade you to give up your army, I'd do just what Charion did. Then I'd have a gang of tough guys waiting over the border for me."

Gordius wagged his head. "I am all confused, Rollin. Charion's arguments still appear logical to me, but if things are as you say . . . Look, it could not be that Charion plans to lead barbarians into Logaia; he has no quality of leadership. They would not follow him."

"Didn't say he was. Just said you want to be careful."

"Yes, yes, I suppose so. I'll tell Valangas to make a search for evidence, and to begin re-enlisting troops . . ."

"What makes you so sure of Valangas?"

"Oh, he is a soldier, my boy, and we can rely on his word."

"Seems to me he acted damned cheerful yesterday, just the way Valturus did."

"O my Nois! You're a most suspicious young man, Rollin. But—very well, then, instead of Valangas I'll put the matter up to Laus—"

"Yeah? What makes you so sure—"

"Rollin!" cried the king, "you're being insufferable! I have to trust *somebody*. What logical reason can you give for suspecting Laus?"

"No logical reason; I was just suggesting that you don't trust anybody until you know better where you stand." He stood up. "Anyway, it's your baby, King. Handle it the way you think best. I'm leaving."

"Leaving? I don't understand!"

"You will." Hobart headed for the door. This time he was going to try the simplest method: to go to his room, get his baggage, and walk out the front door in plain daylight. They could make what they liked of it.

"Rollin, I demand an explanation! You cannot desert me at such a time for no reason at all!"

"Okay," said Hobart. "I'm leaving because—"

He stopped in mid-sentence as Theiax strolled into the room. It would not do to state bluntly, as he had intended, that he simply would not let them make a prince and a king's son-in-law of him—not in front of the social lion, unless he wanted to commit suicide.

"Skip it," he said. "I'll stay. But if you want my advice you'd better take it. First-off, better round up the royal family; they're all in the same boat, so you should be able to trust them. Then collect some really trustworthy palace guards and servants—"

A voice announced through the speaking tube: "Your Altitude, his Superiority the Chancellor of Logaia!"

"Send him away!" hissed Hobart.

"Send—" began the king. But then the door opened without a knock, and Charion stood in the entrance, with a long black cloak over his blue skin-suit.

The king stammered: "I—uh—c-c-cannot see you now, Charion . . ."

The Chancellor frowned. "Is Your Altitude ill?"

"No, but—"

"Then, in my official capacity, I have precedence over Prince Rollin," snapped the Chancellor.

"But—"

"Either I am Chancellor, and have precedence, or I am not and don't. Which shall it be?"

The king almost wept. "Please, good Charion, later . . ."

Charion glared at Hobart, who returned the look stonily. The Chancellor turned on his heel and went out, slamming the door behind him.

"Now," said Hobart, "let's see a list of the people and weapons available in the palace. When we know where we stand . . ."

Thirty minutes later the Xerophi family had been assembled in the study, together with a few hastily collected weapons such as the king's ornamental but still usable swords of state, and a crossbow with which His Altitude had once shot a singularly ferocious wild beast and which had been kept in a glass case ever since. A couple of trusted sentries had been posted in the hall leading to the study with instructions to let nobody by.

The king said: "Won't it be time for lunch soon, Rollin?"

"To hell with lunch. If Charion has half a brain he'll be organizing a palace revolution right this minute. This has been coming up for some time; evidently my arrival forced their hand, as witness that attempt to murder you on the hunt . . . Hello, what's that?"

There were footsteps in the corridor, then voices, louder and louder. *Boom!*

Running steps approached; one of the sentries, Averoves, hurled himself into the study. "They shot Seivus when he stopped them!" he cried.

Queen Vasalina began to weep. Tramp, tramp, and down the hall came a group of men, led by General Valangas with a smoking pistol in his hand. After him came Charion, the Wizard of Wall Street, and three tough-looking parties with swords.

"Come out quietly," roared the general, "or we'll come in and get you!"

There was a blur of movement past Hobart; Averoves the sentry had hurled his spear at Valangas. It struck the brass holder of the plume that towered up from his helmet, knocking the helmet off.

"There's your assassin," said Hobart. Under the helmet Valangas's scalp was smoothly shaven.

The king cried: "A black wig—he must have worn it to hide the fact that he was a blond barbarian—"

He was cut off by a thunderous snarl from Theiax, who slunk into the doorway with his ears laid flat and crouched to spring.

Laus whipped a wand from his robe, pointed it at the lion, and began:

"Beilavor gofarser

"Norpoto wemoilou . . ."

"Where the hell—" breathed Hobart anxiously; then he spotted the crossbow in Prince Alaxius' nerveless fingers; snatched it and discharged it at the wizard. At the twang of the bow Laus screeched and tumbled backwards, though Hobart could not see where the bolt had gone. He reached past Theiax and slammed the heavy door, bolted it, and with

Averoves' help shoved a couch in front of it. A terrific thump told that the attack on the door had begun.

"Alaxius!" cried Hobart. "Take a sword—"

"I c-cannot—I'm afraid—"

"Oh hell, then you barricade the other door before they start coming in that way. A gun, a gun, my kingdom for a gun. Hey, what's that?" He pointed at one of the little cannon that had been turned into a plantholder. Without waiting for an answer he tore the plant out by the roots and dropped it; upended the gun and brought it down on the floor to shake the rest of the dirt out, ignoring a bleat of "My rug!" from the Queen.

"Can I do something, sir?" queried Prince Aites, eyes full of worship.

"Maybe—say, that pile of your old junk! Firecrackers?"

"Yes, sir—"

"That's luck! Get 'em out; break 'em open and pour the powder down this little darling!"

"I have some old iron shot, too—"

"Better and better!" They worked frantically; a double handful of iron balls followed the powder into the gun's maw. The door began to bulge and crack from the battering, and there were voices through the other door, too.

"What'll we mount it on?" mused Hobart. "Got any string?" The king produced a ball of twine from his desk; Hobart lashed the cannon to a chair.

"That string won't hold," said Averoves dubiously.

"Doesn't matter; we'll only fire it once. Look, everybody: Aites, take the crossbow. Argimanda, you and the Queen haul that sofa away and open the door—not now, when I tell you to. I'll fire the gun; Aites, shoot the crossbow at the same time. Then the king and Averoves and I will go after them with our swords—you, too, Theiax. All set?"

He poured the rest of the powder into the touch-hole, twisted up a morning paper, and lighted one end of it with his cigarette-lighter. "Stand clear of the gun, everybody!"

The door opened just as the rebels swung back their improvised battering ram for another blow. They stood uncertainly for two ticks of the clock; then Valangas started to stoop for his pistol. Hobart lowered his torch.

Wham! The room shook to the concussion; gun and chair flew backwards and whanged against the far wall. Hobart and his party charged through the smoke. Hobart struck once, half-blindly; his blade clanged against a brass breastplate; then they were out in the hall pounding after a couple of running figures. They got to the front entrance to see Valangas and two other men vault into saddles and gallop out, bending over their mounts' necks.

"Let 'em go," said Hobart; "there may be some more."

They retraced their steps, passing the sentry Valangas had shot. Between this point and the study door lay three men: Charion and two of the tough strangers. Theiax crouched over one of the latter and crunched.

"Where's Laus?" asked Hobart. Just then a shriek came from the study. They clanked back to it, to find a trembling Alaxius and a fluttering, hysterical Queen.

"The Wizard!" screamed Vasalina. "He took her! Through the window!"

Theiax bounded to the embrasure and reared against it, foaming and filling the room with deafening roars. When conversation was again possible, it was explained that Laus, in the form of a giant pig, had burst open the side-door and scattered Alaxius' barricade; had resumed his proper shape and seized Argimanda. Then his robe developed a pair of wings with which he flew out the window and away.

Queen Vasalina became incoherent at this point. King Gordius said: "Rollin, my son, you must lose no time: while Laus holds my daughter as a hostage, Valangas will be gathering the barbarians!"

"Me?" said Hobart stupidly.

"Of course, it is you who will rescue her! I am too old, and Alaxius thinks of nothing but his own safety. When you have done so, I shall have to give you the other half of the kingdom. So you will be King of Logaia!"

"Oh my God," muttered Hobart through clenched teeth. He turned on the king. "Hadn't you better put off this king business for a while, sir? I haven't any experience—"

"Nonsense, my boy! After all you've done for us; saved my life twice so far—"

"That was just dumb luck—"

"Modesty, son, modesty; anyway the deed transferring my rights to you is all made out, and Argimanda's husband must have a position commensurate . . ."

Hobart clenched his fists to keep from screaming "I don't want your daughter, or your kingdom, or anything to do with you! I'm an engineer and a bachelor, and all I want is to get back . . ." He would have defied the old boy, at that, but for the sight of Theiax moaning in the corner. If he once agreed to try to rescue Argimanda again, he'd go through with it, he knew. If he could stall off this horrible marriage long enough, maybe he'd find another chance to escape. But if they sewed him up on a life contract, he'd be really trapped: his confounded silly scruples would keep him from walking out on his bride, even with a good excuse. He might even get to *like* it, to pile horror on horror . . .

Theiax stood before him, head cocked anxiously. "We go now?" rumbled the lion. "I go with you. You save me from shrinking to pussy-cat size: I do anything you say."

When Hobart withheld his answer, Theiax's tail swung gently right-left. It seemed likely that Theiax would follow the feline rather than the canine tradition as to the meaning of tail wag.

"All right," groaned Hobart.

*   *

With every step in his campaign, its futility seemed more and more patent to Rollin Hobart. He was supposed (a) to rescue Argimanda, and (b) either to enlist a force of barbarian mercenaries to defend Logaia, or, failing that, to create dissention among the barbarian tribes *a la* Col. Lawrence, in order to gum up the invasion long enough to permit the threatened kingdom to re-arm.

But he had said he would, damn it all, and he'd have to go through with it . . .

The first step, which the Logaians would have never, apparently, have thought of taking for all their pride in their logic, was to learn which way Laus had gone with his captive. A number of the citizens of Oroloia, it transpired, had seen the Wizard of Wall Street fly from the palace grounds. By plotting these observations on a map of the city, Hobart got a very good idea of the direction the kidnapper had taken. Comparison of the street map with one of all Logaia showed that the line of flight, prolonged, led straight to the country of the Parathai, one of the barbarian tribes that was worrying King Gordius.

Of course, thought Hobart, gloomily hefting his sword while waiting for the grooms to bring his horse

and other accessories, Laus might change his direction
—circle or zigzag to throw possible pursuers off . . .
But he would have to chance that. And it was not too
unlikely that the wizard would have flown in a bee-
line for his hideout, if he had a hideout. The people
of this world were as utterly un-subtle as they very
well could be.

He swished the sword about. Damn nonsense, he
thought; give me a Tommy gun any day. He didn't
know a thing about sword play and was not anxious
to learn. But since the only firearms available were
matchlocks that took minutes to reload, he might
have to fall back on the fool snickersnee yet.

Finally, having endured the tearful embraces of
the elder Xerophi, Rollin Hobart mounted his horse
with a clank and set out for Barbaria—probably, he
reflected ruefully, the most unwilling knight-errant
that this world of noble heroes and dastardly villains
had ever seen.

9

In the second day of Rollin Hobart's entry into Barbaria, he was winding among the cylindrical mesas that rose on all sides when Theiax growled.

Hobart pulled up. The lion stood with spread feet, yellow eyes fixed and tail twitching.

"Men come," he muttered.

Well, that was all right: he would hoist the Logaian standard—a miniature of King Gordius' own, complete to the word RAIT—and they would understand that he was an ambassador and that his person was inviolate.

Hooves drummed softly on the sand, and a troop of armed horsemen trotted around a mesa. At the sight of Hobart and his companion they broke into shrill barking cries and a gallop. Hobart raised the standard: the men came on the faster. Wait a minute; *maybe* these guys knew about inviolate ambassadors and then again— An arrow whistled overhead, and another. Theiax snarled: "We run or fight, Prince?"

The quick-thinking part of Hobart's mind labored

to convince the rest of it that these men were out to kill him; that they could actually do it—kill *him*, a real person—as his fingers fumbled belatedly for his lighter. He dropped the standard, cocked his piece, lit and blew the match, and swung the barrel to cover the horsemen just before they arrived. Theiax gave a terrible roar that echoed among the mesas, and crouched.

At the last minute the charge split; the men as they pounded past leaned over the far sides of their horses to keep the animals' bodies between them and the musket. Hobart yelled: "Pick up the standard, Theiax!"

The charge came to a skidding, dust-kicking halt; Hobart found himself surrounded by men who bent bows or pointed lances at him, or idly twirled swords. He twisted back and forth in the saddle, swinging the musket, but he obviously could not menace every point of the compass at once. If one of them actually took a swipe at him he would have to fire, and the rest would cut him down in fiftieth of the time necessary to reload. The only scant comfort was the thought that flight would probably not have worked either.

"Envoy!" shouted Hobart. Then: "What's the matter, don't you understand Engl—Logaian?"

The men wore tall hats of black fleece, from under which brassy-yellow hair descended to their shoulders. Long loose pants and soft-leather shoes completed their costume. Instead of answering him, they began to laugh, loudly and yet more loudly. They were looking at Theiax.

The social lion was sitting up on his haunches, holding the standard upright with his forepaws. He rolled a disgusted eye up at Hobart. "What is this, trick?" he inquired. "This is no time for tricks. I am made fool of."

Hobart reached down and took the standard. "Well?" he snapped.

A couple of the men exchanged comments, but in a language Hobart did not understand. Theiax emitted a few low growls. Hobart faced away from the lion, swinging the musket slowly, the butt tucked under his right arm. He took time for a quick blow on the match, at which it brightened.

One of the men spoke unintelligibly to him, and answered in the same tongue his statement that he was the ambassador of King Gordius and demanded to be taken to their big shot. After several repetitions and much pointing at the standard, the barbarians seemed to get the idea. They motioned to Hobart and began to move off the way they had come, still surrounding him.

*   *   *

Khurav, the Sham of the Parathai, was a fine-looking man; a jewelled baldric slanted across his broad bare chest and supported a prodigious sword. He was now putting a question in his own language to Hobart's escort. The engineer could not understand the replies, but he guessed that they ran something like: "O Sham, we found this stranger near the border of Logaia, and this tame lion with him. We would have slain them, but the stranger claimed to be an ambassador . . ." Probably the escort did not add that Theiax's growls and his cocked musket had helped to dissuade them from their intention of carving him into little bits.

Khurav now addressed Hobart directly, in slow and carefully enunciated Logaian—or English: "Do-you-seek-audience-with-me?"

"Yes," said Hobart. "You're the Sham of the Parathai, aren't you?"

Khurav frowned. "Do-you-want-to-deny-it?"

"Not at all; just asked." Hobart identified himself, whereat Khurav frowned some more.

"My men say," remarked the barbarian, "when they found you, this tame lion was holding the standard. How do I know he is not the ambassador?"

Theiax looked bewildered; then he opened his mouth and gave a peculiar roar that started shrill and cascaded down the scale. He repeated this sound several times, and finally rolled over on his back, waving his paws. "I laugh!" he coughed. "I am ambassador! This is funny trick! I laugh some more!" Wherewith he repeated his sliding grunt.

"He means," said Hobart, "that he is not the ambassador."

"So I hear," said Khurav. "But I do not like to be laughed at. Am I being insulted?"

"No, no!" cried Hobart. This fellow was going to be difficult. He remembered King Gordius' last caution: "Watch out for Khurav, son; he's said to be a proud sort of barbarian."

As if the Sham had not sufficiently displayed his pride already, he now bent a hostile glare on Hobart's musket.

He said: "You threaten me with a lighted gun, Prince Rollin. Is it that you wish to challenge me to a duel?"

Hobart wearily pinched out the glowing end of the match. He apologized for the gun, for Theiax's behavior, and for having been born. He finally dampened down Khurav's supicions to the point where the Sham invited him into his huge felt tent. Khurav paused inside the threshold and gestured expansively.

"You are my guest, Prince Rollin. All this is yours. All that is mine is yours."

"You're much too kind," said Hobart, assuming that this was just a formula.

"No, I am not. We Parathai are hospitable. Therefore I am hospitable. Of course," he continued, "it is likewise true that all that is yours is also mine. For instance, I should like the gold chain on that strange-colored garment you wear."

Hobart, mastering his resentment, unsnapped his watch-chain and handed it over. He managed to do it without exposing the actual watch, for fear that Khurav should take a fancy to that, too.

"Sit," said the chieftain, doing so, "and tell me why you come."

"Several reasons," said Hobart, wondering how to begin. "First: I'd like to extradite a fugitive from Logaian justice, one Laus, formerly the court wizard."

"Is he the one who flew over this country three days ago?"

"Guess he is. How about it?"

"He is not in my territory. He continued beyond the border; perhaps he landed in the country of the Marathai."

"Your neighbors?" queried Hobart, who had not yet gotten all the barbarian tribes straight.

"Our immemorial enemies," corrected Khurav. "So I do not see how you can get your wizard."

Hobart mused: "I could visit the chief of the Marathai."

"No," said Khurav flatly.

"Why not?"

"They are our enemies. You are our friend. Therefore you are their enemy. It is obvious. If you were their friend, you would be our enemy and I should have to kill you."

Hobart sighed; no matter how carefully you handled the Sham, the conversation was apt to turn dangerous. Wait, there was a possibility—"Are you at war with the Marathai at present?"

"We are, but there is no fighting."

"How so?"

"They have guns. We warned them long ago that if they ever adopted such an unfair method of warfare, we should refuse to fight with them any longer. They have chosen to disregard our ultimatum."

"Haven't you any guns?"

"One or two, as curiosities. I am much too proud to make use of them."

Hobart began to feel excitement despite himself. He leaned forward and asked: "Any idea where they got these guns?"

"It is believed that they were sent from Logaia, though I do not know why King Gordius should be so stupid as to arm his enemies."

Hobart almost blurted that Gordius' stupidity had been of another order before he remembered that a diplomat should never give anything away without getting something much better in return. He suggested: "Strong as Logaia is, there's no doubt that we'd welcome help from such tough fighters as the Parathai. If you'd like to help us against the Marathai, we could make it worth your while . . ."

But the Sham was leaning forward with a hostile glitter. "Prince Rollin, are you insulting me? Do you not know that I am much too proud to serve as a hired mercenary?"

"N-no—no offense, Sham—"

"Of course," said Khurav relaxing a little, "if King Gordius chose to send me a gift, I should have to repay it; in services, if desired. Though how we could resume normal hostilities with such faithless ones as the—"

"Fine, fine," interrupted Hobart quickly. "Consider it settled; I'll take the matter up with Gordius first thing. By the way, have you heard anything of our runaway general, Valangas?"

"Do you mean the son of the Sham of the Marathai, Baramyash? He but recently returned to his ancestral home."

"Sounds like the same one."

"It could be; he would have Logaianized his name while among you. But come, it is dinner-time." And Khurav rose abruptly and led the way to another compartment of the tent.

The first course consisted of lamb, roasted. It was served by a pair of husky, good-looking blond wenches in beaded finery and things that jangled when they moved. Khurav, mouth full of mutton, waved at the girls. "My wives," he said, and took an enormous gulp of wine. "Which will you have?"

"Uh—*what?*"

"Which will you have? You did not think I lied when I said that all of mine was yours, did you? That would be an insult to my hospitality!"

"I—uh—could I decide later, please?"

"If you wish. You may have both if you insist, but I pray you will leave me one, for I am fond of them."

The next course was lamb, boiled. Hobart had thought he was in a complex predicament when he had learned of the Xerophi family's plans for him. That was all *he* had known about complex predicaments! The fearfully perfect Argimanda would have been trial enough, but a she-barbarian—who according to the rules of this world would be one hundred percent barbarous . . . Let's see; he couldn't protest that he was already married, or about to be; Khurav evidently saw nothing out of the way about polygyny. If he refused the gift, the Sham would be offended and carve him. If he claimed he was . . .

The third course was lamb, fricasseed. Khurav talked ponderously of his people's herds, of the troubles of keeping the wolves from the sheep and the lions from the camels. Hobart foresaw the end of his capacity for lamb; he did not dare stop completely, so diddled with his food. He took a sip of Khurav's excellent wine for every gulp on the part of the Sham.

Khurav crammed the last pound of lamb into his mouth with both hands, and washed it down with a whole goblet. Then he leaned toward Hobart—they were sitting cross-legged on mats—and belched, horrendously.

Hobart, though not normally squeamish, flinched. Khurav looked pleased for the first time since Hobart had met him. "Thad was goode wan," he drawled. "You do battair, Preence!" He suddenly acquired a thick accent, and Hobart was alarmed to see that his host had become quite drunk.

Hobart opened his mouth and stretched his esophagus, but no belch came.

"Cawm," reiterated the Sham. "Like thees!" The rugged face opened again, and out came another collossal burp.

Hobart tried again, with no more result.

Khurav frowned. "Id is rude, not to belch. You do, queeck, now!"

Hobart tried desperately to conform to barbarian etiquette. "I can't!" he cried finally.

Khurav's scowl became Stygian. His lip lifted in a snarl. "So! You insuld my hospitality! You want to fighd, yez? Cawm on!" The chieftain bounded to his feet—he was evidently one of those whose physical reflexes were not disorganized by intoxication. He snatched out his sword. "Ub!" he shouted. When Hobart hesitated, Khurav reached down and yanked him to his feet.

"Theiax!" yelled Hobart as he was marched out the entrance of the big tent.

Khurav jerked him around and stared at his face.

"Thad lion, yez? Ho, ho!" He raised his voice to a bellow: *"Adshar! Fruz! Yezdeg!"*

"Thu, Sham! Thu, Sham!" answered the darkness, and men materialized into the torchlight. Khurav snarled a question at them; they answered. Some ran off. There was a rattle of chains and a startled roar from a freshly awakened Theiax. The roars rose to frenzied volume and the chains clanked, but the Parathai must have trussed him well.

Khurav faced Hobart, who was still protesting innocence of wrong intent. The chief rasped: "You have no shield? Then I nod use either. Draw" He put his left arm behind him like a German *Sabel* fencer and stamped his feet. His eyes reflected little yellow torch-flames.

"But—" screamed Hobart.

Swish! The huge blade clipped a lock of hair from Hobart's head. "Draw!" bawled Khurav, "or I keel you anyway!"

Rollin Hobart drew. He would probably be dead in a matter of minutes, but by God one howling barbarian would know he'd been in a fight!

There was little science on either side. Hobart sprang in with a full-armed slash. The blades clanged, and Hobart backed and parried the Sham's ferocious downright cut. The blow nearly disarmed the engineer, and twisted the blade in his hand. Then his eye fixed itself on a patch of bare skin: Kurav's sword-hand, protected by no more than a cross-bar on the hilt. Hobart swept his blade up and then down in a backhand slash; felt it smack.

Khurav's sword dropped to the sand, and the big man stared at his right hand. It had a weal across the back, but that was all, and Hobart realized in a flash that he had struck it with the flat. Time was wasting, though. The unwilling duellist brought his blade down hard, flat-wise on Khurav's skull, thump!

Khurav reeled under the blow and sat down. He looked up, blinking; tried thickly to speak. Then he dragged himself slowly up. When he was drawn painfully to his full height, he folded his arms, facing Rollin Hobart.

"Kill me," he said shortly.

"Why? I don't want to!"

"Kill me, I say. I am much too proud to live after you have humbled me."

"Aw, don't be silly, Khurav! That was just an accident; shouldn't have been any fight in the first place!"

"You will not? Very well." The Sham shrugged and turned to one of the circle of spectators. Words passed; the man took out a sword. Khurav knelt in front of him and bowed his head and pushed his hair forward from his thick neck.

Hobart stared in horrified fascination. The Parathaian spit on his hands, took a careful stance, and swung his sword up—and *down*—Hobart shut his eyes just before blade met neck; he could not, unfortunately, shut his ears. *Chug, thump!*

A strange sound rose from the circle of watchers, and grew: the sound of men sobbing. The tears were running down into the beards of the barbarians as they reassembled the corpse of the late Khurav and reverently removed it.

And now, wondered Hobart, what would they do with—or to—him? Probably kill him, though for several minutes they had let him stand unmolested with sword in hand. Their attention was on the group carrying off the corpse. Maybe he could slip away in the darkness . . . Wait, he'd have to release Theiax first. Of course it had been Theiax's own idea to come, but still one couldn't walk out on . . .

He began to pick his way toward the direction from which the social lion's roars had come, and were still coming, muted to a continuous snarl. He had taken no more than ten steps among the tents when horny hands grabbed him from behind and hustled him back into the torchlight.

They were all around, shouting and waving lethal weapons. One of them stuck a whiskered face practically against Hobart's own, screaming: *"Fez parethvi ush lokh Sham! Ush Sham Parathen!!"* All were howling *"Ush Sham Parathen!"* No doubt they were telling him what was to be done to him for causing the death of the Sham of the Parathai . . .

A hawk-nosed oldster in a tall felt hat with ear-flaps was trying to hush them. When this had been accomplished, he addressed Hobart in very broken Logaian: "They—say—you—new—Sham."

"I—what?"

"You new Sham; Sham of Parathai."

"But—but I don't *want* to be the new Sham! All I want—"

"Too bad you not like," said the old man complacently, "But too late. You beat Khurav; you Sham anyway. Now we—uh—*yavzi*—you know—elevate you!"

Which they did with rough enthusiasm, hoisting Hobart to a sitting position on a shield carried on stalwart shoulders. For at least an hour they paraded around the camp, the men singing while the women screeched and waved torches and the children bawled.

Hobart's protests and requests to let him unhitch Theiax went unheard and unheeded. The old man was the only barbarian he had met besides Khurav with whom he could communicate, and the elder was lost in the torch-splashed shuffle.

He rematerialized when the shield-bearers finally put Hobart down in front of his tent, saying: "You not go yet; Parathai must swear loyalty!"

The old boy took his place at the head of the line that was rapidly forming. He seized and wrung Hobart's hand vigorously and rattled off a sentence in Parathaian. He moved on, and the next man repeated the performance. And the next and the next. By the time he had shaken a hundred hands, Hobart's own hand began to ache. At two hundred it was swollen and red, and his feet were bothering him. At three hundred his eyes were glassy and he was swaying with fatigue. At five hundred . . .

He never know how he stuck it out, with each handclasp shooting pains up to his elbow. At last, wonder of wonders, the end of the line drew near. Hobart touched the last man's hand briefly, snatching it away before a squeeze could be applied, and thanking God that the women didn't have to swear fealty, too.

He turned dead eyes on the oldster. "May I go now?" The man nodded; Hobart added: "What's your name?"

"Sanyesh, chief of hundred families."

"Okay, Sanyesh; I'll want to see you first thing in the morning." Hobart slouched into the tent—and his arms were seized from the two sides. Hobart gave one more convulsive start—assassins?—and there was feminine laughter and the jingle of ornaments.

Behind him came the reedy voice of Sanyesh:

"These your wives, Sham. Thought you like know, yes?"

"But I don't *want*—"

"Too bad, but you beat Khurav, so they yours. Is all done. They nice girls, so you not disappoint them, no? Good-night."

Rollin Hobart stuffed his handkerchief into his mouth to keep from screaming.

10

KHURAV'S WIDOWS SERVED Hobart breakfast when he awoke. They waited on him assiduously, but with reproachful looks that said as plainly as words: "In what way have we displeased you, lord?" Well, they would have to bear their disappointment as best they could. Even if the spirit had been willing . . .

The breakfast comprised a mess of assorted organs and glands from one of the tribal sheep: probably, thought Hobart, the one whose meat he had eaten the night before. It was no doubt economical, and necessary to keep the barbarians supplied with vitamins. But he'd be damned if anyone would make him like it.

The trouble with him was that he was too easy-going; too readily persuaded into accepting responsibilities, each of which merely led in this crazy world to more responsibilities, so that his goal of return to his own earth and work receded farther the more he pursued it. Well, what else could he have done? Every time he tried to take a firm stand, Theiax came along with his mouthful of teeth, or the barbarians with their swords, and bullied him into further commitments. Perhaps if he began by bumping off Theiax—but no, he couldn't do that. Treachery was not one of his faults, and besides the social lion was an amusing and likeable companion.

He'd have to go through with or evade his present commitments as best he could. The official positions that had been forced upon him should not be entirely disadvantageous; he might be able to use his prerogatives to locate Hoimon the ascetic . . .

He shooed his "wives" out before dressing, a procedure that utterly mystified them, and went in search of Theiax. The lion was duly found and unchained, but, understandably, chose to be one hundred percent sulky. Even when Hobart had explained everything there was to explain, Theiax averted his eyes to the ground, grumbling:

"I am treated badly. I am humiliated. I think you are my friend, but you let these ignorant ones tie me up like pig. I lose my dignity!"

"Aw, come on, Theiax," urged Hobart. "I was practically dead when they finished with me last night. And everything will be okay from now on. Look, would it make you happy if I did a trick for you? Stood on my head, for instance?"

Theiax's mouth twitched, and he burst into one of the high-low roars that served him as laughter. "You are funny, Prince! All right, I be good." And the lion frisked down the path between the tents ahead of Hobart like a puppy.

Shortly after Hobart had returned to the Sham's tent, one of the widows announced: "*Zhizda Sanyesh Veg,*" and sure enough it was the old chief of a hundred families.

Hobart set about, first, methodically questioning Sanyesh about the rights and duties of a Sham. He was slightly shocked at the extent to which the former outweighed the latter. Perhaps if he stayed with the Parathai long enough he could teach them something about constitutional government—no, no, no, Rollin! Keep your eye on the ball! It probably wouldn't work with these illiterates anyway . . .

It transpired that one of his first jobs would be to select a bodyguard of retainers from among the stalwarts of the nation, who would accompany him wherever he went. Why must they? Oh, explained Sanyesh haltingly, a Sham was always accompanied by retainers; that was one of the ways you knew he was a Sham. But Hobart's counsellor agreed that there was no immediate rush about selecting the guard.

"Well," said Hobart, "what would you say to an invasion of the country of the Marathai?" Not that he approved of invasions generally or soldiering by Rollin Hobart in particular, but it seemed the only course open to him.

Sanyesh raised his white eyebrows. "Guns?"

Hm, that was a poser. The Marathai had practically all of Logaia's firearms, and because of distances and poor communications it would take all eternity to collect an equal armament from the other civilized states such as Psythoris. The Parathai had only hand weapons; their prospective foes had these *and* guns *and* probably Laus's magic. Formidable as the Parathai looked, Hobart had heard them and the other barbarians spoken of in Oroloia as "fickle." Assuming that the description applied with the usual literalness, that probably meant that the barbarian warriors could be counted upon to make one reckless attack with fearsome whoops, and then to run away at the first check. Unless, of course, their leader were a second Ghenghiz Khan, which Rollin Hobart emphatically was not.

But if superiority in fire-power were unobtainable, what about superiority in magic? He asked Sanyesh: "Are there any wizards or sorcerers in the tribe?"

"Was," shrugged the old man.

"What do you mean, was?"

"Was shaman and two assistant shamans."

"Where are they now?"

"Dead. They say, Khurav should fight Marathai hard, with guns and everything, or make peace. He think they insult him."

"Are there *any* good magicians in or near Parathaia?"

Sanyesh pondered. "Ikthepeli have medicine-man. Not much good. Ikthepeli just dirty savages, not know anything."

The Ikthepeli lived quite a distance off, so Hobart decided it was too late in the day to set out. He spent the rest of the day trying to learn from Sanyesh the rudiments of the Parathaian language. Here he encountered a practical example of the fact that a good engineer is seldom a good linguist and vice versa. By the end of the day he had memorized perhaps a score of words, but had not gotten to first base on the formidable Parathai grammar, in which there seemed to be almost as many declensions as there were nouns and almost as many conjugations as there were verbs.

The widows, in an effort to propitiate their new lord and master, had prepared him an extra-special dinner: lamb, barbecued. Hobart hurried through the meal; afterwards he gave Sanyesh, who would have liked to sit and drink and talk all night, a polite bum's rush. Then he hastened to the sleeping-compartment of the tent, wanting to begin his slumber early enough not to mind getting up before dawn—only to find the widows planted before it, wreathed in anticipatory smiles that chilled his blood.

He jerked his thumb. "On your way, girls!"

The widows looked blank. The taller one, Khvarizud, said plaintively: "*Bish er unzen math shaliv gvirsha?*"

"I don't understand you, so no use talking. I'm going to sleep, without benefit of quotes. One side, please."

"*A, buzd unzen Sham Shamzi yala?*"

Hobart got enough of this sentence to infer that they were asking whether there was anything wrong with him. He reddened and shouted rudely: "Get out!" They understood the tone, and, scared and perplexed, got.

*   *   *

Sanyesh squinted at the bright sun that had just popped over the horizon, and remarked to Hobart: "Zhav sends hot day."

The news did not cheer the engineer, for he reasoned that the day would be a hundred percent hot—practically incandescent. Fortunately he had left his coat and vest behind. His lips tightened into an even thinner line. Damn this world—or was there something wrong with him, a lack of adaptability that prevented his enjoying even five minutes of the time he had spent here, despite the fantastic honors that the natives insisted on heaping on him? Nonsense! He just knew what he wanted, that was all!

"Who," he asked casually, "is Zhav?" Conversing with Sanyesh was a strain because of the elder's dialect, but the other two Parathaians, Yezdeg and Fruz, who rode with them as a tentative bodyguard, did not speak any Logaian at all. Sanyesh had recommended them, and, after Hobart had agreed to take them, had casually added that they had been cronies of the late Khurav. Though they had so far shown no inclination to avenge the former Sham, their presence made Hobart uneasy, and he kept his musket ready in the crook of his arm.

Sanyesh replied: "Lord of everything."

"A real person, or does he just live in the sky or something?"

"He real. Not live in sky. But lord of all: you, me, lion, weather, everythings."

"Sounds like that Nois the Logaians tell about."

"Same person, different name. Logaians ignorant; not use right name."

Theiax growled: "It is barbarians who are ig—" Hobart turned quickly in the saddle and frowned the social lion to silence. He asked some more about Nois-Zhav, who appeared to hold a position in this world somewhere between the Japanese Emperor and the primitive Jewish Jehovah. Yes, he lived in a real place, in a wild country fifty-four miles beyond the boundaries of Marathaia. Yes, anybody could see him personally about such matters as drouth and pestilence, though not many people did. When asked why more subjects did not take advantage of the accessibility of their god-emperor, Sanyesh shrugged vaguely and said he supposed that Zhav demanded a price for his favors.

They left the sandy mesa-county and crossed a savannah like the one Hobart had hunted the behemoth in, except that this was as flat as a table-top. Later the party stopped and rested for an hour while the horses cropped and Theiax, wrapping his tail around his nose, snored.

When the scorching sun had started down, they crossed another sharp boundary, whereat the savannah changed into a kind of desert. The footing was red sand, with great numbers of spherical black stones lying upon or embedded in it. This desert had some vegetation, in the form of cylindrical cactuslike plants at fifty-foot intervals in neat rows.

They had to walk the horses to minimize the risk of a stumble on the treacherous round stones. Hobart's heart leaped when Sanyesh pointed out to him the shimmer of water ahead. He was sure he had been about to expire of thirst—their water supply was low—and boredom.

"Sure it isn't a mirage?" he asked.

"What is mirage?"

"You know; you see water but it really isn't there."

Sanyesh raised his thin shoulders till they almost touched his ears in a mighty shrug. "No such thing in Parathaia," he said.

He was probably right at that, reflected Hobart; in this world things were always just what they seemed. Sanyesh told him that the body of water ahead was Lake Nithrid. It was a big lake; the far shore was out of sight, or so Hobart thought.

"Can see," said Sanyesh, when Hobart mentioned this. Naturally a barbarian would have keen eyesight. The elder added: "If not, would be sea, not lake."

The cavalcade came to the top of a moderate slope leading down to the lake shore. All at once Hobart saw a lot of little yellow figures moving casually about by the marge. The vision must have been mutual, for as the horses started to pick their skidding way down the slope, the small figures suddenly speeded up their movements like a nest of disturbed ants. Tinny little cries came to Hobart's ears.

The barbarian named Fruz pointed and bellowed something. "He says," translated Sanyesh, "must hurry; Ikthepeli run away."

The horses were encouraged as much as was safe considering the incline. But long before the party reached the bottom, the yellow savages had launched a lot of dugout canoes and were paddling swiftly out over the smiling surface of Lake Nithrid. Fruz and Yezdeg shouted epithets after them as they disappeared into the golden river of reflection painted on the lake by the setting sun.

"Don't seem to trust us, do they?" commented Hobart.

Sanyesh spat his contempt. "Useless ones; no good except to hunt for sport."

If the barbarians were in the habit of killing Ikthepeli for the fun of it, Hobart could see why their reception was not so cordial as it might have been. Holding fast to his determination not to let himself be sidetracked by considerations of moral reform, he asked wearily: "What'll we do now?"

"Find place to sleep," said the hawk-nosed elder. "Sun out soon. Fish-eaters come back."

"When?"

"Tomorrow maybe, maybe not. Nobody know." A shrug implied the unimportance of time.

At the base of the slope were a number of gaping holes; entrances to the caves in which the savages evidently dwelt. The unenthusiastic Sham investigated a couple. They smelled strongly of their recent tenants, and contained a scattering of crude weapons and implements: wooden spears, fish-bone combs, and the like. The afternoon sun had heated them to ovens.

"Look, Sham," said Sanyesh. He indicated another cave across whose entrance a leather curtain was hung. When this was pushed aside, the party gave a simultaneous gasp of delight at the cool air that flowed gently out. At right angles to the curtain, a small groove or trench ran from the floor of the cave and out to lose itself in the sands. A small trickle of water flowed out through this ditch.

"Good for sleep, Sham," said Sanyesh. As he spoke the light dimmed and expired almost as though it had been turned off. The sun had set, and as it was immediately too dark for more exploration, the elder's suggestion seemed the only practical one.

When Theiax volunteered to stand watch, Fruz and Yezdeg looked at the lion for the first time in truly friendly fashion. The human wing of the party made themselves as comfortable as they could in the cool cave and dropped off to sleep as though stunned.

11

LIGHT AND SOUND AWAKENED Rollin Hobart; the former from the cave mouth, where the curtain was thrust aside by Theiax's head, the latter the lion's deep voice: "Yellow men come back, Prince! Wake up!"

The Parathai yawned and stretched themselves out of their respective dreamlands. "What are they doing?" asked Hobart, feeling his teeth with his tongue and wishing for a toothbrush.

The social lion looked back over his shoulder. "Many little boats come. One yellow man gets out, wades, comes on shore. You want I kill him?"

"No, no! I want to see him." Hobart stood up and thrust the curtain entirely to one side. The Ikthepeli canoes were lined up a few yards off shore, packed with yellow humanity with no signs of hostile intent. Across the beach advanced one of the savages: a squat, middle-aged individual with a face like a disk of wrinkled butter and lank black hair. He wore the skull of a small animal around his neck, and a bone skewer through his nose, but was otherwise unclad.

When he saw the group in the cave-mouth he said something in a high-whining voice and dropped to all fours. He crawled thus toward them with every evidence of the most abject humility.

Yezdeg spat and jerked his thumb toward Hobart, snarling: "*Myavam Sham Parathen irs zamath varaliv Logayag vorara math a gvari!*"

The crawling man raised his head toward Hobart with a slightly less hopeless expression, saying: "You wish to speak with me in Logaian?" He handled the language quite fairly himself.

"Uh-huh," said Hobart. "Stand up, man; I'm not going to hurt you!"

"I plead for my poor people, who never hurt Parathai—" began the savage, getting up.

"Okay, okay; tell 'em to come ashore. If they don't bother us, we won't bother them."

The savage turned and shrilled a command to the people in the boats. Gingerly the canoes were brought up to the land, and timidly the occupants, all ages and sizes, climbed out, each one trying to hide himself behind the others. They were a scrawny lot; from the fact that the one who spoke Logaian looked much the best fed, Hobart guessed that he was the boss.

He said: "We're looking for the medicine man of the Ikthepeli."

"Why do you want him?"

"Business; I think he can help us."

"I am him. I am called Kai."

"Fine! How—"

"*Mizam Zhav!*" cried Fruz. He was staring toward the rear of the cave; the other followed his eyes. By the light that now came through the entrance appeared a sight that made Hobart's scalp prickle: great cakes of ice, on each of which reposed a corpse. The light was strong enough to show bright-red skin.

"What are those?" asked Hobart. "Keeping 'em to bury, or what?"

"No," said Kai indifferently. "To eat."

"*Huh?*"

"Sure. They are Rumatzi we killed in this year's battle."

"You mean you—uh—"

"You did not know? Every winter we cut ice from the lake. In spring we arrange battle with the Rumatzi, who live across the lake. Same number on both sides, same weapons, same everything. We take their deads and they take ours, to eat. Good idea, yes?"

"Not according to my way of thinking," said Hobart.

"But what else to do? Too many people otherwise; not enough fish; we starve; Rumatzi starve. Must kill some, so why not have fun of a battle?"

"Maybe I'm prejudiced, but it still seems a pretty gruesome way of disposing of the casualties."

Kai spread his hands. "You mean fight like horse-people and *not* eat the deads? We think that is bad, wicked business, to kill people for no good reason!"

"Okay, you can eat your own grandmothers as far as I'm concerned. Now how—"

Kai's mouth and eyes widened with horror. "You mean eat one of our own tribe? Why, that would be *cannibal!* That is eating *people!* We eat Rumatzi; they eat us; we are always careful not to mix deads up! You horse people have such bad, wicked ideas!"

"Okay, skip it! We need the help of a competent magician against our enemies, the Marathai—"

"Not me!" interjected Kai. "Not my war! My poor people have enough trouble with Parathai, without getting Marathai down on us, too! Anyway I am not a good magician. I am just a poor hungry Ikthepeli, who knows a couple little tricks to protect me and my poor people!"

"What sort of trouble have you had with my outfit?"

"You will not punish my poor people if I tell?" said Kai, looking uneasily at Hobart's companions.

"Of course not!"

"All right. You could not catch me anyway; I would just disappear, fush-whoosh, but my Ikthepeli can not do that. You ask for trouble. What you call trouble. Is it trouble when your horsemens come by on horses and chop up our canoes to make a fire?"

"Yes, I'd say it was," said Hobart judiciously.

"Is it trouble when they take away our only net, that took a year to make, so we have to spear fish until we make another?"

"Undoubtedly."

Kai stood upright now, his former hangdog air gone as his anger rose. "How then, you call it trouble when they rape our women, right here on beach, in front of whole tribe? Trouble when they kill women's men when they try to stop them? Three men killed—let me count—fifteen days ago. Rest not killed because they ran fast. One killed four days ago; we found him dead with Parathai arrow. One of your horse people thought it funny to shoot. What do you say now, Sham?"

Hobart was by this time almost as indignant as the medicine man. He snapped, "I'll soon put a stop to that. But wait—how about your help?"

Kai looked crafty, but so openly and transparently so that the effect was more amusing than sinister. He said at last: "If you will really stop Parathai from hurting us, I will help. But can you? They are proud people."

"I'll do my best. If they commit anything on you, I'll punish them as though it were on a member of their own nation. But what's your help going to consist of? Are you really a poor magician, or was that just a gag?"

"I am not very good, but I will do my best, too. Maybe I know more than just a couple tricks."

"Such as?"

"Oh, I will not tell that. Secret of trade, yes, ha-ha?"

"Ha-ha yourself," smiled Hobart. "You'd better show me at least a sample."

"I can do." Kai turned to the clear sky and extended his hands, palms up. He began an ululating wail:

> "*Marekula eromanga,*
> "*Savaii upolu!*
> "*Maalaea topanga*
> "*Nukunana kandavu,*
> "*Pag pago oamaru!*"

A few hundred feet up, a small cloud formed; at first like one of those that mark an ordinary thermal; then boiling more and more furiously, like a miniature thunderhead. Kai's voice rose to a shriek, and he clapped his hands. At once a narrow shaft of rain poured down from the cloudlet; it was no trouble to watch the dark streamer extend earthward. It took it two or three minutes to reach the surface of the lake, where it churned the smooth surface in a fifty-foot circle tangent to the shore-line.

Kai clapped his hands twice, and the rain was sharply cut off at the source. By the time the drops that had already started down from the cloud had all struck the lake, the cloud itself had evaporated. Kai turned to Hobart with a grin: "I have a couple tricks, yes?"

"Evidently. Want to get your stuff ready to come with us?"

"Me come with you? No sir! Not me! I fear Parathai, and my poor people need me. Look!" He took off his necklace with its little rodent skull, and hung it around the engineer's neck. "When you want me, take hold of the skull and squeeze—not hard, or it breaks—and call me. I come, foosh! But three times only; it will not work after that."

"Well—" said Hobart doubtfully.

"Do not worry; I come! I must protect my people." Kai stiffened, a far-away look coming into his eyes. He pulled several slivers of bone out of top-knot, tossed them into the air, and studied the positions in which they fell to the ground.

"Ha!" he cried tensely. "Now, Sham, you can show me if you mean what you say. I gave you a sample magic; you give me a sample justice. One of your Parathai has just killed one of my poor people!"

"*What?*" Hobart looked wildly around; Yezdeg was plainly missing.

"Yes. He took the wife of Aao. We think it is a bad, wicked thing to take another man's wife. The last time it happened, in my father's days, we gave the bad man to Rumatzi to eat. But that is not all: the wife of Aao fought your horseman, and he got angry and killed her. Now, will you kill your horseman?"

"*Whew!*" whistled Hobart. As usual, just when he had been about to draw a breath of relief, it transpired that his apparent piece of astounding good luck had a catch in it. In this case the worm had contained an exceptionally vicious hook: he was committed to having one of his new subjects executed.

He turned to Sanyesh: "Will you—" But he stopped at the elder's stony expression. He could trust nobody but himself to find Yezdeg, investigate the alleged murder, and deal impartial justice.

He picked up his musket, and said "Come on!" and strode out to where Theiax guarded the horses, to the uneasy displeasure of the latter. There were only three horses, a fact that blasted Hobart's lingering hope that he might find Yezdeg innocently snoozing in the neighborhood. The Ikthepeli gave all the party a wide berth, hovering ready for a dash to their canoes, except for Kai, who followed sticking the skewers back in his hair.

"Better come along and see how this turns out," Hobart told him.

But Kai shook his head stubbornly, and Hobart, intercepting the glares that Sanyesh and Fruz focused on the medicine man, could not blame him. Kai explained: "My bones will tell me, Sham!"

Hobart mounted and led the way to the top of the slope. The flat, cactus-studded desert spread out before them, and Hobart immediately saw in the distance a horseman ambling peacefully toward them on a yellow horse. It was Yezdeg without a doubt.

A muttered conversation between Fruz and Sanyesh behind him made the skin of his back crawl, though he could not understand a word. It would be bad enough to have to kill a man, without risking retaliation by the deceased's friends.

The two Parathai were evidently thinking along similar lines, for Sanyesh cried sharply: "Sham! I heard your talk with savage. You can not shoot Yezdeg for little thing like that! Fruz says so, too."

"What makes you so sure he's guilty?" said Hobart.

"Oh, savage knows. But suppose Yezdeg did? Not crime to kill useless fish-eaters; everybody does. Not like real people."

Rollin Hobart needed just this opposition to make him really determined. "Well, they are real people from now on," he barked. "You heard my agreement."

"But Sham!" persisted Sanyesh. "If she real person, why not act like real person? Real woman like Parathai *never* go around with no clothes if not want man to take. If she real person, then she want man to take, and all her fault. Woman can not say to Parathaian, 'take,' and then hit him when he try to; that insult. If not real person, then no crime to kill anyway."

"Makes no difference," snapped Hobart. "The new law of the Parathai is that the Ikthepeli are real people whether they wear clothes or not, and are to be treated as such. I, the Sham, say so."

But it appeared that the customs of the barbarians were not as easily disposed of as that. Sanyesh continued his argument: "Was not law when Yezdeg killed woman. Can not kill man for breaking law nobody ever heard of!"

It was true; there was even a provision in the U.S. Constitution against *ex post facto* laws. Besides Sanyesh and Fruz were by now gently fingering their sword hilts, the elder apologetically, the young retainer defiantly. The implication was that he might shoot one of the three, but the survivors would make sure he had no chance to reload.

By now Yezdeg was close enough for a hail, the sun gleaming on his yellow hair. He was caroling a song as if he had not a care in the world, and wiping an obviously bloody knife with a piece of thin leather.

The other two Parathai tensed themselves, watching Hobart. But the engineer merely said: "Time to start for home, boys," and led off.

After they had ridden a while in silence, Hobart pulled alongside of Sanyesh and asked: "I ought to know more about the laws of the Parathai. You recognize the right of self-defense?"

"That's so," said the counsellor, not at all chummy.

"How about duels?"

"We have. Depends. If fair fight, same weapons, same everything, no crime. If you pick fight and have big advantage, like gun, counts like murder.

Man's family can take you before tribal assembly and get permission to kill you."

"How about responsibility for agents' acts?"

"What is that?"

"Suppose a man hires another man to kill a third man. Who's the murderer?"

"Each is half murder. Instead of killing one man, we half kill both."

"How would you do that?" asked Hobart, intrigued despite his predicament.

"Easy; cut off heads halfway."

Hobart abandoned a nascent idea of sicking Theiax on the unregenerate Yezdeg. As far as he was concerned there was no distinction between being decapitated halfway and completely. He would have to get Yezdeg killed by some less direct method.

Not that Hobart wanted to kill Yezdeg or anybody else, abhorrent though the young barbarian's act seemed to him. But he'd promised Gordius, and he'd promised Kai . . .

"Damn all promises!" he said aloud.

He jogged along in deep thought for a while. Then he directed Sanyesh: "Tell Yezdeg that he's evidently brave enough to kill a woman."

Sanyesh gave Hobart a glance glittering with suspicion, but spoke a sentence to Yezdeg. The latter seemed puzzled for a while, then answered with a long speech.

"He say," interpreted Sanyesh, "he brave man; killed many Marathai."

"I haven't seen him kill any Marathai, but I do know he killed a woman."

Again the pause for translation; Sanyesh reported: "He say he not kill real woman, only dirty fish-eater."

"Okay," said Hobart amiably. "Then he's brave enough to kill a poor fish-eater woman."

This time Yezdeg frowned. Sanyesh announced: "He say he brave enough to kill fish-eater, or real woman, or real man, or anybody."

"Maybe so. I still haven't seen him kill a real man or even a real woman, but only a poor fish-eater, and a female at that."

When this was reported to Yezdeg, the young man's temper flared. He rose in his stirrups and shouted. When Sanyesh could get in a word, the old man told Hobart: "He say you insult him."

"Not at all," protested Hobart. "I'm just stating facts. You agree, don't you, that I haven't seen him kill any Marathai, and that if he killed the Ikthepeli woman he must obviously have been brave enough to do so?"

"I guess so," said Sanyesh grudgingly.

This time Yezdeg really went off with a bang. He screeched and fingered his hilt menacingly. Hobart had prudently gotten out his cigarette-lighter; he now applied it to the match of his gun.

He remarked as casually as he could manage: "You agree, don't you Sanyesh, that I haven't attacked Yezdeg, and that if he goes for me I'm obviously entitled to shoot him in self-defense?"

"I guess so," muttered Sanyesh.

"Ask Fruz if I'm not right." Fruz agreed in a vague way; the dialectics of the quarrel had gotten beyond his simple mind.

Yezdeg was still shouting. Sanyesh interpreted: "He say he want fight you, but gun against sword no fair."

"Well—" Hobart hesitated; the last thing he wanted was a sword-duel with Yezdeg, who would probably make Salisbury of him. "Tell him that if he's brave enough to kill a fish-eater woman—"

He was drowned by another torrent of speech

from Yezdeg, who had evidently become sufficiently familiar with the sound-sequence "fish-eater woman" to be sensitive to it.

Sanyesh said: "He say swords not fair either. You beat Khurav; he best sword-fighter of Parathai; you must be best sword-fighter. You too good."

That was a break. What should he suggest? Wrestling? A look at Yezdeg's massive shoulders banished that idea. Boxing? It would hardly be fatal, and like most professional workers Hobart had not actually used his fists since he was an adolescent, though like most Americans he had a general impression that his people were a nation of natural-born boxers.

Then his eye fell on the red-and-black desert surface. "Tell him," he said, "that to make everything fair, since he insists on a fight, I'll fight him with stones."

Yezdeg was in a state where he would have agreed to flyswatters in a telephone-booth. They dismounted.

"Hope you know what you do, Prince," growled Theiax. "Want me to—"

"No. Sanyesh, do you and Fruz agree that, since insults are untrue statements and I haven't said anything untrue, I haven't insulted Yezdeg?"

"He say—I not know—"

"A thing is either an insult or it isn't, isn't it?" said Hobart triumphantly. The two mounted men nodded glumly. Hobart continued: "And that Yezdeg has challenged me; practically forced this fight on me? And I've done everything I could to give him his fair chance? And that no matter how it comes out, I haven't violated any of the laws and customs of the Parathai?"

Sanyesh found no way to deny all this, much as he might have liked to.

The combatants each collected a pile of the black

stone balls, placed in front of him about thirty feet from his adversary. Hobart made winding-up motions to limber his arm, which had not thrown a baseball since his college days. Yezdeg tried clumsily to imitate this procedure. Finally each stood with a stone in each hand.

"*Yikhi!*" shouted Sanyesh, acting as referee.

Yezdeg threw his first stone underhand and wildly. Hobart ignored it, swung both arms forward and up, then right down, back, and forward, like the lunge of a snake. The stone whizzed past Yezdeg's right ear; the barbarian threw his second even more wildly and stooped quickly to snatch more ammunition. Hobart waited until he started to straighten up again, estimated where his head would come by the time the stone got there, and let fly. Forehead and stone converged. *Crunch!*

They buried Yezdeg in the desert, quickly, lest his corpse suddenly liquefy in the heat. Kai's bones, if he consulted them, would give him the desired news now.

Hobart remounted, concealing as best he could the fact that he was suffering from a bad case of the shakes. Sanyesh and Fruz followed, looking at him with expressions of apprehensive awe.

As Hobart jogged along with his head bowed, Theiax questioned: "What is matter, Prince? Everything you try to do, you do, but each time you look sadder! You want me to do trick? Look!" And the lion turned three sommersaults in succession.

Hobart grinned wryly. He said: "Thanks, old bean, but if I felt like laughing I'd be rolling in the aisles at my own situation. If you want to cheer me up, you just figure out a way I can be a spectacular, hundred-percent failure!"

12

WHEN HOBART REACHED HIS own tent, his companions started off toward their respective quarters. The engineer called: "Hey, Sanyesh, I'm not through with you yet!"

"What is?" queried the elder, turning back. Hobart led him into the Sham's tent.

"Sanyesh," said Hobart, "I want to start a little war with the Marathai right away."

"War!" cried Sanyesh. The old man jumped up, hand on his sword. Hobart was alarmed until it transpired that the gesture had merely symbolic significance. "War! Ha! Cut! Stab! Shoot! Kill lots Marathai! Gr-r-r." Then the ferocity suddenly left the leathery face; Sanyesh stared blankly. "Sham, cannot start war right away! Must gather men, tell chiefs, plan battle!"

"How long will that take?"

"Five—six days."

"Oh, that's all right."

"Huh," grumbled Sanyesh, sitting down again. "If you not mean right away, why you say right away? Get me all excited for nothing. You fight fair war?"

119

This question puzzled Hobart; he answered with a vague "Yeah, I suppose so."

"Good." Sanyesh went to the entrance and hollered into the darkness. Presently a dapper young barbarian appeared; Hobart supposed him to be some sort of adjutant. Sanyesh spoke to him in Parathaian, then came back to Hobart and asked: "How many men you want take?"

"How many can we raise?"

"Twelve thousand, four hundred, nine," replied the elder promptly.

"Okay, we'll take 'em all."

Sanyesh whistled. "Why you say little war when you mean big war? You terrible hard Sham understand. I thought you meant little battle, one hundred each side."

"No, I'm playing for keeps. But what do you mean, a little battle with a hundred on each side? Do you pick even numbers like a game?"

"Sure, everybody knows that!"

Hobart shook his head wonderingly. "I can see where it might have advantages. You'd settle things without much bloodshed."

"Oh, it is not that," said Sanyesh comfortably. "Brave Parathai not afraid die, and even in big war hardly any get killed. Just in—inconvenient for so many leave during lambing season and things."

"I'm glad your wars are so unsanguiary, but how can that be if you're so brave?"

"Look, Sham," said Sanyesh with the air of explaining two times two to a backward child, "here is company of men, we suppose, yes? All right. Company can fight in formation, yes? Cannot fight if dis—you know, all scattered. All right. Battle start. Men get knocked down, pushed around. One or two get shot. Company not in formation. Cannot fight, so run away. Not cowardly to run when cannot fight, no?"

Hobart thought it was too bad that all the military units in history who had run at the first casualty had not had Sanyesh's logic to excuse themselves with. He abandoned the argument to get down to the material questions of organizing a campaign. The elder drew him a rough map on a piece of hide with charcoal and pointed out several alternative routes for the invasion.

"Really, I don't know," said Hobart. "Which one do you think best, Sanyesh?"

Sanyesh immediately indicated the most direct approach to Marathaia. Hobart shrugged. "Okay, if you say so," he said, though with mental reservations. He thought vaguely that he would have preferred an indirect approach, but since he could not really run the expedition he considered it wise to interfere with Sanyesh's judgment as little as possible.

His next shock came when he was sitting on horseback with Sanyesh outside the tent-city the following afternoon and watching some troops go through evolutions. He asked casually: "Say, Sanyesh, who was that young fellow who sat in with us at our conference last night? Haven't seen him around today."

"Him herald," grunted the elder. "Gone to warn Marathai."

"*What?*"

"I said him gone warn Marathai; tell them when we attack, what route, everything."

"Oh my lord! You mean he's a traitor or a spy?"

"No, no, Sham! You said you want fight fair war. All right. When you fight fair war, you send herald to challenge enemy, arrange battle place. Simple, yes?"

"Too damn simple," groaned Hobart. "Guess we'll

have to change the plans, to provide for an unfair war."

"Cannot do that," said Sanyesh calmly.

"Why the devil not?" snapped Hobart.

"Orders already given out, to get ready for fair war, battle in five days in Uzgend Valley. Now you want to change. So must countermand orders. Will take days to get everything back like was, and six days more get ready for unfair war. So we could not get to Uzgend Valley in time for battle. If we do not come, Marathai will be insulted, say we betray them. Then they invade us before we are ready. Impossible, Sham."

Hobart argued, but the elder was adamant. As he explained it, you prepared either for a fair or an unfair war. The preparations were different in each case, and therefore it was out of the question to prepare for one kind and then wage the other. You simply had to go back to the beginning and start over.

Hobart gave in for the time being, but during the night he had an idea for a daring coup to circumvent Sanyesh's quibbles. The next day he determined the fact that over two thousand men had been mobilized, and armed. He ordered Sanyesh: "Tell 'em to get their blankets and enough food for twenty-four hours. I want to take 'em on an overnight practice march."

"Good," said Sanyesh, and carried out the order. The party got under way by noon. There were 841 infantrymen, sturdy phalangites with twenty-foot pikes, and the rest horsemen.

Hobart endured a desperately dull afternoon, occasionally thanking his stars that he was not a professional soldier and hence did not have to submit to such boredom often. About an hour before sunset they reached a place where the yellow sand they were crossing gave place sharply to white. Along the line of demarcation was a long row of little obelisks, stretching out to the horizon on either side. The army halted, unordered, at the line.

"What's the matter, Sanyesh?" inquired Hobart.

"Border of Marathaia," said Sanyesh.

"I guessed that. But why are they stopping?"

"You say this practice march, not invasion, Sham."

"Okay, I know I did. But here's my idea: if we keep on going we'll reach the Marathaian capital late tonight. We can surprise them—"

"Impossible, Sham. Cannot start training for fair war and change to unfair one in middle."

"Damn it!" cried Hobart. "You tell 'em we're going ahead! That's an order!"

Sanyesh looked surly, but translated the message to the subcommanders. These looked even more displeased, and passed it on to their men. Instead of resuming its march, the army stayed where it was, buzzing with angry talk. Then little groups of men detached themselves and began to trail off toward home.

"Hey!" yelled Hobart. "What's this? Mutiny?"

Sanyesh replied nonchalantly: "They desert. They say you deceived them. Not like deceitful Sham. Pretty soon I desert, too, by damn."

"Tell 'em I just changed my mind—"

"Make no difference. Not like changeable Sham either."

Hobart swore himself blue in the face before he capitulated. "Okay," he groaned. "Tell 'em I was just having a little joke. I'm a humorist, see?"

Sanyesh looked surprised. "You funny man? Good! Fine! Parathai like jokes." He raised himself in his stirrups and shouted: "*Gish!*"

The men wandered back slowly; there was more

palaver, and the soldiers began to grin and laugh in a reassuring fashion. A couple of them sidled up to Hobart, laughing and clapping him on the back and spouting Parathaian.

Then they suddenly seized his arms, twisted them behind his back, and tied his wrists. Another produced a rope whose end was doubled in an efficient-looking hangman's knot. The loop was slipped over Hobart's head, and the other end tossed over a branch of a convenient thorn-tree.

"Hey!" screamed Rollin Hobart, "what's the idea?" But nobody answered him. The soldiers, grinning, tightened the rope; several hefty phalangites anchored themselves to the free end. Hobart saw with horrid clarity what they were going to do: slap his horse into motion, so that it would bound out from under and leave him dangling. His yells of protest made no impression.

Smack! A horny hand came down on the animal's rump. It leaped forward. Hobart braced himself for the shock of the noose. The rope tightened, jerked— and whipped over the branch to trail loosely behind.

A calvaryman cantered up alongside and gathered Hobart's reins; another untied his wrists. When he turned around he saw that the entire army was helpless with laughter, rocking in saddles and rolling on the ground.

"Sanyesh!" gasped the engineer. "What's the idea?"

"Haw-haw-haw!" bellowed the elder, his kalpak tilted over one eye with the force of his mirth. "You like joke, yes? Ha-ha-ha-ho-ho-hoo!"

Hobart kept silent lest a worse thing befall him. It did anyway. As soon as he dismounted, strong arms seized him and dropped him into an outstretched blanket. Those holding the blanket heaved, and Hobart bounced into the air. When he came down they heaved again, and up he went, higher. He churned the air with his limbs, trying not to come down head first and remembering that people had received broken necks that way. Up—down—up—down—he was dizzy and breathless when they finally spilled him out on the yellow sand. He reeled over to Sanyesh and clutched the elder's arm for support.

"Haw-haw-haw," chortled Sanyesh. "More fun. You like more jokes, yes?"

Hobart croaked: "Heh, heh, very funny. But tell 'em that's about all the humor I can stand for one day. We'll march back a couple of miles from the border and set up our tents, and after that I'll follow your advice on the campaign."

The thing that griped Hobart most was the thought that if he had simply let the whole crew desert without interference, he would have been free of this gang of logical lunatics. Damn obligations!

He was not quite through with the Parathaian sense of humor yet. His jangled nerves relaxed, after a frugal soldier's supper, over the thought that at least others would do the Sham's camp chores for him. As Sham, he had a real bed, or at least a mattress. He entered his tent with the hope of forgetting his plight by intimate contact therewith.

Some jokester had carefully piled, in the center of his bed, a bushel of horse-manure.

* * *

It was past noon, days later, when Hobart's scouts brought word to him, the nominal commander of the army of the Parathai, that the Marathai were drawn up in battle-array a short distance up the valley. That was not news to Rollin Hobart, who had already noted the twinkle of sunlight on military equipment. Sanyesh had begun to deploy their own army.

Hobart did not have too much confidence in the

elder, but the only alternative would have been to try to run the war himself, an entirely impractical scheme. Even if he had known something about strategy and tactics, he could not in a few days have trained the barbarians to use any other than their traditional methods of fighting. At that, the terrain was such that the traditional methods were likely to prove as effective as any. They marched between vertical walls of black rock forty feet high, just far enough apart to allow the armies to deploy comfortably, but too close together to permit any wide flanking movements in the style of Subotai or Sherman.

Sanyesh gave all the orders, though he usually unbent far enough to inform Hobart of what he was doing after he had done it. His conferences with Hobart gave the troops the impression that their Sham was really running things as a Sham should. Since they could not understand how a man could be the commander and not be the commander at the same time, they were satisfied for the nonce. Oddly enough they showed no sign of resenting the fact that Hobart was most decidedly not one of them. That, he told himself gloomily, was no doubt due to the fact that they were all keyed up with the excitement of the invasion. How they would act after a defeat was something else; Hobart had his own ideas, and they were not nice.

Meanwhile he had nothing to do but to watch the bloody drama unfold with a certain degree of detachment. These people's actions were so devastatingly consistent, and their motives so childishly simple, that they never seemed quite real. If this attempt failed, he supposed he would have to let his whiskers grow and penetrate Marathaia single-handed, disguised as a repairer of old clichés or something. He might of course have tried that in the first place, but such a piece of romantic knight-errantry was for him the last resort, not the first.

And not a soul among the Parathai had been able to help him in his quest for Hoimon. The late Khurav had, at the beginning of his reign, let it be known that any ascetic who wanted immediate promotion to the rank of martyr had merely to set foot inside his principality. A few had availed themselves of the offer, but after the supply of would-be martyrs had been exhausted there had been no more contact between the brotherhood of ascetics and the Parathai.

He turned to Sanyesh. "Better set up the stepladder."

"That so," said Sanyesh, and gave the order. The stepladder was Hobart's one contribution to the military art, and was just what its name implied, except that it was larger than most stepladders. From its top he could see over the heads of men mounted and men afoot, and thus keep a better tab on the progress of the battle than if he had remained on the flat valley floor.

He climbed the rungs. "Theiax!" he called, but the lion had slipped out of sight among the soldiers, who, once they had gotten used to him, had become inordinately proud of such a formidable ally.

Directly in front of Hobart was the phalanx, six thousand men strong, holding their twenty-foot pikes upright like the bristles of a gigantic brush. On each side of them, small bodies of light infantry were getting into formation; beyond the light infantry, the heavy cavalry. The light cavalry—horse-archers—were strung out in a thin line across the entire front of the army. If the idea was to fool the enemy as to their dispositions, Hobart doubted whether it would work, since the Parathai always fought in one invariable formation.

The enemy were now close enough for individuals

to be distinguished but not recognized. They appeared to have come to a halt, too, in a somewhat different formation. There was a heavy block of cavalry on each wing, and between the wings stretched a chain of infantry—squares of pikemen alternating with oblongs of musketeers.

A couple of gaudy persons were now out in front of the respective armies, shouting at each other. Hobart leaned down toward where Sanyesh sat his placid black horse, and asked what that signified.

"Challenges," said Sanyesh. "You see."

The gaudy men blew on trumpets and returned to their own lines. Presently a horseman rode out from the Marathai army and cantered up and down the yellow sand between the two armies. The Marathai cheered. Another man spurred out from among the Parathai; now the Marathai were politely silent while their foes cheered. The two horsemen drew up at opposite ends of the space between the armies, which were sitting and slouching in the attitudes of relaxed spectators.

The soldiers quieted down, so that the muffled hoofbeats of the duellists came clearly as the challenger and the challengee galloped at each other. They passed each other too quickly for Hobart to see just what had happened, except that one man stayed in his saddle and continued on, reining up, while the other flopped out of his with the first man's lance sticking through his body.

From the cheers Hobart inferred that the Marathaian was the winner. This man now rode closer to the Parathai lines, calling out his challenge. Sure enough, another went out to meet him. This time they met with a splintering crack; pieces of broken lance soared into the air. The riders circled back, dropping the butts of their broken lances and drawing their swords.

There was a brief confusion of swinging arms and whirling blades, and a metallic clatter; then one of them pitched out onto the sand: again, it transpired, the Parathaian.

Sanyesh turned a leathery, worried face up to his lord. "Bad," he growled. "If we lose all challenges, we lose battle."

"Why?"

"Always happens. Ah, look!"

The low yellow shape of Theiax was scudding over the sand toward the hostile cavalryman, tail stiffly erect and swaying like a mast as the lion galloped. There were shouts of warning from the Marathai side, but even as the champion made vague movements to prepare for this sudden assault, Theiax left the ground in a tremendous leap, struck the champion fair and square, and carried him out of the saddle on the far side. The riderless horse snorted and bounded off, circling the rectangle defined by the armies and the valley walls in a frantic effort to escape. Meanwhile the lion stood over the Marathaian and shook him so that his arms and legs flopped limply like those of a doll. Eventually Theiax tired of this amusement and trotted back to his own army.

But now the heralds were at it again. "What's up?" asked Hobart as the Parathaian herald pushed his way through the ranks to Sanyesh and spoke.

Sanyesh explained: "Protest. General Baramyash say his men not challenge lion; no fair; and unless we—"

"So what?" interrupted Hobart.

"If we can not get through challenges, we can not get around to battle!" cried Sanyesh.

"Bunk. It's driving me nuts, sitting around and waiting to get it over with." Hobart reached up and grasped the rodent skull, and called: "Kai!" No result! Hobart raised his voice, "KAI!"

"You need not break my ears," said a shrill voice beside him, and there was the medicine man, grinning like some depraved yellow idol. "What you want, Sham?"

Hobart pointed at the hostile army. "Can you break 'em up?"

"I do not know. Maybe. What you want, rain spell?"

"No! Something with punch in it; a monster, for instance."

At that instant Sanyesh called up: "Watch out, Sham; enemy coming!"

The hostile commander, Sham Khovind's son Baramyash—or Valangas—had evidently lost patience, for sharp commands were ringing up and down his array. The Marathaians cheered and began to move.

Kai frowned. "I can conjure serpent. Look." He made passes and incanted:

> "Borabora tahaa,
> "Totoya manua;
> "Gorontalo morea,
> "Niihau korea,
>   "Kealakekua!"

And a spotted viper a yard long appeared at the base of the stepladder. The immediate effect was to cause a nearby horse to rear and throw its rider.

"Take it away!" cried Hobart. "Not here; can't you plant a few thousand among the Marathai?"

Kai spread his hands. "One is all I can do at one time. What you think, I am great magician? I am just poor starving fish-eater—"

"Shut up!" yelled Hobart in exasperation. Sanyesh had departed to line up his men. The only familiar faces nearby were those of Kai, Hobart's horse standing near the stepladder, and the groom holding the horse. Hobart hated to think of what would happen if

his army started to run away before he had a chance
to climb down and mount. "What else can you do?
Open the earth?"

"A little," whimpered Kai, "like this:

> "*Aia aia alala,*
> "*Walla walla potala*
> "*Nuuanu nukuhiva*
> "*Tokelau kapaaa:*
> "*Rota, haleakala!*"

The earth trembled and groaned; the stepladder
swayed perilously, hung on the edge of an overset,
then settled back. A crack six inches across had appeared in the sand near it. All the soldiers nearby
looked at the crack with horror and aversion.

Hobart, whose fingers had gripped the stepladder
with the violence of reflex, drew breath. He shouted
at Kai: "You damn fool, one more like that and you'll
panic my whole army! Can't you do anything to the
other side?"

Kai waved his hands. "I never said I was a great
magician! Just poor starving . . ."

He was drowned out by a gathering thunder of
hooves as the Marathaian cavalry got under way,
straight for their opposite numbers on the Parathaian
wings. From his eminence Hobart could clearly see
that his own cavalry was badly outnumbered. Perhaps his own cavalry saw it, too, for as the Baramyash's
lancers poured down on them, their formation lost
its sharp corners; horses wheeled this way and that,
and the Parathaian wings dissolved into amorphous
crowds of men riding hell-for-leather to the rear. The
Marathaians shrieked their triumph and tried to catch
up with them. Friend and foe vanished down the
valley in a great cloud of dust. Hobart remembered
Sanyesh's explanation that the barbarians considered
the slightest disorganization an excuse for flight, on
grounds of irrefutable Aristotelian logic.

Flight and pursuit had occurred so suddenly that the infantry on both sides had not even gotten into motion. Hobart called down to Sanyesh: "Think we can smash those guys before the cavalry comes back?"

"How your magician?" parried Sanyesh.

"Lousy."

"I know he that, but does he know any magic?"

"Not enough. Kai, what else do you know?" said Hobart, shaking the medicine-man's shoulders.

"I can make wildflowers spring up. I stopped a pestilence among my poor people last year. I can call fish into the nets . . ."

"All too pacific. You savages are too damn civilized for your own good. Sanyesh, tell 'em to go ahead." He had been mistaken, he saw, in not expending one of his three calls via the rodent-skull for a staff-talk with Kai in advance. He had wanted to save the calls as long as possible—false economy . . .

The phalanx was getting under way. The men of the leading ranks lowered their pikes and tramped forward to the beat of drums; the rest followed with their pikes upright. They would gradually pick up speed until they hit the enemy at a run—if they hit the enemy at all. Something might happen—

Crash! The Marathaian line spilled flame and smoke. Cries of pain and alarm . . . Kai half climbed, half fell down the ladder as a couple of musket-balls whizzed close. Rollin Hobart followed at a more dignified pace. *Crash!* The muskets of the second rank went off; a few pikes toppled. Hobart climbed aboard his horse as the animal began to jitter. *Crash!* The phalanx slowed up and came to a dead stop. *Crash!* They began to retreat. Sanyesh galloped around them, yelling, but they kept on backing until they were out of effective range.

The first rank of the musketeers had not finished

reloading, so there was a pause. Sanyesh called to Hobart: "You do something damn well quick, Sham! Marathai charge soon . . ."

Then an idea hit Hobart like a blinding flash. "Kai! Rain on the enemy, quick!"

He had to repeat it before the medicine-man got the idea; but then the Ikthepel began:

"Marekula eromanga . . ."

A fierce little cloud formed over the Marathai line, and down came the rain with a swish. Sanyesh and his officers got the phalanx back into something like its original square. The Marathai turned angry faces up at the sky, right and left; then in response to commands began to advance, pikes first, muskets in the intervals. The phalanx took a few rippling, uncertain steps forward. Around the brush-bristle of pikes Hobart could see irregular, perplexed movements among the musketeers, who were trying, with no success, to shoot muskets whose matches had been rained out!

Two guns did go off, *pop! pop!* but that salvo merely encouraged the Parathaians, whose leading ranks saw quite clearly what the matter was. With a self-confident roar the phalanx got into its stride again, and clanked ponderously toward the foe, who, however, did not await its coming. With wet muskets, and pikes alone greatly outnumbered, the Marathai performed the same dissolving-act that had previously been exhibited by the Parathaian cavalry. In thirty seconds the whole mass was streaking for the rear, dropping pikes and muskets as they ran, some of them even shedding helmets, cuirasses, and greaves to enable them to run faster.

When the Marathaian cavalry cantered back up the valley just before sunset, they were singing, waving things plundered from the Parathaian supply-train, and feeling pretty good generally. They had chased the hostile force clear out of the lower end of the valley with practically no loss. But when they came to the site of the battle, they found nothing whatever but a few dead and wounded soldiers, and a vast quantity of military equipment, including a couple of thousand muskets, scattered around the valley floor. The Marathai consulted among themselves, came to the same conclusion as to what happened, and quietly departed thence. If your side lost a battle it lost it, and that was that.

The next day Rollin Hobart, firmly established in the Marathaians' main tent-city, brought a force down the valley to collect the booty and such of the wounded as had survived the night. Kai came with him, wearing a curious turban. Some of the Parathaian soldiers, after a night of making extremely free with the women of the Marathai, had sent a delegation to Sanyesh to protest the unseemliness of allowing an utterly naked savage to roam the camp. Sanyesh had found an old pair of trousers, which he had instructed Kai to don; the medicine-man, delighted with the gift, had made what seemed to him the best use of them, to wrap around his wide yellow head.

Kai was watching the interment of the men who had fatally intercepted musket-balls, and remarked: "All those good deads going to waste. What bad, wicked people everybody but my people are! I go now, Sham; you call again when you need me. Goodbye!" With a swish and a swirl, Kai vanished.

13

Rollin Hobart had gone on the sound theory that if he piled enough tasks on old Sanyesh, the counsellor would probably not have time to plot any mischief. That mischief there would sooner or later be, Hobart had no doubt, in view of the fact that Sanyesh, though not particularly friendly, was his only effective point of contact with his alleged subjects. If Sanyesh decided to make himself Sham, there was little that Hobart could do to prevent it. If he liquidated Sanyesh he would be in a worse position than he was now.

His only hope appeared to be to act quickly before any seditions broke out; rescue Argimanda, send her to her father, and then quickly disappear. He'd even forestall any revolts, against him at any rate, by abdicating and putting some other Parathaian in his present hot seat. Otherwise—good lord, if events followed precedent in this continuum, the Marathai might decide that they wanted him as Sham also! They might even fight the Parathai for the privilege; or some local Solomon would suggest the compromise of slicing Hobart in halves and giving one to each tribe.

But by then Hobart hoped he would be far away, disguised, and proceeding with his proper business of finding Hoimon and getting back home. Home! Good old New York; dear, respectable, congenial engineering position; kindly, interesting friends—what if some of them did think he was an opinionated old grind? He was not really obstinate—nonsense! He just knew what he wanted . . .

Thus thought Rollin Hobart of Higgins & Hobart as he jogged back to the main tent-city of the Marathai, followed by creaking wagonloads of pikes and muskets.

When he almost reached the ineffective ditch and rampart, Sanyesh trotted out on a horse, followed by a couple of retainers and a standard-bearer. It was hardly any distance, but as a petty chieftain it was beneath his dignity to walk when he could ride. The old man looked careworn as he reported: "I send man to Logaia, tell Gordius about battle, like you said. Half our cavalry come in, and some Marathai. Say they join us if we give them back families. One of them know about Laus. Speak Logaian good. You want talk?"

"Yes, right away," responded Hobart. "And tell these Marathai we'll gladly give them back their families without obligation, though we'd naturally be glad to have them join us, too."

This generous gesture might or might not be good statesmanship; if it were not, Hobart's successor could worry about the effects thereof.

The informative Marathaian turned out to be a young chief of a hundred families named Gorvath, on whose neck Hobart felt like falling in his relief at being able to converse fluently for a change.

Gorvath asserted: "If you are reasonably careful,

Sham, you can have all of Marathaia in a month. Khovind and Baramyash have their retainers, but the rest of our army is scattered into fragments all over the country. I do not think Sham Khovind will be able to rally many, for the word has gone out that you have the luck of Zhav with you."

"Hm," said Hobart. "You don't seem much concerned about the fate of your late commanders."

Gorvath shrugged, shrewd, humorous wrinkles springing into his weathered-beaten face. "I, too, think you have the luck of Zhav—or Nois, whichever you prefer."

"Just what do you mean by that?"

"I mean that our supreme lord seems to have picked you for a rapid rise in the affairs of the world— how far, none knows yet."

"Literally?"

Gorvath frowned. "I do not understand; I do not lie, if that is what you mean. So, naturally, being a man of sense, I intend to attach my fortunes to yours as early as possible. I shall not be surprised if Sham Khovind and his son come to the same way of thinking."

Oh, yeah? snorted Hobart mentally. They'd have to catch him first. Aloud he said: "What can you tell me about the wizard, Laus?"

Gorvath chuckled. "Rascals always fall out; they could not be rascals otherwise. Laus flew in here last week on those fearsome wings that turn into a cloak, with King Gordius' daughter for a hostage. Shortly after, Baramyash appeared, having spent four years in disguise at Gordius' court. It was learned that their little plot with the Logaian chancellor for the destruction of the royal family and the conquest and looting of the kingdom had miscarried because of the arrival of one Prince Rollin, who, it seems, is now Sham Rollin as well.

"What happened then is not known to me in detail; but I believe that Baramyash and Sham Khovind, reasoning that a wizard who had just betrayed one master might do likewise with the next, decided to destroy this dangerous ally and use Gordius' daughter for a hostage themselves. They believed that, between the possession of the princess and that of most of the muskets in Logaia, they would not need Laus' magic to overcome Gordius.

"Laus, I suppose, was warned of this by his magical arts, for he speedily put on his wings and flew off with the Princess before anything happened to him."

Hobart inquired: "Where did the wizard go?"

"That is not known, though he was flying due south when last seen."

Hobart pondered. Sham Khovind's routed infantry had mostly fled north and east; his cavalry had dispersed in all directions. Probably a good deal of it had gone south, since this course would take it away from Logaia and Parathaia and also away from the Parathaian army to the east of it. If he went south with a small party he risked running into a larger force of Marathai . . . But if he waited till he had everything under control, events would fasten their claws on him—he didn't know just how, but they would . . .

He stood up suddenly, and called: "*Fruz, Sanyesh gvakh!*" The phrase "Fetch Sanyesh" had become to Hobart an almost automatic reaction to every situation involving barbarians. He added, to Gorvath: "If you want to throw in with me, you can come along right now. We're going after Laus!"

As he got ready, his mind clicked off plans and alternatives: They'd take an escort of about a hundred, with the fastest horses available. He'd whistle up Kai—no, better wait till they located Laus; the savage had probably never ridden a horse and would balk at trying. If they were chased they'd simply outrun their pursuers. By now Hobart was, if not an expert rider, at least not a conspicuously bad one. How would they find the wizard? Simple: Hobart remembered a remark to the effect that animals were disturbed by the presence of magic.

Sanyesh, when he had his orders, went off shaking his head at the eccentricities of the new Sham, but in two hours—that is—shortly before sunset—he had the hundred light cavalrymen with horses in duplicate. Hobart left the elder to hold down the lid in the camp and took Gorvath for guide and interpreter. Theiax padded along expectantly. Suppose the Marathaian led them into a trap, or got them lost, or suppose Laus had not flown this way at all . . . Hobart did not care. He was willing to take almost any risk to get this next and last task out of his way; and, judging from his experiences so far, he could afford to take pretty steep ones . . .

They crawled along, steered by the stars, at a slow walk. Hobart estimated that they had covered about thirty miles when the sun popped up. It was pure guess-work, but it seemed likely that Laus had flown farther than this from the tent-city before alighting. He gave orders for spreading out over a front of several miles, with instructions to the men to report to him any signs of uneasiness on the part of their mounts. The horses, after being up all night, looked as if it would take something out of the ordinary to rouse them.

They presently left the savannah they had been traversing and entered a stretch of hill-country. Each hill was low and rounded exactly like the next, even to the clump of dry shrubs on its top. The only animal life was an occasional bird or lizard; there was no sign of Marathaian soldiery.

Hobart yawned with fatigue and boredom. Every piece of this land fitted into such an exact and limited pattern: there were certain number of types of topography, conical mountains, dome-shaped hills, flat plains, and so on; a certain number of types of cover, jungle, grass, or nothing, as the case might be; and a limited number of combinations of these. He had not seen all the possible combinations yet, but he was sure he could imagine them, so what was the use of touring the world to see them? All he asked was a chance to snatch up Argimanda with one quick pounce; to see her safely packed off to her father, and . . . Such questions as who should be Sham of this or that tribe and what should be done with the Logaian muskets did not interest him.

Thus he mused as hour crawled up the back of dull hour. It was nearly noon when a horseman cantered up and threw an unintelligible string of sounds at him. "He says," explained Gorvath, arriving next, "that the horses out on the right wing are balking. Is that what you wanted?"

"Yep; round 'em up," snapped Hobart. Let Laus turn him into a small black cinder; anything would be better than eternally crawling around this loathsome world!

The Parathai quickly guessed the cause of the horses' unease, and themselves showed no eagerness to come to close quarters with the wizard. Hobart supposed he could have roused them to excitement with the right sort of pep talk, but he had never given a pep talk in his life and did not propose to begin now. He told them to spread out as far as possible around the circle of magical influence. Then he dismounted and tied his horse to a bush. Neither nags nor barbarians were likely to be of much help.

He grasped the rodent skull and called: "Kai!"

There was an opacity in the air, as of a whirl of dust, and a swishing sound; then the medicine man stood before him. As Hobart explained what they had to do, Kai's broad saffron face got longer and longer.

"I am not good magician!" he wailed. "I just know a few little spells, keep my people from harm!"

"Anything's better than nothing," continued Hobart implacably. "What could you do to ward off or neutralize Laus' spells?"

"Well—let me see—I can make—*ouf!* Please stop you lion from sniffing my leg, Sham; it makes me n-nervous!"

The thing that Kai claimed he could make was a sort of shield which would deflect all but the strongest spells.

It was made of twigs and fish skins. Twigs could be had from any bush, but fish were something else.

"Conjure 'em up," said Hobart.

"No water," mourned Kai, spreading his hands.

"Oh my God, rain some!" barked Hobart. The fact that Kai knew some real honest-to-gosh magic did not necessarily imply that the savage was any genius. With Theiax's help they scooped out a depression two feet across, and Kai's spell beginning *"Marekula eromanga"* brought down a downpour a yard in diameter, which soon filled the hole. Another spell filled the water with squirming fish. Here Kai's thinking processes broke down again; Hobart had to suggest to the rattled necromancer that he could conjure up his magic bone skinning knife to complete the operation.

The shield was of the general size and appearance

of a child's home-made kite, with fish skin instead of paper. Kai explained: "You hold it in front of you like a real shield. Careful; it is not strong like real one."

Hobart asked Kai what else he knew in the way of spells. Kai seriously counted them off on his fingers; the only one that was at all promising was a hornet-conjure.

"Okay," sighed Hobart. "Come on."

"What? Oh, no, not me! I could not stand against great Laus; I never went to college of magic; just poor fish-eater—"

"Come on!" roared Hobart, "if you want to save your people from something really nasty!"

They trudged cautiously among the low hills, until Theiax halted with one forefoot raised, laid back his ears, and gave an infinitesimal growl. Hobart peered and sighted a small projection on the top of the farthest hill within their field of vision.

Hobart lit the match of his musket. He explained in a low voice: "I'm going to try to sneak up for a shot. If that doesn't work we'll rush him. I'll hold the shield up until I'm close enough to get at him with the sword; you two stay behind me so it'll protect you, too."

Theiax objected: "Suppose he flies away?"

"That's so." Hobart fingered his chin. "What sort of wings does that robe of his develop "

"Vulture, I think," said Theiax.

"Fine! Kai, if he starts to fly, you rain on him, hard! If you can soak his feathers it ought to bring him down."

When there was but a single hill between them and the one on which Laus' tower stood, they crept slowly up to the top and looked through the bushes. Hobart heard a sharp intake of breath from Theiax;

he looked again and caught sight of a human figure on top of the tower, in a gauzy garment—Argimanda.

"Where's Laus?" whispered Hobart.

"I can feel his presence," muttered the lion. "Ah, there, around base of tower!"

The tower itself was a ruinous old structure, practically a simple cylinder with a single opening—the doorway. This entrance was partly blocked by the heads and necks of two enormous snakes, lying one over the other, with bodies extended out of sight around the base of the structure.

"Amphisbaena," rumbled Theiax.

"What's that?"

"Snake with two heads, one each end. Alaxius says Laus could be one, but I never see it done."

"Ready everybody?" murmured Hobart. He propped the shield up in front of him and extended the musket through the bushes. He should be able to hit one of the heads at this distance—but which one? Did Laus's human intelligence reside in one, or both, and if the former how was one to know?

Get it over with, he thought, heart pounding. He sighted and squeezed. *Boom!* The butt kicked his shoulder; by moving his head quickly to get the puff of smoke out of his line of vision, he was able to catch a spurt of dust, twenty feet short of the reptilian heads and to the right. Hell, he should have remembered that a smoothbore matchlock wasn't a Winchester automatic.

"Rain!" he barked over his shoulder to Kai.

Kai began at once. The snake heads had reared at the shot. One of them swung slowly, like a man panoraming a movie camera; the other darted about aimlessly. Then the slow-moving head ducked into the tower door; the whole monstrous creature flowed after it. The other head disappeared around the tower and presently reappeared on the other side, bringing up the rear.

The rain-cloud boiled and dropped its contents. When a few seconds later Laus, in his usual dark gown and conical hat, came out on the roof, it was into a miniature cloudburst. The two small figures on the tower-top twinkled about, dark chasing light.

Hobart thrust the hot musket-barrel into Kai's hands. "Use this for a club!" he shouted. "Come on!" They burst out of the shrubbery and pounded down the hill they were on, Hobart drawing his sword and holding the little kite stiffly in front of him.

"Look!" cried Theiax in an anguished roar. Laus had caught up with the princess. Still struggling, she was carried aloft in the arms of the wizard, who soared from the tower on immense black vulture's wings. "Aloft" is not quite the right word, for despite desperate flaps the pair flew lower and lower, slanted across the gap between the tower-hill and an adjacent one, and came down on the latter's gentle stony slope.

Hobart angled toward them. Laus, holding the kicking and beard-pulling Argimanda under one arm, whisked out a wand with the other.

"Theiax!" yelled Hobart. "Come back here!" But the lion had bounded out from the protection of the shield and charged straight for the wizard with an earthshaking roar. Hobart was just near enough to see the wizard's face working and catch a whisper of his incantation. Theiax in mid-leap shrank to the size of an alleycat; bounced and sprawled on landing.

Hobart kept running. He could hear Kai's panting behind him, growing fainter, either because the short savage could not keep up or did not wish to. Laus went to work on Hobart, crying:

> *"Faborle dyor murtho*
> *"Tarwuzei kounovir!*

"Worngord houdorzhar
"Meveiler shaibaudir!
"SIRVZASHTAUI!"

Nothing happened, except that Hobart's left hand, holding the shield, tingled as though from a slight electric shock. Laus started another:

"Wargudviz vlapeisez
"Thorgwast tha zistal . . ."

But he stopped when it became obvious that Hobart would reach him before he finished. He dropped Argimanda, and in a twinkling changed from venerable wizard back into amphisbaena.

Hobart heard a squeal of fright from Kai, behind, as the monster poured down the hill toward them with the irresistible deliberation of a lava-flow. The leading head was undoubtedly the dominating one; it stared at Hobart with wicked intelligence, and even looked a little like Laus. The other, thrashing about futilely on the after end, was just the head of a big snake.

Hobart instinctively put up the shield to protect himself as he swung his sword down on the horny snout. The sword bounced up with a clang, and the jaws clomped on the shield. Hobart snatched his hand back just in time. The head crunched the shield and spat out the remains, then lunged at Hobart again. The engineer skipped back out of range, swung, missed, and whirled himself clear around. He got a glimpse of Kai, dancing with terror thirty feet off. "Get busy!" he yelled, then had to leap to avoid another lunge. He was, not, he feared, built for the part of Rikki-Tikki-Tavi. He got in a crack on the amphisbaena's snout as it recovered, but without apparent effect. Have to try for an eye . . .

"Watch out!" shrilled Kai. "He turn back into wizard, you have no shield!" Wish to God he would turn back, thought Hobart. While Laus could obviously not recite cantrips and make passes in his present form, the engineer was sure that if he returned to the human one, he, Hobart, could cut him down before he could get out another spell.

A toy-sized Theiax had bounded up onto the middle of the serpent's back and was vainly trying to rip it open with his little teeth and claws. Kai, gathering his courage, ran in and wacked the snake's back once with the butt of the musket; but then the other head came slithering around with open jaws, and the medicine-man scuttled back out of the way of imminent head.

"I make spell!" he called.

Hobart, wielding his sword in both sweaty hands, heard the incantation going off behind him. The air was filled with a vicious hum and then with hundreds of yellow-and-black striped insects: hornets!

In a twinkling the amphisbaena's scaly hide was dotted with them. But they did not stay there long, once they found the job of stinging through the horny scales hopeless. They rose in a menacing cloud . . . Hobart yelled as a dozen fiery stabs of pain lanced through his skin; stumbled back, away from the monster, as he swatted at his new tormentors. That guy Siegfried had had a cinch. He heard a scream of real agony behind him; a glance showed that the hornets had gone as one hornet for the most inviting target on the Marathaian landscape: Kai's unprotected skin. The savage dropped the musket and ran as Hobart had never seen a man run before. Then the amphisbaena was pouring down again.

Hobart spread his feet and waited. If he could only get an eye . . . The monster waited also for a few seconds, while it caught its sluggish reptilian breath. The dominating head reared back, threatening. Hobart quailed at the sight of unmistakable venom-fangs as the jaws opened halfway. Out of his lateral field of vision he saw the other half looping lowly around, and the second head getting ready for business. Like a boxer's two fists . . . The dominating head made a tentative stab forward; halted as Hobart jerked back his sword—*clunk!* Hobart had a flashing vision of the musket-butt swung by Argimanda's arms, come down squarely between Laus' eyes.

"Look out!" screamed the princess.

Hobart glanced to the other side just as the second head began to lunge. He dove to one side, landed on his shoulder, and rolled to his feet again as the head shot through the air he had just displaced. It kept on going—and caught the dominating head squarely by the muzzle!

The part of the snake adjacent to the dominating head writhed in protest, but now the secondary head had worked its jaws over the whole of the dominating one. Once begun, the process knew no stopping. The secondary head's loosely-hinged lower jaw moved, right side forward and then left. As Hobart watched in fascinated amaze, the great reptilian loop shortened and thickened till the whole had the shape of an inner-tube; then that of a doughnut. When Hobart did not see how it could swallow itself any further, the doughnut coalesced into a scaly globe the size of a pushball; it shrank swiftly—and vanished.

Argimanda stood with her thin wet garment clinging to her and little Theiax cradled in her arms. Hobart looked at her foolishly.

"Where'd he go?" he finally asked.

"He swallowed himself," replied the princess.

"How?"

"When I hit the thinking head I must have dazed it for the moment, so that it no longer controlled the other. And the other, being a simple serpent's head, had to obey its instincts; once it had caught the thinking head it could do naught but swallow."

"I see that, but where did it *go?*"

Argimanda said patently: "How long would you say the whole amphisbaena was?"

"Oh, about fifty feet."

"And how fast did the inferior head swallow?"

Hobart thought. " 'Bout five feet a minute."

"Well then, what would you expect to happen at the end of ten minutes?"

He took her hand and led her down the rest of the hillside and back the way he had come. "Young lady," he said at last, "you can thank your Nois the androsphinx didn't ask that one!"

14

THERE WAS NO SIGN OF KAI, though they looked. Hobart surmised: "Probably remembered to disappear. These stings are the very devil. Any get you?"

"No, they didn't touch me," said Argimanda. "Can I do aught for yours, dear Prince?"

"Thanks, but I'll stand them until we get back to camp."

"Camp? You mean one of the tent-cities of the Marathai?"

"Uh-huh." Hobart gave the princess a brief account of recent events. He finished: "I'm taking you back there now, and I'll ship you off to your father first thing."

She sighed a little. "I owe you life a second time, Rollin. There is nothing I would not do for you if I could. But—you have not changed your mind?"

"Nope. Sorry," muttered Hobart, becoming suddenly very busy at reloading his musket. But she did not embarrass him by discussing their relationship further. Not the least painful part of his predicament was the fact that Argimanda was so considerately obliging that she never gave him an excuse for getting angry with her.

She put down Theiax, who trotted mournfully behind them, misjudging distances and bumping into things. His voice was a shrill wail as he protested.

"I am insulted! I am humiliated! Prince, can you no get my size back?"

"Nope, old fella; not my department."

"You should not kill Laus! He could restore me."

"Didn't kill him, really. He committed suicide. Matter of fact," Hobart continued, turning to Argimanda, "I haven't done any of the noble deeds that you and the other people of this cockeyed world insist on crediting me with. It's been just dumb luck, plus my ignoble and selfish efforts to save my own neck."

Argimanda smiled. "Your fairy godmother must have given you modesty along with your heroism, Rollin."

"I'm not a hero!" cried Hobart despairingly. "I'm just an ordinary, practical engineer, and not a very nice guy at that! I'm self-centered and set in my ways; my friends think I'm dull and pedantic—"

"A scholar as well as a hero!" breathed the princess rapturously. "I would not have believed such a combination of virtues possible! If you would only let me serve you, however humbly—"

"Please, let's not discuss it!"

"Very well, my prince." There was a trace of moisture in her eye, but she blinked it away and smiled with heartrending bravery. "I shall be happy enough, just being near you for a few hours!"

Hobart clenched fists and teeth, torn between desires to yell "Shut up!", to run off and leave this infuriatingly lovely person, and to grovel in apologies. In the end he marched briskly straight ahead, musket on shoulder and glower on face. His pace did not bother Argimanda, who swung along easily on her superb long legs. Thus they reached the escort in less time than it had taken Hobart and Kai to find the wizard's lair.

Somebody called "Hi!" from the top of one of the hills and clumped down toward them. It was Gorvath. "I did not expect to see you so soon; or ever, for that matter! You have the lady?" The barbarian doffed his kalpak and bowed to Argimanda. "I am dazed by her beauty!" Gorvath staggered a little to show that when he said dazed, he meant dazed. He recovered and said to Hobart in a stage-whisper: "She would make a wonderful Shami!"

"No doubt," answered Hobart drily. "But we're in a hurry; round up the boys."

Gorvath started to go; then caught sight of Theiax, who tried to hide behind a shrub. The Marathaian stared, then burst into uncontrollable laughter. "Hahahahaha—the noble beast has shrunk! Did you wash him in too hot water, or what?" Gorvath staggered off, still laughing and holding his midriff.

Theiax caterwauled: "If I get my size back, I teach that ignorant one not to rickidule me!"

When Hobart had seen Argimanda mounted, he swung aboard his own horse, and called down to Theiax: "Think you can hold on without scratching me or the horse? Okay; jump!"

When Theiax had settled himself across the saddle, he turned his small yellow eyes up to Hobart, and asked: "What is this about you not marrying Argimanda?"

"That's right." Hobart repeated the protest that had now become automatic from frequent use, about not giving a damn for all the pomp an alien world had to offer.

Theiax glowered, and spat: "If I get my size back, you do not walk out on my Princess so nanchaloncy!"

"I know it," chuckled Hobart. "Look here, old man, you wouldn't want to force Argimanda into a loveless marriage, would you?"

"Not loveless. She loves *you*."

"An unhappy one, then."

"If she loves you, she is happy with you no matter. You should make her happy, just as I make happy lionesses who love me. But not any more," he concluded mournfully, twisting his head to inspect his diminutive shape.

"Well, damn it, an inequitable one then!"

"Inetiquable—ineq—oh, tea-leaves! You are too smart man for me. Where do you go after you leave my Princess?"

"Back to my own world, I hope."

"Are there lions in that world?"

"Yes, but not where I live. They're not allowed in the streets and houses."

Theiax made a gentle buzzing noise that presumably indicated thought, then came out with: "I love Argimanda, but I love my dignity, too. I must not go back to Oroloia; every dog in city hears about my new size and waits to chase and humiliate me. Could I go with you?"

"I'll think about it," replied Hobart. "I'd have to pass you off as just an unusual kind of pussy-cat, you know."

"I know." The social lion dropped the subject, and spent the rest of the trip reminiscing about his love-affairs with assorted wild lionesses. Hobart found the stories very rare indeed, for Theiax, being a feline, had no inhibitions in such matters. But the engineer tried not to laugh, not wishing to insult his little friend's melancholy. Come to think of it, a confirmed bachelor ought to have some sort of pet, and Hobart's last dog had died a couple of years previously. Theiax would have to be taught to confine his conversation to the privacy of the apartment . . .

"Sham!" cried Gorvath. "Somebody has a preceded us to the camp. Look!" He indicated a swath of trampled grass that even Hobart could see marked the passage of a large body of horsemen.

"What do you make of it?" the engineer inquired.

"I do not know, but it might be Sham Khovind and his son."

"Suppose they attacked the camp?"

"They might have, though they could hardly have surprised it in daylight." Gorvath with a sweep of his arm indicated the featureless plain whose grass would not have concealed anything larger than Theiax.

"Guess we'll have to go see," Hobart announced. Another hour's ride brought the tent-city up over the skyline, in the form of a little dark irregularity between the blue sky and the yellow sea of grass.

"Should we scout?" asked Gorvath.

Hobart privately wished the barbarians would not consult him on matters of military strategy and tactics, but he replied: "If we go any closer they'll see us sure. And I don't propose to crawl ten miles on my belly through the grass. Suppose we send Theiax. He's small enough—ouch! You little devil—"

The social lion had dug a claw sharply into Hobart's thigh, then jumped down. He mewed: "You make fun of me! I do not let people make fun of me! I am lion, even if small!"

"Okay, okay, I wasn't making fun of you. I was saying that your size makes you just perfect for reconnoitering the camp; there's not another man or beast in this world that could do it as well!"

"Oh, that is different. I am sorry I scratch." Mollified, Theiax set off at an easy lope through the grass, with which he blended to invisibility after a few leaps.

The rest of the party disposed themselves to await the lion's return; some dismounted, others remained slouched in their saddles, eating, smoking, or snoozing. The horses cropped contentedly. Hobart pointedly avoided conversation with Argimanda and Gorvath, fearful lest he should somehow get committed to more deeds of derring-do. He snatched some sleep, but as the hours dragged by, he became concerned. The sun was well down when Theiax reappeared, trotting with lolling tongue.

"Horses!" gasped the pussy-lion. "Horses, horses, all around camp! Parathai horses, Marathai horses, even some horses from Logaia! I reckonize bridles."

"Now what," Hobart asked the clear atmosphere, "would Logaian horses be doing there? Any sign of fighting, Theiax?"

"No; everything is peaceful. People sing in camp."

Hobart sighed with bafflement. "Guess we'll just have to go see for ourselves. Hey, everybody, mount! When we get near the tent-city, stand by to run like hell if they act hostile."

They had to skirt several herds of stock whose herdsmen waved languidly to them. There was certainly no sign of blood and tumult here. As Theiax had described, there were horses all around the camp, pegged out in orderly rows. As they threaded their way among the herds, Hobart recognized one of the royal Logaian grooms.

"Hi!" he called. "What are you doing here, Glaukon?"

"I don't know, lord," responded the youth. "I came with King Gordius as I was told to, that's all."

Hobart continued toward the main gate at the

head of his party. As he approached it he must have been sighted, for there were trumpet-blasts from within. The singing and other sounds of revelry within ceased, and out from the gate boiled a crowd of people on foot.

Hobart tightened his grip on the reins, prepared to whirl his animal around on its haunches; but the people were evidently not hostile. In the front rank were four: Sanyesh, King Gordius, ex-General Valangas in barbaric costume, with short blond fuzz sprouting from his scalp, and a very old barbarian who limped forward on a stick. They were flanked and followed by assorted retainers and standard-bearers. Then what Hobart feared worse than a fight came to pass: the four dignitaries with one voice bellowed: "Hail, Rollin, King of Kings!"

Hobart had a chance of perhaps five seconds to bolt, but he lost it while making up his mind. Then they were all around him, Argimanda in her father's arms, the others fairly hauling him off his horse.

When the tumult of acclaim died, King Gordius wrung Hobart's hand, explaining: "I knew you'd save her, my boy! And since you're now King of all Logaia, and Sham of the Parathai, Sham Khovind—this is he," (he indicated the old man on the stick) "Sham Khovind and his son agree that the only sensible thing to do is to make you King of Kings, Sham Shamzen, over all three realms!"

"But," wailed Hobart, "I don't *want* to be King of Kings—"

"Nonsense, son! You're just the man for it!" The king took Hobart's arm and began to walk him back through the gate. "You see we could never manage it before, because the Marathai wouldn't accept a Parathaian or Logaian ruler; a Logaian wouldn't take a Parathaian or Marathaian, and so on, heh heh. But

you're neither one thing nor the other: a stranger
with barbarian hair and civilized manners; as my son
Alaxius rudely put it, an impossible person, wearing
clothes of a non-existent color, and a puissant hero to
boot. You're the one man who can take charge of our
countries, stop these silly internal wars, and make
one mighty realm out of them!"

Sham Khovind added in a gutteral voice: "We can
make it beeger than just the three keengdoms, Sham
Shamzen; we can conquer the wild Theoiri—"

"And," Gordius broke in, "I'm sure the Psythoris
will join us if invited—"

"And eef they do not, we take them anyway—"

"And we really should seize the golden city of
Plakh; it controls the trade-routes to Gan Zheng—"

"And we need the Buryonoi Mountains, for a—how
you say eet—strategic frontier—"

Hobart heard in thin-lipped silence. When they
reached the Sham's tent, he asked with quiet grim-
ness: "While you men plan how I can conquer the
whole planet, will you excuse me? I want to be alone
for a while."

Of course, they clamored, he could be alone as
long as he wished; he was King of Kings, and what
he said went. Hobart retreated to one of the smaller
compartments which he had used as sleeping-quarters
the night after the battle. He grasped the rodent
skull and called for Kai.

The yellow man popped into view, glancing about
nervously at the sounds of celebration that filtered
through the tent-walls. His bare hide bore a score of
large red lumps.

"Hornets get you?" asked Hobart sympathetically.
"Too bad, old boy; can't you cure 'em by magic?"

Kai spread his hands helplessly. "I buy spell from
magic-peddler; does not work. Peddlers always cheat

us poor fish-eaters. Can you stop them, Sham Shamzen?"

"Maybe. I see you've kept up with the news. Look, when you do that disappearing act, can you take somebody else with you?"

"Sure; you take me by the hand, I pull you along, foosh-whush."

"Okay. Know where Nois hangs out?"

"You mean Baaa, master of all?"

"Nois or Zhav or Baaa, whichever you prefer."

"I know," said Kai, apprehension growing on his dishface.

"Well, I want you to take me there. Now!"

Kai was siezed with violent trembling, and sank to his knees. "Oh, Sham Shamzen Shamzen! I am afraid! Baaa is lord of everything! Very powerful! Why you want to see him?" he wailed.

"He's been up to some more tricks, and I don't like it. He and I are going to the mat. Come on, give me your hand!" As Kai continued to ululate his fears, Hobart snatched one dirty hand and shook the savage roughly. "Get going!" he roared.

"Y-you take care of my poor people when I am gone?"

"Yes! Damn it, get—" At this instant Kai dissolved into dusty opaqueness; Hobart felt a violent tug on the hand he held. He gripped it more tightly, and felt himself pulled along; though he knew not what. Everything was roaring confusion.

"Here we are," squeaked Kai. The surroundings crystallized into shape, and Hobart gasped.

They were standing in a huge bowl of sleek black rock, miles across. There were no steps or other irregularities in the sides of the bowl. Hobart did not see how anyone, having once slid into the depression, could get out with neither wings nor magic.

The floor of the bowl was circular and flat; they stood at its edge, where the obsidian-like rock began to curve up. In the center of the floor, which was perhaps half a mile across, rose a great white pyramid, unnaturally bright, since the rays of the evening sun slanted across the bowl above the pyramid's apex.

15

"THAT IS IT," SAID KAI, POINTING superfluously. "I go now, quick. Will you give me the skull? Will not work for you any more."

Hobart handed over the necklace. Kai said: "Goodbye, Sham Shamzen Shamzen Shamzen. You are great man; you do not need me any more. But remember your promise to protect poor fish-eaters. If you want me, I shall be with my people at Lake Nithrid." And the medicine man was gone.

Hobart turned toward the pyramid, wishing he had remembered to bring his musket. There was no substitute for the confidence conferred by possession of a loaded gun, even a muzzle-loading matchlock.

The sun dipped below the edge of the bowl, and the skylight went out with a rush. Hobart was standing in star-spangled blackness, facing the pyramid, which sprang into vivid luminescence, glowing with a cold ghostly white light. He hesitated for a second, then walked firmly toward it.

It grew larger and larger until it towered over

him. He stopped and shouted: "Hey!" After a pause he added: "Does Nois live here?"

An entrance appeared silently in the white surface, in which stood a tall majestic old man who intoned: "What dost thou seek, Rollin Hobart?"

"I'm looking for the big boss, if you don't mind. You him?"

"Nay; I am but a servitor of our lord, Psylleus by name. Dost know what that which thou askest implieth?"

"No, but I want to see Nois anyway. They told me anybody could."

"Very well, if thou hast duly considered—"

"Skip it," snapped Hobart irritably. "This thing has gone far enough, and it's cold out here. Does this Nois of yours really exist?"

Psylleus' brows went up. "Of course! The most perfect being necessarily exists; Nois is the most perfect being; therefore Nois exists. Q.E.D."

Hobart waved a weary hand. "Lead on, Aristotle."

The priest bowed and motioned Hobart in. It was hard to make out the features of the interior because of the ubiquitous dead-white glow. There seemed to be passages—Hobart almost ran into a wall at a turn—and then they were out in a lofty chamber. As Hobart's eyes accustomed themselves to his surroundings, he made out another, smaller pyramid—of the step kind—in the middle of the chamber. Instead of a sharp apex it was crowned by a glowing white chair of stiff straight lines. In the chair sat a dimly-seen white-robed figure.

"He has come," boomed Psylleus.

"Ah," replied a voice from the top of the pyramid. It was a strong voice, but very old and a bit creaky. "Stand forth, Rollin Hobart. Why dost thou seek me?"

Hobart said boldly: "I've been told that you had a hand in some of the things that have happened to me during the past couple of weeks."

"Ah. That may be. But first the questions, then the audience."

"What questions?"

"Didst not know? All who seek me must answer three questions, or failing, render up their souls that their Nois may continue."

"Hey, I thought anybody could see you—"

"So they may, but nothing is said about leaving my presence afterward, ha ha."

"What happens to 'em if they don't answereth?"

"They are placed below the throne on which I sit."

"You mean inside that pyramid?"

"Exactly, Rollin Hobart."

"What then?"

"Then? Why they cease to exist as separate entities."

This was all sufficiently ominous, if vague, to make Hobart sweat. He continued impatiently: "Now look here, Mr. Nois—"

"Ah, Rollin Hobart, the questions! Nay, think not of escape, nor wish for thy musket; both thoughts are futile, and thou wilt need thy brain for more constructive enterprise. Art ready?"

"Art," snapped Hobart. Just let them try to stick him into the electric oven or whatever was under the throne of Nois!

"Question the first: If everything is in space, as is generally believed, then space itself must be in space; and the space wherein the space is must also be in space, and so on to infinity. But this is absurd, for there is but one space by definition. How explainest thou this paradox?"

Hobart knitted his brows, then grinned in the ghastly light. "Simple, your Highness or whatever you like to be called. There's no paradox; only a confusion between two meanings of the little word 'in.' Things are in space in the sense of 'are surrounded by,' but space is in space in the sense of 'is congruent or identical with.' Get it?"

There was a moment of silence from the steppyramid, then came the voice, lower: "O Rollin, thou hast solved the problem of space, which for centuries hath baffled the wise wits of the world. But the problem of time thou shalt not perchance find so easy.

"Question the second: Before a body in motion can reach a given point, it must needs first traverse half the distance; before it can traverse the half it must first traverse the quarter, and so on to infinity. Hence before it can pass from one point to another, it must needs traverse an infinite number of divisions. But an infinite number of distances cannot be traversed in a finite time. Hence motion is impossible; yet it taketh place every day. How explainest thou this paradox?"

Hobart squared his shoulders. "Say, who sold you that as a hard problem? Who said a distance with an infinite number of divisions is the same as an infinite distance? If you take a finite distance, which is what I suppose you started out with, and divide it into an infinite number of parts, the parts will be infinitely small, so it'll take an infinitely *short* time to pass any one of 'em, so your infinities cancel out."

"I do not quite see, Rollin Hobart—"

"That's because you never took calculus at M.I.T. Anyway infinities are just mathematical concepts, because nobody ever walked an infinite distance or divided an inch into an infinite number of parts. By the way, these problems sound vaguely familiar. Didn't a Greek philosopher named Zeno think them up?"

There was a stir of the dim white robes. "It is not strange that I should know thy name, Rollin Hobart, but how dost thou know mine?"

"You mean to tell me *you're* Zeno of Elea?"

"I was, before I became Nois. I even visited thy world, the three-value world, in an attempt to find the answers to these questions. I failed then, but I see that thy world progresseth."

"What do you mean, three-value world?"

"Why, there do be an infinite number of worlds, according to the logic whereon they are built. Know that this is the world of two-value logic—everything either is or is not something—whereas thy world is the world of three-valued logic—everything is something, or is not something, or is partly something."

"Sounds as if this world were the world of Aristotelian logic," said Hobart.

"Ha ha, thou wilt be the death of me, Rollin Hobart! Know that shortly after I returned hither and became Nois, we had a learned doctor, one Aristoteles by name, who swore to go to your world and teach the inhabitants thereof the true logic, by which he meant that of this world. I never heard what became of him, but it appeareth that he made his mark."

Hobart asked: "What would a world of one-valued logic be like?"

"Monotonous; verily I do not recommend it unto thee. But come; thou hast solved the problem of time; perchance thou mayst not find the problem of motion so easily disposed of, for a truly knotty problem it is. Question the third: Two bodies moving with equal speed traverse equal spaces in the same time. But when two bodies move with equal speed in opposite directions the one passeth the other in half the time in which it passeth it when at rest. How solvest thou this paradox, Rollin Hobart?"

Hobart laughed aloud. "Didn't you ever hear of the relativity of motion? Look, the term 'motion' doesn't mean a thing except with respect to something else, which we call the frame of reference . . ." And Hobart launched into an impassioned ten-minute lecture.

When he ended, the figure replied slowly: "Thou hast solved the problems, Rollin Hobart, as I was sure thou wouldst. My term is passed." And the figure heaved itself out of its throne and tottered down the steps of the pyramid. As it approached Hobart saw that it was merely an old, old man with a scanty wreath of white chin-whiskers.

"Hey," he said, "what are you going to do?"

"Do?" quavered the ancient. "Why, die, of course, and verily it is about time. There is no more need for me, since thou art the new Nois."

"*What?*"

"Certainly, Rollin Hobart; thou hast answered the questions. Is it not simple? Long have I sought thee, for I am utterly weary of my exalted state. When my dust hath been removed, take thou my robe and ascend unto my place. Food thou wilt not need; the soul-stuff of visitors who are unable to answer thy questions will suffice thee. The priests will explain thy powers and duties unto thee. And now farewell. Oh, Psylleus, come hither!"

Hobart exploded: "By God, I won't do it! I don't want to be a prince or king or emperor, or a god either! I'll see you all in Hell first—"

"Yes, master?" said the priest from the entrance, ignoring Hobart's fist-waving dance of fury.

"I die, good Psylleus," said Nois. "Rollin Hobart hath been the death of me, as I said he would. Take thou good care of him. Farewell!" With which the little wizened figure sagged and collapsed to the glowing floor. The white robe settled down over it, lower, lower, until there was no visible space between it and the floor.

Psylleus picked up the robe and shook out a little silvery dust. He held it up for Hobart to don. "Thy robe, Nois," he intoned when Hobart seemed disinclined to slip into it.

"To hell with it," shrieked Hobart. "I'm not your Nois! Get me out of here; get that guy Hoimon!"

"Thou art the next Nois, lord of all," persisted Psylleus. "Wilt thou not take thy robe and thy throne, that thy servant may prostrate himself in adoration?"

"NO! If you prostrate yourself I'll give you a boot in the rump! Where's that damned entrance—ah, here! So long, Whiskers, I'm going!"

"Oh, but my lord!" cried the priest. "Thou canst not leave the pyramid!"

"Why not?"

"Without a Nois, actual or inchoate, verily our world would crumble!"

"Let it." Hobart started for the door again, when Psylleus gave such a pitiful shriek of terror that he stopped. "Well, if you don't want me to go, you get Hoimon! If you're such a hot high priest, you ought to be able to locate one skinny ascetic!"

"Very well," babbled the priest. "It shall be as my lord wisheth. Oh, Chidelas!"

"Coming," rumbled a sleepy voice. Presently a short fat priest, younger than the other, appeared. "I was just getting to sleep—goodness gracious, is this now our Nois-elect?"

"It is."

"Why doth he not ascend his throne?"

"I know not," muttered Psylleus. "It is against all

precedent. Go thou, Chidelas, and seek Hoimon the ascetic, for our Lord desireth his presence forthwith."

"Yeah, and I mean damn quick," snarled Hobart.

Chidelas protested: "If my lord will take his high seat, he can summon Hoimon himself!"

"Yeah? Could I leave the throne once I'd sat in it?"

"Well—uh—" hesitated Psylleus, "thou wouldst not wish to leave, verily—"

"Ha! Thought there was a catch! We'll do it the hard way: one of you will go fetch Hoimon, right now!"

The fat priest went out, shaking his head. Hobart sat down on the floor wearily, and said: "You might get me some grub, Psylleus."

"Dost thou mean the larva of an insect?"

"No, I mean food!"

"If my lord will but ascend—"

"YEEOW! I won't ascend your damned throne, and that's that! I'd rather sit in an electric chair with a lunatic fooling around the switch! And when I say food I mean food! Plain ordinary human fodder!"

Psylleus scuttled out, and returned in a little while with a loaf of bread, a lump of cheese, a pot of jam, and a bottle of wine. Hobart relaxed a little. "Nothing funny about this food, is there? I'd put an awful curse on you if there were. Here, sit down; make yourself comfortable."

"But—my lord—it is against all precedent—"

"To hell with your precedent! Sit down and help me consume this stuff. Mmmm, not bad. Guess you priests do pretty well by yourselves, huh?"

Psylleus ate sparingly, with the expression of one who wonders whether he or his companion is crazy.

After the meal, Hobart had nothing to do but wait.

It would be easier if he could just sit on the lowest step of the throne-pyramid—but, no, he was as near the infernal thing now as he wanted to be. After a while he got sleepy. Despite the omnipresent light he stretched out on the floor and dropped off.

When he awakened, undivinely stiff and sore, he was relieved to find that the devout Psylleus had not carried him up the step-pyramid while he was asleep. Day was breaking—or exploding, which would better describe its action in the two-value world. The big pyramid was translucent. Despite the glow of the white material Hobart could follow the motion of the sun through the walls. Was it an optical illusion, or was the sun rising at an abnormal rate?

Psylleus appeared with breakfast, at which the sun immediately halted its swoop zenithward. Hobart ate, and when he relaxed afterward the sun started its dizzy soar again.

"Psylleus!" he called. The sun stopped.

"Yea, lord?" the priest stuck his head out of the entrance, plate and dishrag in hand.

"Am I seeing things, or can I stop the sun by speaking, the way that fellow Joshua did?"

"The sun hath pursued its wonted course, lord."

Hobart scratched his head, and explained the phenomenon in more detail.

"Oh," said Psylleus. "My lord forgetteth that when he but thinketh his own vast thoughts, time passeth for him at a far greater rate than for us humble mortals, so that a thousand days are to him as one."

That explained how Zeno, the former Nois, had lasted so well since the Fifth Century B.C. It also suggested that there would be no particular advantage to such an existence, even from the point of view of longevity, since the Nois would not have the consciousness of any more elapsed time of life than an ordinary person. On the other hand it was an excellent preventive of boredom, for the day whizzed past before Hobart had a chance to fidget—much. He was still worried; this time-phenomenon made things look as though he had already acquired some godlike powers, which of all things he wished to eschew.

The day raced past; so did the next, during which Hobart did not budge from his place on the floor of the temple. The merest suggestion from Psylleus that his lord might find it more comfortable . . . brought an explosion of temper from Hobart, who instantly suspected sinister motives.

On the third day the fat priest, Chidelas, returned, and after him trudged a gaunt, half-naked figure at whose sight Hobart's heart jumped.

"Hoimon!" he shouted, and sprang forward to pump the ascetic's horny hand.

Hoimon started back with a scandalized expression. "My lord! It is not seemly that a Nois-elect should fraternize so familiarly with a humble ascetic!"

"To hell with that! And to hell with the Nois business! Have you any idea what you got me into when you snatched me from good old New York? Have you heard the things they've done to me?"

"Rumors have come to me, O Nois-to-be," admitted Hoimon, a slight twinkle in his frosty blue eyes. "It seems to your humble disciple that the people of this world have tendered you a degree of recognition of your virtues that were denied you in your own."

"Yeah, that's what they think. But all *I* want is to get back. I don't like it here; I don't fit; and, finally, I won't stay. And *you're* going to take me back through that tunnel!"

The ascetic sighed gustily. " 'Tis true, you do not fit, O Nois-elect. For look you: You denied yourself carnal knowledge of Khurav's widows—"

"You heard about that?"

"I hear many things. As I was saying, you forebore to take advantage of them, which would lead one to think you were an ascetic, yet I know full well that you are not."

"Huh! Think I wanted a couple of little Rollins to come around crying: 'Don't leave us, Daddy'?"

"As I was saying, your motives were not at all those of an ascetic. You went to great trouble and risk to carry out obligations that you had incurred, which would lead one to think you a man of honor. Yet in several minor matters you displayed a carelessness with promises and with the strict truth that are inconsistent with truly honorable behavior. In short you are neither good nor bad, pure nor depraved, honorable nor dishonorable, but something between. That is a type of person which simply does not exist in this world."

"I know it!" cried Hobart. "That's one of the things I can't stand about this world!"

Hoimon smiled. "You are consistent in one respect only, and that is your stubbornness. But I fear that I cannot assist you in your determination to return to the three-value world."

"Why not?" squawked Hobart. "Is the tunnel blocked, or what?"

"Not at all, O lord. But know you not that our world would crumble without a Nois? I could not bring such a disaster on its innocent inhabitants!"

"Even if I order you to, as Lord High Boojum?"

"Not even then. Slay me if you will, or feed me to your soul furnace; it will be all the same."

"I can just plain walk out of here and let it crumble. Damn it all, that's what I'll do, too!"

"The result would be the same, but I should not be responsible." Hoimon folded his skinny arms, obviously prepared to endure the worst.

Hobart pondered, then his eyes lit up. He said insinuatingly: "Tell me something about my new job. Can I get up there on the throne and pass miracles?"

"The powers of the office are unlimited, at least as regards this universe, O lord."

"Can I say anything I want, and have it so?"

"Yes, so long as you do not limit the powers of Nois."

"What do you mean?"   •

"Oh, you could not say that something shall be so forever more. If it were so, your successors could not change it, and you would have limited the powers of the office of Nois, which by definition are unlimited."

"But look, Hoimon, either I'm Nois or I'm not, to use your own screwy logic; so if Nois is omnipotent, then I must be omnipotent—"

The ascetic interrupted: "Entreating my lord's pardon, I do not understand these fine points of philosophy. I merely seek spiritual perfection in my humble most."

"Hm. What do you value most?"

"My spiritual perfection," answered Hoimon promptly. "Neither death nor torment can touch that!"

"I don't want to be hard on you, old man," grinned Hobart. "But after all you're responsible for getting me into this. Tell you what. Either you take me home and let the priesthood worry about getting another Nois, or I'll get up on that throne and turn you into the most lecherous old libertine this Aristotelian world has ever seen! You'll have a raging thirst for firewater; you'll drool and twitch at the mere sight of a woman, and want to tear the dress right off her—"

Swift horror flooded the ascetic's face; his composure was not only cracked but shattered.

"Not that!" he cried. "I hear and obey, O Nois-elect! You are too strong for me!"

"That's better," said Hobart. "Now—guess we'll have to make a dash for it."

"I will conduct you," groaned Hoimon, broad shoulders drooping. "But I shall have to prepare the way whilst you remain here, so that the people shall have time to settle their affairs. I go!" And the ascetic, loin-towel sagging, hastened out.

16

MORE DAYS PASSED, MERCIFULLY swift, while Hobart waited. A hundred times a day he told himself that it was all set now, and a hundred times a day reminded himself that there would be a catch in it somewhere.

When Chidelas announced the return of Hoimon, Hobart flung a hasty farewell at the priests, notwithstanding their final wail of protest. "Come on!" he barked, catching Hoimon's elbow and dragging the ascetic along.

As soon as they emerged from the pyramid, the bright sun was blotted out by gray mist that sprang up from nowhere and turned everything the color of damp blotting-paper, and made all outlines fuzzy at twenty feet.

"It is the interregnum," moaned Hoimon, "When the laws of nature are void, and things neither are nor are not!"

"Doesn't bother me," grinned Hobart. "I only hope you don't lose your way in the fog."

They walked swiftly to the edge of the floor of the bowl, and began to climb the curving wall. At first it was easy; then the slope became too steep for comfortable negotiation. Hobart's shod feet skidded on the obsidian, though Hoimon's bare ones continued to make progress.

Then another factor entered the picture; the rock under the pressure of Hobart's feet began to spall and chip off. While he made a couple of bad slips, losing ground each time, the resulting unevenness of the surface provided traction.

"You see, O Rollin," groaned Hoimon, "it is beginning."

"The crumbling?"

Hoimon nodded somberly, and gave Hobart a hand up the last few feet. On the rim of the bowl were standing two animals: a horse and a donkey. The horse was indicated as Hobart's mount, while Hoimon took the ass. "More in keeping with my humility," explained the ascetic. Hobart's saddle included a pair of holsters in which were stuck two matchlock pistols.

"Come," said Hoimon, clucking to his mount. The little animal started off with negligible urging; Hoimon seemed to have a way with animals. They skirted the rims of a succession of bowls like that which contained the temple. As they rode, the evidence of pitting of the smooth black surface became more and more obvious. When these people spoke of their world's crumbling, they meant crumbling!

The riders came out on another savannah, and pushed their mounts hard, Hoimon apparently steering by instinct. They passed a peasant's hut, briefly visible in the grayness, which had just collapsed into a heap of rubbish. The peasant and his family were standing in a row in front of it and cursing with verve.

Hobart shouted: "Won't the houses in the big cities collapse?"

"Aye," retorted Hoimon. "What suppose you I was doing whilst you awaited me? I spread word to abandon all cities, so that the people might survive the plague of rot until by some miracle another Nois be found! Hold, not so fast; here are the Conical Mountains."

"So soon?" asked Hobart.

"It was not far."

As far as Hobart could see, the sharp, uniform cones had begun to slump and slide, too, so that they looked almost like real mountains. When the riders entered the defiles between the cones, their animals sank up to the hocks in soft crumbly debris.

"Hasten!" shouted Hoimon, "ere the tunnels collapse!"

The agonizing journey went on and on; Hobart chewed his lips until they bled, and hoped to Nois that Hoimon knew where he was going.

"Off!" bellowed the ascetic, suiting the action to the word. "Bring your pistols, if they have not rusted away!"

Hobart snatched them out; the barrels showed a film of red rust, but they looked as if they would still shoot.

"What are they for?" he shouted after Hoimon, who was already leaping up the switchback trail that led to the tunnel opening.

"The cave-folk," Hoimon flung back. "They may be so maddened by the fall of rock that they will attack even me, who has lived among them! And the worst of it is that I shall have to defend myself from them—offer violence to living creatures!"

Hobart struggled up the hill until his heart was going like a tommy-gun and each breath was agony. At the cave entrance he could barely stagger, and felt like flinging himself prone and letting the world crumble away. But Hoimon barked: "Your flame-device, O Rollin! Quickly!"

Hobart snapped the cigarette-lighter open. Hoimon lit a torch he had placed in readiness at the cave entrance, and then the matches of the pistols. "Come!" he shouted again.

Hobart staggered after him, gasping deeply through his open mouth. As he entered the darkness he could hear faint rumblings; little bits of the tunnel-roof dropped on him and got in his hair. He almost had to run, tall as he was, to keep up with Hoimon's gigantic strides. A grinding thump behind told of a larger fall from the roof.

Hoimon suddenly halted, the torch throwing twisted shadows. He held up a warning finger. Hobart heard again that shrill inhuman cry; he was sure that all his hair was standing straight on end. The warbling shriek came closer, and something moved in the corridor ahead.

It was so much worse than anything Hobart had anticipated that the engineer came close to passing out. It was manlike, but dead white and eyeless and covered with long sparse tactile hairs like cats' whiskers. It exposed its fangs, repeated its unearthly scream, and ran toward them with long arms reaching.

Hobart thrust one pistol past Hoimon and pulled the trigger. The flash blinded him and the roar brought down a cascade of fragments from the roof, but when his vision cleared he saw that the thing was lying supine and still.

Hoimon cleared the body of the cave-man in one great bound. Hobart struggled after, and then they halted as the whole tunnel was blocked by the white things. Hobart fired the other pistol, handed it wordlessly to Hoimon, drew his sword, and plunged ahead.

He cut down one, then another; then they were all around him, and something fastened its teeth in his leg . . . He hacked and thrust in a frenzy, and heard the hard breathing of Hoïmon behind him and the thump, thump of Hoimon's pistol-butt on white skulls. Hoimon shot that wonderful extensible arm past Hobart and knocked over a couple facing him, while through the engineer's head ran an inane little syllogism:

Cave-dwelling organisms (cave-shrimps, cave salamanders, etc.) are white and blind.

These cave-folk are genuine cave-dwellers.

Therefore these cave-folk are white and blind.

Something shot past Hobart's head with an audible swish: the body of a cave-man, which crashed into the crowd in front, mowing them down like a cannon-ball. Hoimon dashed past him, swinging the pistol by the barrel and still holding the torch; then halted and backed, almost stepping on Hobart. He called over his shoulder: "Back! The Tunnel col—" The rest was drowned in a deep grinding roar; in the dim torchlight Hobart could see, down the tunnel ahead, masses of rocks moving, pouring into the corridor, and then thick dust billowing toward them. The footing shook, and the two human beings took to their heels.

Behind them came the shrieks of more cave-men, pouring into the uncollapsed part of the tunnel from some obscure side entrance. Hobart heard their feet pattering, and swung his sword blindly behind him as he ran. He was rewarded by hitting something and hearing a scream. The little gray spot that was the outer world seemed to get no nearer; then it expanded suddenly. Both men went straight down the mountainside in long, slithering leaps. Hoimon had finally lost his towel, and was bleeding from a dozen bites and scratches.

Hobart asked: "Will they follow—"

"There is no sun to stop them," answered Hoimon, mounting his ass. Hobart sheathed his sword and swung atop his horse just as the pallid horde poured out of the tunnel mouth and spilled down the slope like popcorn.

The animals hurried off without urging, and were immediately out of sight of the ghastly tribesmen. However, the thin piercing screams followed after and did not grow appreciably fainter.

"Are they coming after us?" asked Hobart.

"Yes, by scent. When we get out of the Conical Mountains we can outrun them."

"Hey, Hoimon, if the tunnels have collapsed, how'll I get back to my world?"

"You cannot, my friend."

"Isn't there any other place—"

"Not that I know! The tunnel-end is the only point where the barrier is thin enough for my spiritual perfection to penetrate. We must return to the pyramid of Nois."

"What? I'll be damned if—"

"You have no choice, O Rollin. Know that you alone can end the interregnum and bring back the sun. Until you do, the cave-folk will pursue us across half the world if need be. It will probably not be necessary, for they can run down the swiftest horse in time. Now save your breath, for we come to the open land."

They trotted out between the last pair of cones and broke into a gallop. The screams pursued and became gradually fainter. But they did not die altogether.

After several briskly running miles, they passed the collapsed peasant's hut. It occurred to Hobart that the cave-folk would not be too nicely discrimi-

nating in their appetite. He pulled up and shouted to
the peasant:

"Run for your lives! The cave-men are coming!"

The man stared at him stupidly. Hoimon remarked:
"They can never escape afoot, O Rollin. The cave-
folk will hunt them down by scent and devour them,
as they will many another unless thwarted."

"How far to the pyramid?" snapped Hobart.

"Perhaps two miles more."

"Okay, we'll give these folks the animals. Get off!"
Hobart dismounted and repeated his warning with
more detail. Thin shrieks wafting through the fog
carried conviction, and the family mounted with stam-
mering thanks and rode off.

Hobart went through the pockets of the jacket of
his conservative brown business suit—now a much
wrinkled, stained, and faded garment—and discarded
the coat itself and his necktie. Then he set out at an
easy long-distance stride, gripping his scabbard in
his left fist. Hoimon trotted beside him.

The ululation of the cave-men came faintly for a
long time. Then they waxed little by little. Hobart
and Hoimon exchanged glances but said nothing,
saving their wind. Hobart was pretty tired from his
previous exertion, but had some miles of running left
in his legs if he were not forced to sprint.

The cries were a lot louder when they reached the
area of the black rock bowls. Hoimon led the way,
trotting around arc after arc. In one glimpse back
Hobart could barely make out a crowd of little figures moving in the grayness behind them.

"Hasten," breathed Hoimon, lengthening his co-
lossal stride. Hobart pumped after him, realizing
that the pursuers were gaining continuously.

He was debating whether to throw away his sword
when they arrived at the bowl containing the glow-

ing white pyramid, one definite thing in that world of half-light. Hoimon ran right down the side with enormous strides. Hobart took four such leaps and turned his ankle and finished the slope rolling over and over with the scabbard banging his shins and prodding his ribs. He stopped rolling at the bottom and tried to get up, but the outraged foot would not support him. Screams drew his regard up; the cave-men appeared on the rim of the bowl.

Hoimon picked Rollin Hobart up, tucked him under one arm, and trotted heavily to the pyramid. Hobart was inside in the presence of Psylleus and Chidelas before he knew it.

The two priests and the ascetic shouted at him all at once: "Quickly, lord, ascend thy throne! Else the cave-folk will do us to shameful death!"

"But they can't come in *here*—" protested Hobart.

"Aye, but they can!" replied Hoimon. "Whilst the throne is vacant this is but a pyramid of curious luminous rock, no more! Hasten!"

"Damn it, why don't one of you guys do it? You'd make a better Nois than—"

They interrupted with simultaneous shouts of protest: "My humility forbids—" ". . . we priests are chosen precisely because we lack such ambitions . . ." "Oh lord, do thy duty!"

They would rather argue till the cave-men at them than ascent the throne, thought Hobart. The shrieks came near through the stone walls; the cave-folk had reached the floor of the bowl . . .

With a silent curse Hobart snatched the robe that Psylleus proffered, and hobbled up the steps of the throne. With each step the ascent became easier. He made the last two in one leap, and jumped into the square, uncomfortable-looking seat as if he were playing musical chairs.

At once the grayness outside vanished. The fog whirled away (Hobart did not know how he could see it do so, but he could) and the sun burst out bright and glorious. The cave-men crowding outside burst into chattering squeaks of dismay.

Hobart shouted: "Let the cave-folk be immobilized in their present positions until I decide what to do with them!"

At once the squeaks ceased. The pyramid was ringed by white, eyeless, fanged statues.

Hm, not so bad, being Nois! Hobart leaned back, finding to his surprise that the throne was perfectly comfortable. There was a lack of bodily sensation, as when one is floating in a saline bath at just body temperature. The pain in his ankle faded away, and the ache in his overtaxed lungs disappeared.

Down on the floor below, three figures, two white-robed and one clothed in nothing but holy dirt, prostrated themselves in adoration.

Hobart relaxed for a full minute, enjoying the sensation. Then he tensed himself again. He called: "Let there be a new and adequate set of cages in the Royal Zoological Gardens of the City of Oroloia! Let the cave-folk, restored to their normal activity, be placed therein! All right, you guys down there, get up! You embarrass me. And I've played God all I'm gonna. Ugh!"

Hobart had tried to rise from his seat and had found to his consternation that he could not. He braced his muscles and heaved. "Unh!" he grunted, but still could not rise.

"Hey!" he called to his worshippers. "What's the idea? I want to leave!"

Psylleus looked honestly amazed. "O Nois, verily—what thou sayest is against all reason! It is unprecedented that thou shouldst wish to depart thy glory!"

"That's just because you never tried to make a Nois out of a Rollin Hobart before. Get me out of this!"

"O lord," muttered Psylleus, oozing reverence, "verily thou canst not leave until thy successor is at hand, for to do so would be to lower the dignity of thy office, which is eternal. Thy servants know no way to release thee."

"Oh, yeah?" Hobart pondered blackly for a few seconds. So they thought they had him at last, eh? He called: "Hoimon!"

"Yes, lord?"

"How'd you like to be Nois?"

"Ow!" yelled Hoimon in sudden anguish. "Spare your servant, O Nois! What would become of my humility, my self-abasement? What of my spiritual perfection? For lo these many years have I striven to erase all personal desires, to abandon all material pleasures! To me, the occupation of such a lofty seat would be the worst fate imaginable! Destroy me if you will, or transmute me to the vilest of hedonists: that is one thing I cannot, will not do! And now, if my lord pleases, I go to resume my solitary life of service and humility, free of all joys save those of the spirit!"

Hobart grinned: "Well, if you want misery, and being Nois is the worst thing you can think of, it's just the ticket for you! Hey, *come back here!*" Hoimon cowered back to the foot of the throne. Hobart continued:

"This is going to be a dirty trick in a way, but after all you started it." He filled his lungs and cried: "When I say 'bang,' let the following things be accomplished: First, that all the damage done during the recent crumbling of this world shall be repaired. Second: that Hoimon the ascetic shall be not only the kind of guy that would make a good Nois, but the kind that would be glad to take the job. Third: that the said Hoimon, otherwise known as the party of the first part, shall be Nois, in the throne and everything. Lastly: that I, the present Nois, shall be just plain Rollin Hobart again, and back in my own apartment in New York City, in the three-value world!

"BANG!"

* * *

He was standing in his own living-room.

He ran his eyes hungrily over every detail, and almost cried at the sight of his old textbooks and other unglamorous but highly individual possessions.

He stepped to the door, wincing as he realized that he had a sprained ankle again, and looked cautiously out through the crack. No rock tunnel; just the good old apartment-house corridor . . .

He unbuckled his sword—nice souvenir—and lowered himself into his big armchair. He pulled up the left leg of his shabby brown pants. The cave-man's bite had left a double row of blue-black bruises, but the teeth had not actually pierced the skin, which was a blessing. His right leg deserved more attention. He pulled off his shoe and then the sock, whose pattern was stretched all out of shape by the swelling of the ankle. He could move the foot a little without pain, so the sprain was not so bad as he had thought at the time. But he'd been stupid not to fix those injuries while he was Nois . . .

He reached over to his battered smoking-stand and got out a cigar. Nois, it felt good to relax!

Perhaps half the cigar had gone up in smoke when a sound from the kitchenette made Hobart prick up his ears. He had thought he heard movement before, but dismissed the idea as imagination. Now however came a definite sound: the *shlink, shlink* of a cocktail shaker. Who the devil would be mixing drinks in his apartment?

"George?" he called. "Say, George, remember my saying you couldn't even conceive of a world run on Aristotelian logic? Well, I was wrong. I've just been there, and it's the damnedest thing you—"

The cocktail-mixer appeared, shaker and glasses on a tray. It was the Princess Argimanda, clad, not in a gauzy whatnot, but in Saks' best.

"Ugk," said Hobart. When his wits returned from their vacation, he got out: "Thanks—I can sure use this—you look like a million dol—say, Argimanda, what are you doing in my apartment anyway?"

She smiled with a trace of mischief. "Hoimon brought me, three days ago. I wanted to see your world, so I prevailed on the old dear to take me through his tunnel. Good heavens, what's the matter with your foot?"

"Turned it. If you could get something full of cold water to soak it in, it'd be just dandy. Oh yeah, and you'll find some epsom salts in the bathroom. You dump 'em into the water."

Argimanda departed and presently returned with a stove-pot full of solution. She continued: "So-o-o, your little country girl looked your world over, and decided she'd like to live there. Hoimon said you'd be along in a few days."

"I almost wasn't," said Hobart.

"What happened? Hoimon spoke of danger."

"Ouch!" He lowered his foot. "Tell you some other time; it's a long story and I'm tired."

"Mad?" She looked slantwise up at him.

"N-not exactly—"

She patted his knee. "Don't worry about me, *Mister* Hobart. I'm moving right away, to the Y. W. until my job starts."

"Job?"

"Sure thing. I'm with Funk & Wagnalls. I'm a lexicographer, you know, though I had a time convincing them of the fact without any references."

Hobart took another drag on his butt, and said: "You've changed, Argimanda."

"How?"

"Clothes—and slang—and everything; you're actually human!"

"Thanks for the compliment. But I really haven't. It's merely the application of Kyzikeia's first gift to her fairy god-daughter: intelligence."

Hobart shook his head wonderingly. "You know, I'll be kind of helpless for a couple of days, and there won't be anybody to get my meals, and—ah—"

"You'd like me to cook them for you?" snapped Argimanda. "Sorry, Rolly, but I shall be busy, I'm afraid. I'll tell the nearest restaurant to send a man up, if you like." She finished her cocktail and set the glass down in a marked manner. "I'm leaving right now."

She clicked decisively into the bedroom, and reappeared with a traveling-case.

Hobart said anxiously: "Argimanda, you know I've been thinking. Maybe I was—uh—hasty—uh—"

"Rollin Hobart!" said Argimanda dangerously. "I've tried to treat you nicely, because after all you did save my life. But if you're going to offer me another chance, allow me to inform you that I don't accept other chances from gentlemen, including you for the sake of courtesy. I'm doing very nicely, thank you; I've got six dates for the next two weeks already."

"You're actually angry!" he gauped.

"You're jolly well right I'm angry! The very sight of you makes my hot Logaian blood boil. If you want to call me up at the end of a year, look for Argimanda

Xerophus in the 'phone book. I may be able to endure your society by then, if I haven't married a college president or a munitions manufacturer. Good bye!"

"A year! Wait a minute, please," pleaded Hobart. "I know I'm a heel and a stuffed shirt. But I do love you. I don't know for how long, but I suspect from the first time I saw you, though I wouldn't have admitted it. I worship the ground you walk on. All I'll do for the next year is watch the calendar. When the time's up I'll come running to offer heart and hand, for whatever they're worth, of one self-centered old bachelor. And I'll bring a spanner to use on your college president if necessary."

She sighed. "Well, in that case, Rolly—wouldn't a year be an awful waste of time?"

Then they were in each other's arms, whispering long-withheld endearments.

"*Miaow!*" It was Theiax, pushing the door open. The social lion cocked an eye at the spectacle, then complacently sat down and began to lap tea out of a cup on the floor.

Argimanda, over Hobart's shoulder, caught the pussy-lion's eye and winked.

Theiax smiled into his mane. He purred: "Prince, you need not worry about my size any more. I have my dignity even if I am small. I just chase biggest dog in New York clear into Hudson River!"

* * * *

THE ENCHANTED BUNNY
Homage to L. Sprague de Camp

by David Drake

JOE JOHNSON GOT INTO THE LITTLE CAR OF THE AIRPORT'S People Mover, ignoring the synthesized voice that was telling him to keep away from the doors. Joe was trying to carry his attaché case—stuffed with clothes as well as papers, since he'd used it for an overnight bag on this quick trip to see the Senator—and also to read the wad of photocopy the Senator had handed Joe in front of the terminal "to glance through on the flight back."

The Senator hadn't wanted to be around when Joe read the new section. He must have thought Joe wouldn't be pleased at the way he'd handled the Poopsi LaFlamme Incident.

The Senator was right.

Joe sat down on a plastic-cushioned seat. At least the car was empty except for Joe and the swarthy man—was he an Oriental?—the swarthy Oriental at the far end. When Joe flew in the day before, he'd shared the ride to the main concourse with a family of seven, five of whom—including the putative father—were playing catch with a Nerf ball.

The doors closed. The People Mover said something about the next stop being the Red Concourse and lurched into gentle motion.

Joe flipped another page of the chapter over the paperclip holding it by the corner. *It was about that time that I met a Miss LaFlamme, a friend of my wife Margaret, who worked, as I understand it, as a dancer of some sort. . . .*

Good god almighty! Did the Senator—did the *ex*-Senator, who was well known to be broke for a lot of the reasons that could make his memoirs a bestseller—really think he was going to get away with this?

The publishers hadn't paid a six-figure advance for stump speeches and homilies. They'd been promised scandal, they *wanted* scandal—

And the Senator's rewrite man, Joe Johnson, wanted scandal, too, because his two-percent royalty share was worth zip, zilch, *zero* if *The Image of a Public Man* turned out to be bumpf like this.

". . . stopping at the Red Concourse," said the synthesized voice. The car slowed, smoothly but abruptly enough that the attaché case slid on Joe's lap and he had to grab at it. More people got on.

Joe flipped the page.

—helping Miss LaFlamme carry the bags of groceries to her suite. Unfortunately, the elevator—

The People Mover shoop-shooped into motion again. Joe tightened his grip on the case. One of the new arrivals in the car was a crying infant.

Joe felt like crying also. Senator Coble had been *told* about the sort of thing that would go into the book. He'd *agreed*.

An elevator repairman at Poopsi LaFlamme's hotel had lifted the access plate to see why somebody'd pulled the emergency stop button between floors.

He'd had a camera in his pocket. That had been the Senator's bad luck at the time; but the photo of two goggle-eyed drunks, wearing nothing but stupid expressions as they stared up from a litter of champagne bottles, would be *great* for the back jacket. . . .

Except apparently the Senator thought everybody—and particularly his publishers—had been living on a different planet when all that occurred.

"In a moment, we will be stopping at the Blue Concourse," said the People Mover dispassionately.

Joe flipped the page. *Unfortunately, pornographic photographs, neither of whose participants looked in the least like myself or Miss LaFlamme, began to circulate in the gutter press—*

And the Washington *Post*. And *Time* magazine. And—

The car halted. The people who'd boarded at the previous stop got off.

Joe flipped the page. *—avoided the notoriety inevitable with legal proceedings, because I remembered the words of my sainted mother, may she smile on me from her present home with Jesus. "Fools' names,"* she told me, *"and fools' faces, are always found in public—"*

Damn! Joe's concourse!

The People Mover's doors were still open. Joe jumped up.

The paperclip slipped and half the ridiculous nonsense he'd been reading spewed across the floor of the car.

For a moment, Joe hesitated, but he had plenty of time to catch his plane. He bent and began picking up the mess.

The draft might be useless, but it wasn't something Joe wanted to leave lying around either. The swarthy man—maybe a Mongolian? He didn't look like any of the Oriental races with which Joe was familiar—watched without expression.

The car slowed and stopped again. Joe stuffed the papers into his attache case and stepped out. He'd cross to the People Mover on the opposite side of the brightly-lighted concourse and go back one stop.

There were several dozen people in the concourse: businessmen, family groups, youths with back-packs and sports equipment that they'd have the dickens of a time fitting into the overhead stowage of the aircraft on which they traveled. Nothing unusual—

Except that they were all Japanese.

Well, a tourist group; or chance; and anyway, it didn't matter to Joe Johnson. . . .

But the faces all turned toward him as he started across the tile floor. People backed away. A little boy grabbed his mother's kimono-clad legs and screamed in abject terror.

Joe paused. A pair of airport policemen began running down the escalator from the upper level of the concourse. Joe couldn't understand the words they were shouting at him.

The policemen wore flat caps and brass-buttoned frock coats, and they were both drawing the sabers that clattered in patent-leather sheaths at their sides.

Joe hurled himself back into the People Mover just as the doors closed. He stared out through the windows at the screaming foreign crowd. He was terrified that people would burst in on him before the car started to move—

Though the faces he saw looked as frightened as his own must be.

The People Mover's circuitry shunted it into motion. Joe breathed out in relief and looked around him. Only then did he realize that he wasn't in the car he'd left.

There were no seats or any other amenities within the vehicle. The walls were corrugated metal. They'd been painted a bilious hospital-green at some point, but now most of their color came from rust.

Scratched graffiti covered the walls, the floor, and other scribblings. The writing wasn't in any language Joe recognized.

Joe set his attache case between his feet and rubbed his eyes with both hands. He felt more alone than he ever had before in his life. He must have fallen and hit his head; but he wasn't waking up.

The car didn't sound as smooth as a piece of electronics any more. Bearings squealed like lost souls. There was a persistent slow jarring as the flat spot in a wheel hit the track, again and again.

The People Mover—if that's what it was now—slowed and stopped with a sepulchral moan. The door didn't open automatically. Joe hesitated, then gripped the handle and slid the panel sideways.

There wasn't a crowd of infuriated Japanese waiting on the concourse. There wasn't even a concourse, just a dingy street, and it seemed to be deserted.

Joe got out of the vehicle. It was one of a series of cars which curved out of sight among twisted buildings. The line began to move again, very slowly, as Joe watched transfixed. He couldn't tell what powered the train, but it certainly wasn't electric motors in the individual cars.

There was a smell of sulphur in the air, and there was very little light.

Joe looked up. The sky was blue, but its color was that of a cobalt bowl rather than heaven. There seemed to be a solid dome covering the city, because occasionally a streak of angry red crawled across it. The trails differed in length and placement, but they always described the same curves.

The close-set buildings were three and four stories high, with peak roofs and many gables. The windows were barred, and none of them were lighted.

Joe swallowed. His arms clutched the attache case to his chest. The train clanked and squealed behind him, moving toward some unguessable destination. . . .

Figures moved half a block away: a man was walking his dogs on the dim street. Claws or heel-taps clicked on the cracked concrete.

"Sir?" Joe called. His voice sounded squeaky. "Excuse me, sir?"

They were very big dogs. Joe knew a man who walked a pet cougar, but these blurred, sinewy forms were more the size of tigers.

There was a rumbling overhead like that of a distant avalanche. The walker paused. Joe looked up.

The dome reddened with great blotches. *Clouds*, Joe thought— and then his mind coalesced the blotches into a single shape, a human face distorted as if it were being pressed down onto the field of a photocopier.

A face that must have been hundreds of yards across.

Red, sickly light flooded down onto the city from the roaring dome. The two "dogs" reared up onto their hind legs. They had lizard teeth and limbs like armatures of wire. The "man" walking them was the same as his beasts, and they were none of them from any human universe.

A fluting *Ka-Ka-Ka-Ka-Ka* came from the throats of the demon trio as they loped toward Joe.

Joe turned. He was probably screaming. The train clacked past behind him at less than a walking pace. Joe grabbed the handle of one of the doors. The panel slid a few inches, then stopped with a rusty shriek.

Joe shrieked louder and wrenched the door open with a convulsive effort. He leaped into the interior. For a moment, he was aware of nothing but the clawed hand slashing toward him.

Then Joe landed on stiff cushions and a man's lap, while a voice said, "Bless me, Kiki! The wizard we've been looking for!"

"I beg your pardon," said Joe, disentangling himself from the other man in what seemed to be a horse-drawn carriage clopping over cobblestones.

It struck Joe that he'd never heard "*I beg your pardon*" used as a real apology until now; but that sure wasn't the *only* first he'd racked up on this trip to Atlanta.

The other man in the carriage seemed to be in his late 'teens. He was dressed in a green silk jumper with puffed sleeves and breeches, high stockings, and a fur cloak.

A sword stood upright with the chape of its scabbard between the man's feet. The weapon had an ornate hilt, but it was of a serviceable size and stiffness. Joe rubbed his nose, where he'd given himself a good crack when he hit the sword.

A tiny monkey peeked out from behind the youth's right ear, then his left, and chittered furiously. The animal wore a miniature fur cloak fastened with a diamond brooch.

The monkey's garment reminded Joe that wherever he was, it wasn't Atlanta in the summertime. The carriage had gauze curtains rather than glazing over the windows. Joe shivered in his cotton slacks and short-sleeved shirt.

"I'm Delendor, Master Sorceror," the youth said. "Though of course you'd already know that, wouldn't you? May I ask how you choose to be named here in Hamisch?"

Kiki hopped from Delendor's shoulder to Joe's. The monkey's body was warm and smelled faintly of stale urine. It crawled around the back of Joe's neck, making clicking sounds.

"I'm Joe Johnson," Joe said. "I think I am. God."

He clicked open the latches of his attache case. Everything inside was as he remembered it, including the dirty socks.

Kiki reached down, snatched the pen out of Joe's shirt pocket, and hurled it through the carriage window at the head of a burly man riding a donkey in the opposite direction.

The man shouted, "Muckin' bassit!"

Joe shouted, "Hey!"

Delendor shouted, "Kiki! For shame!"

The monkey chirped, leaped, and disappeared behind Delendor's head again.

"I *am* sorry," Delendor said. "Was it valuable? We can stop and . . .?"

And discuss things with the guy on the donkey, Joe thought. "No thanks, I've got enough problems," he said aloud. "It was just a twenty-nine-cent pen, after all."

Though replacing it might be a little difficult.

"You see," Delendor continued, "Kiki's been my only friend for eight years, since father sent my sister Estoril off to Glenheim to be fostered by King Belder. I don't get along very well with my brothers Glam and Groag, you know . . . them being older, I suppose."

"Eight years?" Joe said, focusing on a little question because he sure-hell didn't want to think about the bigger ones. "How long do monkeys live, anyway?"

"Oh!" said Delendor. "I don't—I'd rather not think

about that." He wrapped his chittering pet in his cloak and held him tightly.

Joe flashed a sudden memory of himself moments before, clutching his attache case to his chest and praying that he was somewhere other than in the hell which his senses showed him. At least Kiki was alive. . . .

"Estoril's visiting us any day now," Delendor said, bubbly again. Kiki peeked out of the cloak, then hopped to balance on the carriage window. "It'll be wonderful to see her again. And to find a great magician to help me, too! My stars must really be in alignment!"

"I'm not a magician," Joe said in a dull voice.

Reaction was setting in. He stared at the photocopied chapter of the Senator's memoirs. *That* sort of fantasy he was used to.

"After you help me slay the dragon," Delendor continued, proving that he hadn't been listening to Joe, "I'll get more respect. And of course we'll save the kingdom."

"Of course," muttered Joe.

Kiki reached out the window and snatched the plume from the helmet of a man in half-armor who carried a short-hafted spontoon. The spontoon's ornate blade was more symbol than weapon. The man bellowed.

"Kiki!" Delendor cried. "Not the Civic Guard!" He took the plume away from his pet and leaned out the window of the carriage as the horses plodded along.

"Oh," said the guardsman—the cop—in a changed voice as he trotted beside the vehicle to retrieve his ornament. "No harm done, Your Highness. Have your little joke."

"Ah . . ." Joe said. "Ah, Delendor? Are you a king?"

"Of course not," Delendor said in surprise. "My father, King Morhaven, is still alive."

He pursed his lips. "And anyway, both Glam and Groag are older than I am. Though that wouldn't *prevent* father. . . ."

Joe hugged his attache case. He closed his eyes. The carriage was unsprung, but its swaying suggested that it was suspended from leather straps to soften the rap of the cobblestones.

God.

"Now," the prince went on cheerfully, "I suppose the dragon's the important thing . . . but what I *really* want you to do is to find my enchanted princess."

Joe opened his eyes. "I'm not . . ." be began.

But there wasn't any point in repeating what Delendor wouldn't listen to anyway. For that matter, there was nothing unreasonable about assuming that a man who plopped out of mid air into a moving carriage was a magician.

The prince opened the locket on his neck chain and displayed it to Joe. The interior could have held a miniature painting—but it didn't. It was a mirror, and it showed Joe his own haggard face.

"I've had the locket all my life," Delendor said, "a gift from my sainted mother. It was the most beautiful girl in the world—and as I grew older, so did the girl in the painting. But only a few weeks ago, I opened the locket and it was a *rabbit*, just as you see it now. I'm sure she's the princess I'm to marry, and that she's been turned into a bunny by an evil sorceror."

Delendor beamed at Joe. "Don't you think?"

"I suppose next," Joe said resignedly, "you're going to tell me about your wicked stepmother."

"I beg your pardon!" snapped the prince, giving the phrase its usual connotations.

Delendor drew himself up straight and closed the locket. "My mother Blumarine was a saint! Everyone who knew her says so. And when she died giving birth to me, my father never *thought* of marrying a third time."

"Ah," said Joe. "Look, sorry, that's not what I meant." It occurred to him that Delendor's sword was too respectable a piece of hardware to be only for show.

"I'm not sure what father's first wife was like," the prince went on, relaxing immediately. "But I think she must have been all right. Estoril more than balances Glam and Groag, don't you think?"

"I, ah," Joe said. "Well, I'll take your word for it."

"They say that mother had been in love with a young knight in her father's court," Delendor went on. "Her father was King Belder of Glenheim, of course. But they couldn't marry until he'd proved himself—which he tried to do when the dragon appeared, in Glenheim that time. And it almost broke mother's heart when the dragon ate the young man. King Belder married her to my father at once to take her, well, her mind off the tragedy, but they say she never really recovered."

Kiki leaned out of the window and began chittering happily. Delendor stroked his pet's fur and said, "Yes, yes, we're almost home, little friend."

He beamed at Joe once more. "That's why it's so important for me to slay the dragon now that it's reappeared, you see," the prince explained. "As a gift to my sainted mother. And *then* we'll find my enchanted princess."

Joe buried his face in his hands. "Oh, God," he muttered.

Something warm patted his thumb. Kiki was trying to console him.

The measured hoofbeats echoed, then the windows darkened for a moment as the carriage passed beneath a masonry gateway. Joe pushed the curtain aside for a better look.

They'd driven into a flagged courtyard in the center of a three-story stone building. The inner walls glittered with hundreds of diamond-paned windows. Servants in red and yellow livery bustled about the coach, while other servants in more prosaic garb busied themselves with washing, smithing, carpentry— and apparently lounging about.

"The Palace of Hamisch," Delendor said with satisfaction.

Joe nodded. A real fairytale palace looked more practical—and comfortable—than the nineteenth-century notion of what a fairytale palace should be.

A real fairytale palace. God 'elp us.

The carriage pulled up beneath a porte cochere. Servants flung open the doors with enthusiasm to hand out the prince and his companion.

Joe didn't know quite how to react. He let a pair of liveried youths take his hands, but the whole business made him feel as though he were wearing a corsage and a prom dress.

Kiki jumped from Delendor's right shoulder to his left and back again. Joe noticed that each of the nearest servants kept a hand surreptitiously close to his cap.

The carriage clucked into motion. There was a stable on the opposite side of the courtyard.

"Your Highness," said the fiftyish man whose age

and corpulence marked him as the palace major domo, "your father and brothers have been meeting in regard to the, ah, dragon; and King Morhaven specifically asked that when you arrived, you be sent—"

"Is my sister here yet?" Delendor interrupted.

"Yes," said the major domo, "the Princess Estoril has been placed in her old rooms in—"

As the carriage swung into the stables, the driver turned and smirked over his shoulder at Joe. He was the swarthy maybe-Mongolian who'd shared Joe's car in Atlanta.

"*Hey!*" Joe bawled as he took a long stride. His foot slipped on the smooth flagstones and he fell on his arse.

The coach disappeared into the stables.

Instead of making another attempt to run after the man, Joe stood and used the attention that his performance had just gained him to demand, "Prince! Your Highness, that is. Who was driving us?"

Delendor blinked. "How on earth would I know?" he said. "I just called for a coach, of course."

The nods of all the servants underscored a statement as obviously true as the fact the sun rose in the east.

Did the sun here rise in the east?

"Well, anyway, Clarkson," the prince went on, turning again to the major domo, "find a room for my friend here in my wing. I'll go see Estoril at once."

"Ah, Your Highness," the major domo replied with the fixed smile of an underling caught in the middle. "Your father did specifically ask that—"

"Oh, don't worry about that, Clarkson!" Delendor threw over his shoulder as he strode into the palace. "My friend Joe here is a mighty magician. He and I will take care of the dragon, never fear!"

Clarkson watched as his master disappeared, then

sized up Joe. "No doubt . . ." the major domo said neutrally. "Well, we're used to His Highness' enthusiasms, aren't we?"

Joe nodded, though he was pretty sure that the question wasn't one which Clarkson expected him to answer.

Joe's room was on the third floor, overlooking the courtyard. Its only furnishings were a bed frame and a cedar chest. There were two casement windows and, in one corner against the outer wall, a fireplace which shared a flue with the room next door.

The fire wasn't set, and the room was colder than Hell.

Clarkson watched with glum disdain as a housekeeper opened the cedar chest with a key hanging from her belt. She handed out feather comforters to lower-ranking maids. They spread them over the bed frame in what looked like a warm, if not particularly soft, arrangement.

"Why isn't the fire laid?" the major domo demanded peevishly. "And there should be a chamberpot, you *know* what happens when there isn't a chamberpot. And on the courtyard side, too!"

"I don't know where the girl's gotten to," the housekeeper said with a grimace. "I'm sure it'll be seen to shortly, sir."

"Ah," Joe said. "Ah, Clarkson? I wonder if you could find me some warmer clothes? A fur coat would be perfect."

The major domo stared at Joe disdainfully. "That's scarcely my affair," he said. "I suppose you can talk to the chamberlain. Or to the prince, no doubt."

Enough was enough.

Joe set his attache case down and stood with his hands on his hips.

"Oh?" he said, letting the past hour of terror and frustration raise his voice into real anger. "Oh? It doesn't matter to you, then? Well, Clarkson, does it matter to you if you spend the rest of eternity as a fat green frog in the castle moat?"

The maids and housekeeper scurried out of the room, their mouths forming ovals of silent horror. Clarkson's face set itself in a rictus. "Yes, of course, milord," he muttered through stiff lips. "Yes, of course, I'll take care of that immediately."

The major domo dodged through the door like a caroming pinball, keeping as far from Joe as he could. He bowed, spreading his arms—and grabbed the handle to pull the door closed behind him.

Which left Joe alone, as cold as fear and an all-stone room could make a man.

He stared out one of the diamond-paned windows. It was clean enough, but there was frost on both sides of the glass. Maybe one of the half-seen figures in the rooms across the courtyard was the maybe-Mongolian, who'd maybe brought Joe—

His door opened and banged shut again behind a slip of a girl in drab clothing. She shot the flimsy bolt and ran two steps toward the cedar chest before she realized Joe had turned from the window and was watching her in amazement.

Joe thought she was going to scream, but she choked the sound off by clapping both her hands over her own mouth. Through her fingers she whimpered, "Please help me! Please hide me!"

"Coo-ee!" called a man's deep voice from the hallway.

"Here chick-chick-chickee!" boomed another man.

A fist hammered Joe's door. "Better not make us come in for you, chickie," the first voice warned.

Great.

"Sure," Joe whispered.

The girl was short and rail-thin. Mousy brown hair trailed out from beneath her mob cap. She started for the chest again.

Joe grabbed her by the shoulder. "Not there," he said, raising his voice a little because the banging on the door had become louder and constant. He threw back the top comforter.

"*There*," he explained, pointing. She gave him a hopeful, terrified look and flattened herself crossways on the bed.

Joe folded the thick feather quilt over her. Then he slid up one of the windows—it couldn't possibly make the room colder—and drew open the bolt just as the doorpanel started to splinter inward under the impacts of something harder than a hand.

Two black-bearded men, built like NFL nose guards, forced their way into the room. They'd been hammering the door with their sword pommels.

Delendor's weapon had looked serviceable. The swords *this* pair carried would have been two-handers—in hands smaller than theirs.

They didn't even bother to look at Joe. "Where are you, bitch?" one shouted. "We were just gonna show you a good time, but by god it'll be the *last* time fer you now!"

"Look, I'm here as a guest of—" Joe began.

"*There* we go!" the other intruder boomed as his eyes lighted on the cedar chest as the only hiding place in the room.

He kicked the chest with the toe of his heavy leather boot. "Come out, come out, wherever you are!" he shouted.

His fellow rammed his big sword through the top of the cedar chest and splinteringly out the back. Its point sparked on the stone flooring.

Both men stabbed repeatedly at the fragile wood until it was quite obvious that the chest was empty.

They'd thought she was inside that, Joe realized. His body went cold. He'd already put his case down. Otherwise his nerveless hands would've dropped it.

"We saw 'er come in, so she musta got out the . . ." one of the men said. He peered through the open casement. There was no ledge, and the walls were a smooth, sheer drop to the flagstone courtyard.

The two men turned toward Joe simultaneously. They held their bare swords with the easy naturalness of accountants keying numbers into adding machines.

"And just who the hell are you, boyo?" asked the one who'd first stabbed the cedar chest.

In what seemed likely to be his last thought, Joe wondered whether the FAA kept statistics on the number of air travelers who were hacked to death by sword-carrying thugs.

"He's the magician who's going to help your royal brother slay the dragon, Groag," said a cold voice from the doorway.

Which would make the other thug Glam; and no, they didn't show much family resemblance to Delendor.

Joe turned. The brothers had jumped noticeably when the newcomer spoke; and anyway, turning his back on Glam and Groag wouldn't make them *more* likely to dismember him.

"I'm Joe Johnson," he said, holding out his hand to be shaken. "I'm glad to see you."

Classic understatement.

The newcomer was tall, gray, and fine-featured. He wore black velvet robes, rather like academic regalia— though heavier, which this damned unheated building made a good idea. He stared at Joe's hand for a moment, then touched it in an obvious attempt to puzzle out an unfamiliar form of social interchange.

"My name is Ezekiel," he said. "I—"

"I think we'll go now," muttered Glam, bouncing off the doorjamb in much the fashion that the major domo had done minutes earlier. Groag followed him on the same course. Joe noticed that the brothers had sheathed their swords.

The room returned to normal size with Glam and Groag out of it. There were *some* advantages to being mistaken for a magician.

"Ah, thanks," Joe said. "I, ah . . . didn't like the way things were going."

"They're not bad lads," Ezekiel said with what seemed to be his universal air of cool detachment. "A little headstrong, perhaps. But I couldn't have you turning the king's elder sons into . . . frogs, I believe I heard?"

He raised a quizzical eyebrow.

Joe shrugged. Before he spoke—before he decided *what* to say—a train of servants streamed into the room, carrying furs; charcoal and kindling with which they laid a fire; and a chamberpot.

"I suppose," Ezekiel pressed, "you have your apparatus with you? You don't—" he paused "—plan to deal with the dragon unaided, do you?"

"I was wondering," Joe temporized, "if you could tell me something about this dragon?"

Ezekiel blinked. "I'm not sure what it is you want to know," he said reasonably enough. "It's a dragon more than thirty yards long and invulnerable to weapons except at one point on its body . . . which no one in recorded history has discovered."

He smiled coldly. "It digs a burrow deep in the rock and sleeps twenty years of twenty-one, which is good . . . but in the year the beast wakes, it does quite enough damage to ruin a kingdom for a generation. Glenheim has barely recovered from the most recent visitation . . . and this time, the creature has chosen to devour a path through Hamisch. As no doubt your friend Prince Delendor has explained."

The servants were leaving with as much dispatch as they'd arrived. They carried out the scraps of cedar chest with a muttered promise of a replacement.

The fire burned nicely and might even have warmed the room, except that the window was still open. Joe shut it.

"Delendor was too occupied with seeing his sister to give me much of the background," he said neutrally.

Ezekiel's face twisted with disgust, the first emotion he'd shown since he arrived. "Prince Delendor's affection for his sister is, I'm sorry to say, unnatural," he said. "The king was well advised to send Estoril away when he did."

His lips pursed, shutting off the flow of excessively free words. "I wish you luck with your difficult task," Ezekiel concluded formally. "It's of course an honor to meet so powerful a colleague as yourself."

He left the room, and Joe closed the door behind him.

Joe took a deep breath. Well, he was still alive, which he wouldn't've bet would be the case a few minutes ago.

"Ah," he said to the bed. "You can come out now."

The folded comforter lay so flat that for an instant Joe thought the girl had been spirited away—which fit the way other things had been happening, though it wouldn't've improved his mood.

"Oh, bless you, sir," said her muffled voice as the feathers humped. The girl slipped out and stood before him again.

She wasn't really a girl. Her face was that of a woman in her mid-twenties, maybe a few years younger than Joe. Her slight form and, even more, her air of frightened diffidence made her look much younger at a glance.

"I'll . . ." she said. "I think it's safe for me to leave now. Bless—"

"Wait a darn minute!" Joe said. He put out his arm to stop her progress toward the door, then jerked back—furious with himself—when he saw the look of terror flash across her face.

"Look," he said, "I'd just like to know your name—"

"Mary, sir," she said with a deep curtsey. When she rose, she was blushing.

"For *god*'s sake, call me Joe!" he said, more harshly than he'd meant.

Joe cleared his throat. His new fur garments were stacked in a corner. He donned a cloak as much to give his hands something to do as for the warmth of it. "And, ah," he said, "maybe you can give me a notion of what's going on? I mean—"

He *didn't* mean Glam and Groag, as Mary's expression of fear and distaste suggested she thought he did.

Joe understood the brothers well enough. They were jocks in a society which put even fewer restrictions on jock behavior than did a college dorm.

"No, no," Joe said, patting her thin shoulder. "Not that. Just tell me if what Ezekiel said about the dragon's true. And who *is* Ezekiel, anyway?"

"Why, he's the royal sorcerer," Mary said in amazement. "And a very powerful one, though nowhere near as powerful as you, Master Joe. It would take Ezekiel weeks to turn somebody into a frog, and I'm sure he doesn't know how to deal with the dragon."

"Oh, boy," Joe said. From the look behind Ezekiel's

eyes when they talked, the magician had been contemplating the start of a multi-week project that would leave him with one fewer rival—and the moat with one more frog.

"I'm sure he must really hate you, Master Joe," Mary said, confirming Joe's guess. "Of course, Ezekiel doesn't really like anybody, though he does things for Glam and Groag often enough."

Does this palace even have a moat?

"Look, Mary," he said "is Delendor the only guy trying to kill this dragon, then? Isn't there an army or—you know, something?"

"Well, many brave knights have tried to slay the dragon over the years," Mary said, frowning at the unfamiliar word "army." "And sometimes commoners or even peasants have attacked the beast, but that didn't work either. So now there's . . . well, Glam and Groag say they've been spying out the dragon's habits, but I don't think anybody *really* wants to get near it."

A look of terrible sadness crossed the woman's face. "Except for Prince Delendor. He's serious. Oh, Master Joe, you *will* save him, won't you?"

Joe smiled and patted the woman's shoulder again. "We'll see what we can do," he said.

But dollars to doughnuts, there was damn-all a freelance writer *could* do about this problem.

Joe waited in his room; at first in the expectation that Delendor would be back shortly . . . and later, because Joe didn't have anyplace better to go. Anyway, the scatter-brained youth *might* still arrive.

Joe carried the *Fasti* to read on the airplane. Ovid's erudite myths and false etymologies had at least as much bearing on this world as they did on the one from which the People Mover had spirited Joe away.

After an hour or so, Joe snagged the first servant to pass in the hallway and asked for an armchair. What he got was solid, cushionless, and not particularly comfortable—but it arrived within fifteen minutes of Joe's request. The men carrying the chair panted as if they'd run all the way from the basement with it.

The frog story seemed to have gotten around.

But nobody else came to Joe's room until a servant summoned him to dinner in the evening.

"It's so brave of you to return to Hamisch to show solidarity when the dragon threatens, Estoril," said Delendor. "Most people are fleeing the other way."

Kiki sat on the prince's head. When Delendor leaned forward to see his sister past his two huge brothers and King Morhaven, the youth and monkey looked like a totem pole.

Estoril was black haired, like Glam and Groag, but her fine features were at least as lovely as Delendor's were boyishly handsome.

"Or into the city," said the king gloomily. "We're going to have a real sanitation problem soon, especially because of the herds of animals."

"I don't think that will be a serious difficulty, Your Highness," said Ezekiel, beside Estoril at the far end of the table from Joe. "The creature demolished the walls of Glenheim within minutes on its previous appearance . . . and, as I recall, made short work of the cattle sheltering there."

"Well," said Delendor brightly, "*that* won't be a problem here, because I'm going to slay the dragon. Right, Joe?"

"Actually," said Estoril, giving Delendor a look that Joe couldn't fathom, "my visiting now had nothing to do with the dragon. Katya—that was Blumarine's old nurse—died. In her last hours, she told me some things that . . . well, I thought I'd visit again."

Ezekiel took a sip of wine that Joe thought could double as antifreeze. "I met Katya once," he said. "She was a wise woman of some power. Did *you* know her, Joe?" the magician added sharply.

Joe choked on a mouthful of stewed carrot.

"Uh-uh," he managed to mumble without spraying. The meal ran to grilled meat and boiled vegetables, both of which would have been okay if they'd been taken off the heat within an hour or so of being thoroughly cooked.

Estoril turned. Joe couldn't see her face, but there was steel in her voice as she said, "According to Katya, Blumarine herself was a powerful magician. Was that the case, Master Ezekiel?"

"My mother?" Delendor blurted in amazement.

"My understanding, dear princess," Ezekiel said in a deliberately condescending voice, "is that your stepmother may have been a student of wisdom; but that if she ever practiced the craft, it was on the most rarified of levels. At any rate—"

The magician paused to drink the rest of his wine with apparent satisfaction. "At any rate," he went on, "it's certain that she couldn't prevent the young knight with whom she was romantically linked from being killed and eaten by the dragon."

The table waited in frozen silence.

"I believe," Ezekiel concluded, "that his name was Delendor, too, was it not, princess?"

King Morhaven hid his own face in his winecup. Glam and Groag chuckled like pools of bubbling mud.

The hell of embarrassment was that it only afflicted decent—or at least partially-decent—people. "I wonder if any of you can tell me," Joe said loudly to change the subject, "about the kind of guns you have here?"

Everyone stared at him. "Guns?" the king repeated.

Well, they'd been speaking English until now. "I mean," Joe explained, "the things that shoot, you know, bullets?"

This time it was Delendor who said, "Bullets?"

Ezekiel sneered.

Right, back to words of one syllable. After all, Joe had worked with the Senator. . . . "What," said Joe, "do you use to shoot things at a distance?"

"Distance" was two syllables.

"Arbalests, of course," said Morhaven. He pointed to a servant and ordered, "You there. Bring Master Joe an arbalest."

"Or you can throw rocks," Delendor noted happily. "I met a peasant who was very clever that way. Knocked squirrels right out of trees."

"From what I've been told," Joe said, "I doubt that slinging pebbles at your dragon is going to do a lot of good."

"What?" Groag said to Delendor in honest horror. "You're going to throw rocks at the dragon instead of facing it with your sword?"

The servant was returning to the table, carrying a massive crossbow that looked as though it weighed twenty pounds.

And that meant, just possibly, that Joe *could* arrange for Delendor to kill the dragon!

"Why, that's disgusting!" Glam added, echoing Groag's tone. "Even for a little shrimp like you!"

"Hang on—" Joe said. Everybody ignored him.

"I said nothing of the sort!" Delendor spluttered, his voice rising an octave. "How dare you suggest that I'd act in an unknightly fashion?"

Joe snapped his fingers and shouted, "Wait a minute!"

The room fell silent. Servants flattened. Delendor's brothers flinched as if ready to duck under the table to preserve themselves from frogness.

"Right," said Joe in a normal voice. "Now, the problem isn't knightly honor, it's the dragon. Is that correct?"

Morhaven and all three of his sons opened their mouths to object. Before they could speak, Estoril said, "Yes, that *is* correct."

She looked around the table. Her eyes were the color of a sunlit glacier. The men closed their mouths again without speaking.

"Right," Joe repeated. "Now, I know you've got charcoal. Do you have sulphur?"

The proportions were seventy-five, fifteen, ten. But Joe couldn't for the life of him remember whether the fifteen was charcoal or sulphur.

Everyone else at the table looked at Ezekiel. The magician frowned and said, "Yes, I have sulphur in my laboratory. But I don't see—"

"Wait," said Joe, because this was the kicker, the make-or-break. He swallowed. "Do you have potassium nitrate here? Saltpeter? I think it comes from. . . ."

Joe *thought* it came from under manure piles, but unless the locals had the stuff refined, he was damned if he could find it himself. He wasn't a chemist, he just had slightly misspent his youth.

"Yes . . ." Ezekiel agreed. "I have a store of saltpeter."

"Then, by god, I *can* help you kill this dragon!" Joe said in a rush of heady triumph. "No problem!"

Reality froze him. "Ah . . ." he added. "That is, if

Master Ezekiel helps by providing materials and, ah, equipment for my work?"

"And *I'll* slay—" Delendor began.

"Father," Estoril interjected with enough clarity and volume to cut through her brother's burbling, "Delendor is after all rather young. Perhaps Glam or—"

"What?" roared Glam and Groag together.

"What?" shrilled Delendor as he jumped to his feet. Kiki leaped from the prince's head and described a cartwheel in the air. "I *demand* the right to prove myself by—"

"*Silence!*" boomed King Morhaven. He stood, and for the first time Joe was reminded that the hunched, aging man *was* a monarch.

The king pointed at Delendor and dipped his finger. The youth subsided into his chair as if Morhaven had thrown a control lever.

King Morhaven transferred his gaze and pointing finger to Joe. "You," he said, "will prepare your dragon-killing magic." He turned. "And you, Ezekiel," he continued, "will help your colleague in whatever fashion he requires."

The magician—the real magician—nodded his cold face. "I hear and obey, Your Highness," he said.

Morhaven turned majestically again. "Delendor," he said, "your sister is correct that you are young; but the task is one at which seasoned heroes have failed in ages past. You have my permission to try your skill against the monster."

The king's face looked haggard, but there was no denying the authority in his voice as he added, "And if you succeed in saving the kingdom, my son, then there can be only one suitable recompense."

Joe blinked. If he understood correctly (and there couldn't be much doubt about what Morhaven meant), then the king had just offered the crown to his youngest son for slaying the dragon.

No wonder everybody was staring in amazement as King Morhaven seated himself again.

The regal gesture ended with a thump and a startled gasp from the king as his fanny hit the throne six inches below where it had been when he stood.

Kiki, chirruping happily, ran for the door. The monkey dragged behind him the thick cushion he'd abstracted from the throne while Morhaven was standing.

Joe, wearing an ankle-length flannel nightgown (at home he slept nude; but at home he didn't sleep in a stone icebox), had just started to get into bed when there was a soft rapping on his door.

He straightened. The fireplace held only the memory of an orange glow, but it was enough for him to navigate to the door past the room's few objects.

"Yes?" he whispered, standing to the side of the stone jamb in memory of the way the brothers' swords had ripped the cedar chest.

"Please, sir?" responded a tiny voice he thought he recognized.

Joe opened the door. Mary, a thin wraith, slipped in and shoved the door closed before Joe could.

"Please, sir," she repeated. "If you could hide me for a few nights yet, I'd be ever so grateful."

"What?" Joe said. "Mary, for Pete's sake! I'd like to help, but there's nowhere—"

And as he spoke, the obvious thought struck him dumb. *No! She was the size of an eight-year old, she was as helpless as an eight-year old, and the very thought—*

Ick!

"Oh, Master Joe, I'll sleep at the foot of your

bed," Mary explained. "I'll be ever so quiet, I promise. I'm just so afraid."

With excellent reason, Joe realized. If the dragon
was half as real and dangerous as Glam and Groag,
then this place was long overdue for the invention of
gunpowder.

And anyway, there wasn't much time to spend
thinking about the situation, unless he wanted them
both to freeze.

"Right," Joe said. "We'll, ah—"

But the girl—the woman!—had already eeled between the upper and lower comforters, lying cross-
wise as she'd hidden this afternoon. Joe got in more
gingerly, keeping his knees bent.

"Ah, Mary?" he said after a moment.

"Joe sir?"

"Could King Morhaven make Delendor his successor under, ah, your constitution?"

"Oh, yes!" the muffled voice responded. "And
wouldn't it be wonderful? But only when Delendor
shows what a hero he is. Oh, Master Joe, sir, you're
a gift from heaven to all Hamisch!"

"Or something," muttered Joe. But now that he'd
thought of gunpowder, he was pretty confident.

Arnault, the royal armorer, was a husky, sooty
man wearing a leather apron. His forearms were the
size of Joe's calves; blisters from flying sparks gave
them an ulcerated look.

"Yaas, maaster?" he rumbled in a voice that suggested that he was happier in his forge than being
summoned to the new magician's laboratory.

Joe wasn't thrilled about the laboratory either. He
was using the palace's summer kitchen, built in a
corner of the courtyard and open on all sides to vent
the heat of the ovens and grills during hot weather.

The weather now was cold enough that Joe wore fur mittens to keep the brass mortar and pestle from freezing his hands. On the other hand, the light was good; there was plenty of work space . . . and if something went wrong, the open sides would be a real advantage.

"Right," said Joe to the armorer. "I want you to make me a steel tube about three feet long and with a bore of . . ." *Forty-five caliber? No, that might be a little tricky.*

Joe cleared his throat. "A bore of about a half inch. Somewhere around that, it doesn't matter precisely so long as it's the same all the way along."

"Whazat?"

"And, ah," Joe added, beaming as though a display of confidence would banish the utter confusion from the armorer's face, "make sure the tube's walls are thick. Maybe you could use a wagon axle or something."

After all, they wouldn't have to carry the gun far.

"What?" the armorer repeated.

"I thought you wanted the tube to be steel, Joe," said Estoril. "Or was that one of the paradoxes of your craft?"

There were at least a hundred spectators, mostly servants. They crowded the sides of the summer kitchen to goggle at the magical preparations. He'd ordered them away half a dozen times, but that just meant the mass drew back a few yards into the courtyard . . . and drifted inward as soon as Joe bent over his paraphernalia again.

Of course, Joe could demand a closed room and bar himself in it until he'd finished the process—or blown himself to smithereens. That still didn't seem like the better choice.

Joe didn't even bother telling the members of the royal family to leave him alone. But if he had to do this over, he'd keep a couple frogs in his coat pockets and let them out at strategic times. . . .

The spectators weren't the immediate problem, though.

"Right," Joe said with his chirpy face on. "How thick are your axles here?"

"Waal," said the armorer, "they's aboot—" He mimed a four-inch diameter with his hands.

"But they're wooden!" said Delendor. "Ah, aren't they?" He looked around at the other spectators.

Ezekiel nodded silently. Joe thought he saw the magician's mouth quirk toward a smile.

"Right," said Joe. "Wood."

He swallowed. "Well, all I meant was that you need to get a round steel rod about this thick—" he curled his middle finger against the tip of his thumb, making a circle of about two inches in diameter "—and a yard long. Then—"

"Naow," said the armorer.

"No?" Joe translated aloud. His control slipped. "Well, why the hell *not*, then?"

"Whaar's a body t' foind so much stale, thaan?" the armorer demanded. "Is a body t' coot the edge fram avery sword in the kingdom, thaan?"

The big man's complexion was suffusing with blood and rage, and Joe didn't like the way the fellow's hands knotted about one another. The armorer wouldn't have to strangle a man in the normal fashion. He could just grab a victim's head and give a quick jerk, like a hunter finishing a wounded pheasant. . . .

"And after you have provided Arnault with the billet of steel, Master Joe," Ezekiel interjected—and thank goodness for the sardonic magician for a change, because he directed Arnault's smoldering eyes away from Joe. "Then I think you'll have to teach him your magical technique of boring the material."

The armorer didn't deign to nod.

"Right," said Joe, as though the false word were a catechism. Black gloom settled over his soul.

Joe didn't know anything about metalworking. If he *had* some background in metallurgy, he still wouldn't know how to adapt modern techniques to things Arnault could accomplish . . . which seemed to mean hammering bars into rough horseshoe shapes.

"Perhaps Arnault could weld a bundle of iron rods into a tube?" Estoril suggested. "About a yard long, you said?"

"Yaas, loidy," agreed the armorer with a massive nod.

"*No!*" gasped Joe.

Even Joe could visualize the blackened mass of weak spots and open holes that would result from somebody trying to weld a tube on a hand forge. Arnault wouldn't be making a gun, it'd be a bomb!

Joe's face cleared while the others stared—or glowered, in the cases of Arnault and Delendor's brothers —at him. "Estoril," he said, "you're brilliant! Now, how fast does this dragon move?"

"Yes, not only beautiful but wise beyond imagining," Delendor said, turning toward the princess. "I—"

"Del!" Estoril snapped, glancing fiercely toward Delendor, then looking away as if to emphasize that she'd' never seen him before in her life.

"For the most part, not very quickly," Ezekiel answered. Joe had already noticed that the magician was carrying out the spirit as well as the letter of King Morhaven's orders. "And it sleeps for long periods."

He smiled again. You didn't have to know Ezekiel

for long to know what kind of news would cause him to smile.

"When the beast chooses to run, though," Ezekiel went on, "it can catch a galloping horse . . . as I understand *Sir* Delendor of Glenheim learned in times past."

Joe stared at Ezekiel and thought, *You cruel son of a bitch*.

Ezekiel scared him, the way looking eye-to-eye at a spider had scared him once. There wasn't anything in the magician that belonged in human society, despite the man's undoubted brains and knowledge.

"Right," said Joe as though he still thought he was speaking to a human being. "Would the dragon go around, say, a cast-iron kettle—" *did they have cast-iron kettles?* "—if it had a fuze burning to it?"

"The dragon walks through walls of fire," Delendor said. "I don't think we'll be able to burn it, Joe."

He sounded doubtful. Doubtful about his choice of a magician, Joe suspected.

"We won't try," Joe said in sudden confidence. "We'll blow the thing to hell and gone!"

His enthusiasm—the foreign wizard's enthusiasm— drew a gasp of delight and wonder from the assembled crowd; except, noticeably, for Ezekiel and Delendor's brothers.

"Now," said Joe, "we'll need to test it. What do you use for pipes here?"

"Poipes?" said Arnault.

"You know," Joe explained. "Water pipes."

"Pipes for water?" said Delendor. "Why, we have wells. Don't you have wells in your own country, Joe?"

"I have tubing drawn of lead, left over from my clepsydra," said Ezekiel.

He held up his index finger. "The outer size is

this," he explained, "and the inner size—" he held up the little finger of the same hand "—is this."

"Perfect!" Joe said, wondering what a clepsydra was. "Great! Fetch me a six-inch length, that'll be enough, and I'll get back to making something to fill it with. Boy, that dragon's going to get his last surprise!"

Ezekiel stayed where he was, but Joe had more important things to deal with than enforcing instantaneous obedience. He hadn't gotten very far with his gunpowder, after all.

Joe had made gunpowder when in he was in grade school, but he'd never been able to make it correctly because of the cost. Now it *had* to be right, but cost didn't matter.

Charcoal was easy, then as now. As a kid, he'd ground up a charcoal briquette, using the face of a hammer and a saucepan abstracted from the kitchen.

Here, Ezekiel provided a mortar and a pestle whose sides sloped to a concave grinding surface which mated with the mortar's convex head, both of brass. Pieces of natural charcoal (which looked disconcertingly like scraps of burned wood) powdered more cleanly than briquettes processed with sawdust had done.

Joe poured the black dust into one of Ezekiel's screw-stoppered brass jars. He didn't bother wiping the pestle clean, because after all, he was going to mix all the ingredients at some point anyway.

Lumps of sulphur powdered as easily as bits of dried mud. Sulphur had been a cheap purchase at the drugstore also. The only complicating factor was that you didn't want to buy the jar of sulphur from the same druggist as sold you the saltpeter.

Saltpeter was the rub. Saltpeter was expensive, and it was supposed to provide seventy-five percent of the bulk of the powder; so Joe and his friends had changed the formula. It was as simple as that.

After all, they weren't trying to shoot a knight out of his armored saddle—or blow a dragon to kingdom come. They just wanted spectacular fireworks. Mixing the ingredients in equal parts gave a lot more hiss and spatter from a small jar of saltpeter than the "right" way would have done.

With his powdered sulphur in a second jar, Joe got to work on the saltpeter.

Ezekiel's store of the substance amounted to several pounds, so far as Joe could judge the quantity in the heavy brass container. He didn't know precisely how much gunpowder it was going to take to blow up a dragon, but this ought to do the job.

The saltpeter crystals were a dirty yellow-white, like the teeth of Glam and Groag. They crushed beneath the mortar with a faint squeaking, unlike the crisp, wholesome sound the charcoal had made.

The spectators were getting bored. Kiki had snatched a hat and was now more the center of interest than Joe was. Servants formed a ring about the little animal and were making good-natured attempts to grab him as he bounced around them, cloak fluttering.

The spectators who weren't watching the monkey had mostly broken up into their own conversational groups. Delendor and his sister murmured about old times, while Glam and Groag discussed the fine points of unlacing a deer.

It had bothered Joe to feel that he was some sort of a circus act. He found that it bothered him more to think that he was a *boring* circus act, a tumbler whom everybody ignored while the lion tamer and trapeze artists performed in the other rings.

Almost everybody ignored him. As Joe mixed his

test batch of powder—three measures of saltpeter and a half measure each of charcoal and sulphur (because he still couldn't for the life of him remember which of the pair was supposed to be fifteen percent and which ten)—he felt Ezekiel's eyes on his back. The magician's gaze was cold and veiled, like a container of dry ice.

And Ezekiel wasn't quite the only one watching with unabated interest as Joe went on with the procedure. Joe lifted his head to stretch his cramped shoulders. In a third-floor room across the courtyard—Joe's room, he thought, though he couldn't be sure—was a wan white face observing at a safe distance from Glam and Groag.

Mary's features were indistinct, but Joe felt the poor kid's concern.

He went back to mixing his ingredients. He felt better for the glimpse at the window.

"All right, Ezekiel," Joe said loudly to call *everybody's* attention back to him. "I'll need the tube now."

Ezekiel smiled and extended his hand with the length of lead pipe in it.

Joe was sure Ezekiel hadn't left the summer kitchen. The piece could have been concealed in the magician's sleeve all the time, but that left the question of how he'd known what Joe would want before Joe himself knew.

Being thought to be a magician in this culture was fine. Knowing a *real* magician was rather like knowing a real Mafioso. . . .

"Right," said Joe, staring at the pipe and thinking about the possible remainder of his life—unless he could find a People Mover going in the opposite direction. "Right. . . ."

Time for that later. He needed to close one end of

the pipe before he filled it with powder. He could use Ezekiel's mortar to pound the soft metal into a seam, but that wasn't the job for which the piece of lab equipment had been designed.

Besides, the mortar's owner was watching.

"Arnault," Joe said briskly to the master armorer. "I need to close the end of this pipe. Do you have a hammer with you?"

"This poipe . . .?" Arnault said, reaching out for the piece. When the armorer frowned, wrinkles gave his face almost the same surface as his cracked, stained leather apron.

He took the piece between his right thumb and index finger. When he squeezed, the metal flattened as if between a hammer and anvil.

Joe blinked. Arnault returned the pipe to him. The flattened end was warm.

Arnault didn't speak, but a smile of pride suffused his whole pitted, muscular being.

"Ah," said Joe. "Thank you."

Joe looked at the pipe he held, the glass funnel set out in readiness, and the brass container of gunpowder. Either the cold or the shock of everything that'd been happening made his brain logy, because it took ten seconds of consideration before he realized that he was going to need a third hand. He glanced at the crowd.

Ezekiel was used to this type of work; Delendor was the guy whose life and career most depended on the job—

And Joe, for different reasons, didn't trust either one of them. "Estoril?" he said. "Princess? Would you please hold this tube vertical while I pour the powder into it?"

Joe's eyes had scanned the window across the courtyard before settling back on the princess; but that was a silly thought and unworthy of him, even in his present state.

Estoril handled the pipe with the competence Joe already knew to expect from her. The spout of the funnel fit within the lead cylinder, so he didn't have to tell her not to worry if some of the gunpowder dribbled down.

The brass powder container was slick, heavy, and (when Joe took off his glove for a better grip) shockingly cold. He shook the jar as carefully as he could, dribbling a stream of the dirty-yellow gunpowder into the funnel and thence the pipe.

It sure didn't look black. Maybe he should've used more charcoal after all?

Drifting grains of sulphur gave the air a brimstone hint that reminded Joe of the immediately-previous stop on what had begun as a People Mover.

The tube was nearly full. Joe put down the items he held and took the tube from Estoril. "Arnault," he said, holding the almost-bomb to the armorer, "I'd like you to close this down to a little hole in the end. Can you do that?"

Arnault stared at the piece. It looked tiny in his hand. "Roight," he said. "Doon to a coont haar."

Joe pursed his lips. "A little larger than that, I think," he said. "About the size of a straw."

Though, thinking about the sort of women who would willingly consort with the master armorer, Arnault's description might have been quite accurate.

Granted that lead wasn't armor plate, it was still amazing to watch Arnault force the tube into the desired shape between the tips of his thumbs and index fingers. When he handed the result back, Joe couldn't imagine a machineshop back home improving on the job.

Nothing left to do but to complete the test.

Joe had been planning to take the bomb outside the walls of the palace, but now he had a better idea. The summer kitchen's three ovens were solid masonry affairs; and this was, after all, only a little bomb. . . .

Joe arranged it at the back of the center oven.

"Now, I want all of you to keep to the sides," Joe said, his voice deepened and multiplied by the cavity. When he straightened, he found everybody was staring at him from wherever they'd been standing before . . . except that Delendor and his brothers had moved up directly behind "the magician" to stare into the oven.

Ezekiel grinned.

Joe stuck his thumbs in his ears and waggled his fingers. "Back!" he shouted.

Kiki's four limbs gripped Delendor's head, completely hiding the youth's face. Glam and Groag hurtled into the crowd like elephants charging butt-first, doing a marvelous job of clearing the area in front of the oven.

"Right," said Joe, breathing heavily. "Now, if you'll all just keep it that way while I set the fuze."

From what he remembered, you were supposed to make your fuze by soaking string in a solution of gunpowder and letting it dry—or some damned thing. For this purpose, a bare train of powder would do well enough.

Joe dribbled a little pile of the foul-looking stuff at the base of the bomb, then ran the trail out to the mouth of the oven. Granted that he wasn't being graded on aesthetics, he still sure wished his black powder looked black.

"Now—" he said with his hand raised for a flourish.

Oops.

Joe screwed down the top on the powder container and set it carefully on the ground to the side of the bank of ovens. All he needed was for a spark to get into *that*.

"Now," Joe repeated as the crowd watched him. "I'm going to light the fuze and—"

And neither he, nor any of the people around him, had a match.

"Ah," he said, changing mental direction again. "Would somebody bring me a candle or—something, you know? I want to light the fuze."

"You want to light it *now*?" asked Ezekiel.

Joe nodded. He didn't understand the emphasis. "Ah, yeah," he said. 'Is there some reason—"

Ezekiel snapped his fingers. Something that looked like a tiny—no, it had to have been a spark—popped from his pointing index finger. The spark flicked the end of the train of gunpowder.

"Ge' back!" Joe shouted, waving his arms as he scrambled aside also. "Get clear, y'all!"

Ezekiel was smiling at him in cold satisfaction.

The pops and splutters of burning gunpowder echoed from the oven. Stinking white smoke oozed out of the door and hung in the cold air like a mass of raw cotton, opaque and evil looking.

Joe put his hands over his ears and opened his mouth to help equalize pressure against the coming blast. He wished he'd remembered to warn the locals that the bang would—

There was a pop. A stream of orange-red sparks spurted through the open oven door. Joe heard a whanging sound from within, a *whee*!—and the would-be bomb came sailing straight up the flue of the oven. It mounted skyward on a trail of white smoke and a rain of molten lead.

The crowd scattered, screaming in justified terror. Delendor picked up his sister and ran for the nearest doorway in a cloud of skirts. Even Ezekiel fled, though he did so with more judgment than any of the others: he flung himself into one of the cold ovens.

The rocket began to curve as the wall of the lead tube melted unevenly. The only two people still watching it were Joe, in utter dismay; and Arnault, who stared out from the haze of his smoldering hair with a rapturous look on his face.

The rocket punched through one of the third-floor windows across from Joe's room. There was a faint *pop* from within. The remainder of the damaged window shivered outward into the courtyard.

Maybe a boxcar load of this "gunpowder" would daze a dragon. But probably not.

Arnault turned to Joe. The armorer's spark-lighted beard had gone out, but a wreath of hideous stench still wrapped him. "Moy, but yoor a cooning baastaard!" Arnault bellowed happily as he hugged Joe to him.

Joe squealed. His mother had always told him that if he persisted in playing with gunpowder he'd surely be killed, though he doubted she'd expected him to be crushed in an elephantine expression of joy. . . .

Arnault threw open his arms. Joe sprawled on the flagstones. He took a deep breath of the cold, sulphurous air and began coughing it out again.

Ezekiel crawled from the oven. His face was livid where it wasn't smudged with soot. For a moment, the magician stared upward toward the missing window, a gap in the array of diamond-paned reflections. A tiny wisp of smoke came out of the opening.

"You may think you're clever, destroying my laboratory that way!" he cried to Joe. "But it won't help your protegé against the dragon, you know. And *that's* what you're sworn to do!"

The magician turned and strode toward the door

into the palace. His robes were flapping. The wisp of smoke from his room became a column. As Ezekiel reached the doorway, he flung dignity to the winds and began to run up the stairs.

Delendor reappeared, looking flushed and joyful. "Wow!" the prince said. "That's tremendous, Joe! My mother's spirit certainly led me right. Why, that dragon won't have a chance!"

"I'm glad you feel that way," said Joe as he got to his feet.

Joe's belly felt cold. What he'd done was sure-hell impressive . . . but it proved that he couldn't make gunpowder that would explode.

And that meant that Delendor was a dead duck.

There was a faint tap on Joe's door.

"Sure, come in," he mumbled without looking away from the window. The sun was still above the horizon, but in the shadowed courtyard beneath, servants and vehicles moved as if glimpsed through the water of a deep pool.

Mary slipped into the room. For a moment she poised beside the door, ready to flee. Then she asked, "Master Joe, am I disturbing you? If you need to plan all the little details of how you'll destroy the dragon, then I—"

Joe turned. The room was almost dark. The charcoal fire gave little light, and the low sun had to be reflected many times to reach Joe's leading-webbed windows.

"I *can't* destroy the dragon!" he said savagely. "I can't kill it, and I can't go home. And none of it's any fault of mine that *I* can see!"

Mary cowered back against the door. Her eyes were on Joe's face, but her thin fingers fumbled to reopen the door.

"Aw, child, don't do that . . ." he said, reaching out—then grimacing in self-disgust when he saw her wince at the gesture. "Look," he said, "I'm just frustrated that . . . well, that I made things worse."

Mary began fussing with the fire, adding small bits of charcoal from the terra cotta container beside the fireplace. "And so now you want to leave?" she asked.

"I always wanted to leave," Joe said. He tried to keep the force of his emotion out of his voice. "Mary, I never wanted to *come* here, it just happened. But it doesn't look like I'll ever be able to leave, either."

"But Joe," she said, lifting her big frightened eyes to his, "only a great magician could have done what you did this morning. I don't see why you think you're failing."

"Because I'm not a chemist," Joe explained.

He turned away from the pain in the maid's expression. The courtyard was still deeper in shadow. "Because I'm not much of anything, if you want to know the truth. I did the only thing I know how to do—from when I was a kid. And that's not going to help a damned bit if the dragon's half what everybody tells me it is."

Mary touched the hem of Joe's cloak diffidently. "I think you're something," she said.

"What I am," said Joe, "is the guy who told Delendor he'd fix it so he'd kill the dragon. Which was a lie. And Delendor's a decent kid who deserved better 'n that."

A four-horse carriage drove out of the stables across the courtyard. The streets would be pitch dark soon, so the lanterns on the vehicle's foreposts were lighted. They waked glimmers of vermilion lacquer and gilt on the carriage's polished sides.

"I'm sure you'll find a—" Mary began.

The carriage driver looked up at Joe's window. *Great god almighty! It was the Mongolian!*

Joe spun to his door. He had barely enough control to jiggle the latch open—it was simple but not of a present-day familiar type—instead of breaking off the slender handle that lifted the bar. His shoes skidded as he ran to the nearest staircase, but he managed not to fall.

At the back of Joe's mind was the knowledge that somebody—fate, the Mongolian, sunspots, *whatever*—might be playing with him. He could reach the courtyard and find that the coach had driven out the main gate and into the city . . . or simply had disappeared.

But Joe had to try. He should've had better sense to begin with than to think he could do any good in a world with dragons and real sorcerers. Since he'd screwed things up even worse, the only honorable course was to get himself the hell out of the way at the first chance that was offered.

Sure, that was honorable. And besides, it was survivable.

This was a servants' staircase, helical with stone steps that were just as slick as the floors. There wasn't any namby-pamby nonsense about stair railings, either. By god, there were things Joe knew that he could teach these people . . .

Unfortunately, none of those things included dragon-slaying methods; and nobody in Hamisch was going to be much interested in staircase and bathroom designs from the guy who got Prince Delendor killed.

Joe swept down on a trio of maids. They flattened to the curving walls in terror when "the new magician" galloped past them.

The two long flights took him—well, Joe didn't know how long it took him. He knew if he slipped, he'd knock himself silly for sure; and he suspected that was just the sort of joke the Mongolian had in mind to torment a perfectly innocent ghostwriter.

He reached the ground floor between the laundry room and the buttery. A liveried servant dozed on a chair beside the courtyard door. Joe slammed past him, startling the man shriekingly awake as though the morning's rocket had been set off again between his coattails.

The carriage waited in the twilit courtyard. The swarthy driver smirked past the coachlamp toward Joe. Vague voices drifted between the stone walls, and concertina music came from somewhere in the servants' quarters.

Joe put his foot on the carriage step and gripped the silver doorlatch. It was warmer than the surrounding air, but it wouldn't have stopped Joe if he'd thought the cold metal would flay the skin from his palm.

"Stop, Master Joe!" somebody wailed.

The carriage door started to swing open. Joe looked over his shoulder.

Mary had followed him down the stairs. Her eyes were streaming tears.

Her arms held out to him the attache case he'd abandoned when he saw his chance to go home.

Much the way Joe had abandoned Mary and his promise to Delendor.

"Right," said Joe. He hopped down from the carriage step and took the case from the maid.

"I don't think I'll need this for a while," he said to the sobbing woman. "But it may as well stay in my room for now. With me."

The driver clucked something to his horses. The coach began to move toward the archway, but Joe didn't look back as he guided Mary into the palace.

As a result, Joe didn't see the clawed, skeletallythin hand that pulled shut the carriage door from the inside.

A horde of minuscule demons was sweeping shattered equipment from Ezekiel's workbench. They suddenly froze in place, then formed a flying arrowhead which curved halfway around the laboratory before vanishing into the dimension from which the creatures had come. Their voices made a tiny eeping that persisted several seconds after the demons themselves disappeared.

"What's that?/What happened?" Glam and Groag blurted together in high-pitched voices. Each brother slapped one hand to his swordhilt and covered his face with the other, as though they thought the swarm of demons might flee down their throats—

As indeed the panicky demons might do, and much good the outflung hands would be in that event.

Ezekiel made one attempt to regain control by gesturing. Then he *heard* what the demons were wailing and stepped to an undamaged window—the center of the three casements was boarded up—to glance down into the courtyard.

"Great God!" he muttered as he jumped back again from the glass—and much good a stone wall would be if the *being* below chose to act against Ezekiel.

"What's going on?" Glam demanded in his full, booming voice. He'd regained confidence now that the flying demons were gone, and there seemed to be no room within his thick skull for wonder at what had frightened the horde away.

"I saw a . . ." the magician said. "A being. A being from the 7th Plane."

Groag strode over to the window Ezekiel had vacated and looked out. "You mean Delendor's tame wizard?" he said. "He don't look any great shakes to me."

"Joe Johnson is down there?" Ezekiel asked sharply. "You see him?"

"Yeah, sure I see him," Groag said, testy with his sudden fear and his present, false, assumption of safety. "He's getting into a carr—no, he ain't. He's going—" the big man squinted for a better look in the twilight "—back inside."

Ezekiel swallowed. The lingering smell of brimstone seemed sharper. "What is the—carriage doing?" he asked with as much nonchalance as he could muster.

"Huh?" Groag answered. "It just drove off, out the gate. Why?"

"Whadda ya mean, 7th Plane?" Glam asked. "You mean a demon?"

As though the word had been a summons, one of Ezekiel's pack of demons thrust its head back into the laboratory, then followed with its entire body. The creature was blue and more nearly the size of a gnat than a fly.

The demon gripped a shard of broken alembic and tried to lift the piece with a metallic shimmering of its wings. After it quivered vainly for several seconds, hundreds more of its fellows poured through the hole in the continuum and resumed their duties. Bits and pieces of wreckage rose and vanished.

"Not a demon," the magician said, speaking as much to himself as to the pair of humans with him in his laboratory. "Demons are beings of the 3d Plane, below rather than above ours. The inhabitants of the 7th Plane are—"

"But it's not this Joe character that we're supposed to worry about, then?" Glam interrupted.

"If he communes with creatures of the 7th Plane,

then you'd *better* worry about him!" Ezekiel snapped. The magician's vehemence straightened the two hulking princes like a slap. "The—folk of the 7th Plane don't meddle in human affairs, precisely . . . but they offer choices. They have terrible powers, but they won't be guided by humans. *Nobody* deals with them."

"Well then, what—" Groag said, his brow furrowing.

"Except," Ezekiel continued, "that the Princess Blumarine is said to have done so."

"You mean Delendor's mother . . .?" Glam said in what was for him a considerable mental stretch. "But she's dead. Ain't she?"

"Blumarine couldn't save her beloved knight," Ezekiel said savagely. "And she won't be able to save her son, either. Do you hear?"

He glared around the room. "*Do you hear?*"

The waves of tiny demon wings rose and trembled with the amplitude of the magician's voice.

"Ah, good morning, Joe," said Delendor. "I was just wondering how preparations for my dragon-slaying are coming?"

Joe looked at the prince sourly. "You're up bright and early," he said.

"Well, ah, yes," Delendor agreed, looking around Joe's room with vague interest. "I *do* get up early, you know; and besides, Estoril and I are going on a picnic today."

Mary, wearing a sturdy pair of boots in place of her usual slippers, curtsied. She was blushing furiously. Kiki hopped from the prince's shoulder and chirped at Mary's feet, but the maid seemed unwilling even to admit the monkey was there.

"Ah, you're going on a picnic also, Joe?" Delendor added. His lips pursed. "But with an arbalest?"

"What we're doing," Joe said, "is taking a look at your blasted dragon."

"Really?" said Delendor. "Goodness. Why?"

"Because I haven't got a clue as what to do about a damned dragon!" Joe snarled. "Because I'm not a magician! But I *might* be able to help if I had the faintest notion of what I'm supposed to be dealing with."

He didn't so much calm as run through the temporary enthusiasm that anger gave him. "And I, well, I'd really like to help things out here. Mary said she'd guide me. Apparently the dragon's pretty close to the city already."

Delendor nodded with his lips still pursed. "Yes," he said, "I wanted to go to the glade north of the walls where we picnicked when we were little, but Clarkson says that's not a good idea. But why the arbalest?"

The youth's expression grew tight and angry. "You're not planning to—"

"No, I'm *not* planning to shoot the dragon with a crossbow!" Joe blazed. "Though I sure as hell would if I thought it'd do a damned bit of good."

"*Oh!*" squealed Mary.

The maid had stuffed rags in her boots to line them down to the size of her tiny feet. Kiki grabbed the end of one and ran around in a circle, attempting to bind Mary's ankles together. Joe snatched at the monkey with his free hand.

Kiki bounded up the wall, off the ceiling, and back onto Delendor's shoulder in an impressive display of acrobatics—and judgment, given the fury that bent Joe's groping hand into a claw.

"Bad, bad monkey!" Delendor chided.

"Look, Delendor," Joe continued in an attempt to

sound calm. "I just figured I ought to be armed if I'm going to look for this thing."

"Oh, well," the prince said, his face clearing. "Well, I'll loan you a sword then, Joe. It's more fitting to your position, though I suppose technically a magician isn't a—"

"No, I don't want a sword," Joe interrupted. "I don't know anything about swords except they're long enough to trip me if I need to run . . . as I figure I'll want to, pretty soon now."

"Ah," said Delendor. He didn't look as though he would have approved if he understood. His eyes wandered; focused on Mary, who'd taken off her boot to restuff it; and snapped back to Joe.

"Delendor," Joe said, "I don't know anything about crossbows either. Or guns, if it comes to that. Arnault had to crank this—" he hefted the weapon in his right hand with some difficulty "—up for me."

Joe tried to smile as though he meant it. "Mary," he went on with a nod to the maid, "warned me not to put an arrow in the thing until I was out in open country. It's just a security blanket, but the good lord knows I need some security."

Delendor reached a decision. He nodded enthusiastically. "I understand," he said. "A very noble, if I may say so, undertaking. I'll tell Estoril that we won't be able to picnic today, because I'm going with my magician to view the threat to the kingdom first hand."

"Ah," Joe said. "Ah, are you really sure you want to do this?"

"I certainly do," the prince responded firmly. "And not only that, but we'll go on foot. The—fate—of Sir Delendor, my namesake, suggests that horses aren't to be trusted in the vicinity of the dragon."

Joe nodded. It just might be, he thought, that Delendor wasn't a complete airhead.

"Well, it's certainly a beautiful day to be out in the country, isn't it?" Delendor gushed. "Bright sun, crisp breeze . . . just cool enough to be bracing."

Joe sneezed. "No people around," he said. "Not a soul."

He looked back over his shoulder. The pennoned turrets on the city walls were still visible every time the road rolled upward. They'd set out on the main turnpike between Glenheim and Hamisch, so there should've been *some* traffic.

Unless the dragon was a lot closer than the farmers from outlying districts, now thronging the streets of Hamisch, had insisted.

It occurred to Joe that the farmers might be more than a little upset about the lack of progress in dealing with the beast that was devastating their lands. If some of the nobles who were supposed to slay such threats could be enticed into proximity to the dragon, then one or the other was going to be killed.

And the farmers might think either result was a good one.

"I don't think we should be walking right up the road," Mary said, echoing Joe's next thought as it formed.

Delendor looked at the brush fringing the sides of the highway, then tapped the road's cobblestone surface with his green leather shoe. The edges of the road were apparently cut back every few years, but at the moment they were a tangle of saplings, bushes, and creepers—thick enough to provide concealment for somebody a few yards in, but not too dense to get through without a machete.

"Well, it might be more comfortable for walking,"

he said judiciously. "But my sword would catch. I don't think we'll do that."

"We'll do that," said Joe grimly as he forced his way into the brush.

Joe's legs were holding up—they'd walked less than a mile—but his arms were aching with the weight of the crossbow. The nut that held back the thumb-thick cord had a slot in it to grip the nock of the bolt. At least Joe didn't have the bolt falling off every time he let the weapon point down, the way he'd expected.

The bolt—the quarrel—had a thick wood shaft and three wooden feathers. The head was square and steel, with a four-knobbed face instead of a point. It looked dangerous as hell—

And if the dragon had shrugged off showers of similar missiles, as everybody assured Joe the beast had, then the dragon was Hell on four legs.

Kiki was having the time of his life, swinging around the three humans. He was so light that the branches of saplings, none of which were more than twelve feet tall, were sufficient to support his cheerful acrobatics.

Delendor, last in the line, had rotated his swordbelt so that the weapon in its scabbard hung behind him like a stiff tail. It didn't get in his way after all.

The prince's tasseled fur cloak, his ruffed tunic, and his ballooning silk breeches, on the other hand, seemed to cling and fray on every thorn. Delendor became increasingly—vocally— irritated about the fact.

"Joe," he called, "this doesn't make any sense at all. We could never escape if the dragon charged us, but the thorns wouldn't slow the beast a bit."

"We couldn't outrun it anyway," Joe said, doggedly forcing his way between a clump of saplings. "All we're trying to do is stay out of sight."

"The dragon stops when it makes a kill," Mary said. "The others will have time to get away while it eats."

The careless, matter-of-fact statement contrasted unpleasantly with the maid's timid voice.

"Well, perhaps in that case I should be in the lead," Delendor suggested. "Because my rank is— drat! Where do all these blackberry vines come from?"

If the prince had paid attention to what he was doing rather than to his concept of *noblesse oblige*, he'd 've gone around those vines the way his companions had.

"You know," Delendor resumed a moment later, "this makes even less sense than I'd thought. We're making so much noise that we'll never sneak up on the—"

Joe froze with one foot lifted. He hissed, "Hush!"

"—dragon. I've done enough hunting to know—*ulp!*"

Mary had turned and clamped her hand over Delendor's mouth with surprising strength. "Oh, please, Prince!" she whispered. "*Please* obey Master Joe."

Joe put his foot down very carefully. Something that clanked and wheezed like a steam locomotive was coming up the road toward them. There wasn't much doubt about what the something was.

The dragon came around a sweeping bend only fifty yards away. Its color was the red of glowing iron.

The dragon probably wasn't any longer than the thirty-odd yards Ezekiel had claimed for it . . . but seeing a creature of that unimaginably great size was very different from hearing the words spoken.

No wonder the knights—and the crossbowmen— had been unable to harm the thing.

The dragon was covered with bony scutes similar to those of a crocodile, and the beast's general shape was crocodile-like as well: so low-slung that the long jaws almost brushed the cobblestones, with a massive body carried on four short legs. The upper and lower rows of the dragon's teeth overlapped like the spikes of an Iron Maiden.

The dragon's claws sparked on the roadway. Its breath chuffed out a reek of decay which enveloped Joe as he peered from the brush in amazement.

Well, he'd come to look at the dragon to determine what were its weak spots.

There weren't any.

They'd have to get back to Hamisch as fast as they could—making the necessary wide circuit to avoid the dragon. The beast would reach the city in a few tens of minutes, and the only hope of the people inside was to scatter. The walls wouldn't last a—

"*Kikikikiki!*" shrieked the monkey. It hurled a bit of seedpod as it charged the dragon.

"Kiki!" cried Delendor in a voice almost as high-pitched as his pet's. The prince whisked his sword from its sheath and crossed the expanse of brush between himself and the highway in three deerlike leaps.

With Mary running after him, an equally athletic, equally quixotic, demonstration.

"For god's sake!" Joe screamed. He tried to aim his arbalest. A loop of honeysuckle was caught around the right arm of the bow. "Come back! Come back!"

The dragon didn't charge, but its head swung with horrifying speed to clop within a finger's breadth of Kiki. The monkey's cries rose into a sound like an electronic watch alarm.

Kiki hurled himself back into the brush. Delendor continued to run forward, with Mary right behind him—casting doubt on the evolutionary course of intelligence.

"Get down!" Joe cried. *"Don't,* for god's sake—"

He slipped his bow loose of the vines and raised the weapon. He'd fired a rifle a couple times, but the crossbow had a knob rather than a shoulder stock.

There weren't any proper sights. Joe tried to aim along the bolt's vertical fin, but the weapon's heavy muzzle wobbled furiously around a six-inch circle. The dragon was only twenty feet away, and Joe was going to miss it if he—

Delendor swung his sword in a swift, glittering arc. It rang on the dragon's snout as though it had struck an anvil. The blade shattered and the hilt, vibrating like a badly-tuned harmonica, flew out of Delendor's hand.

Delendor yelped and lost his footing. He hit the cobblestones butt-first, which was just as well in the short run because the dragon's jaws slammed where the prince's torso had been.

"Get out of the—" Joe shrieked.

"Take me!" Mary cried, waving her arms to catch the monster's attention as she stepped on Delendor's swordhilt.

Mary's foot flew in the air. She hit the ground in a flurry of skirts.

The dragon paused, faced with two victims ten feet apart. It opened its jaws wider. The maw was the size of a concert grand with the lid up. The interior of the dragon's mouth was as white as dried bone.

I'll never have a better chance, thought Joe as he squeezed the under-lever trigger of his crossbow. The muzzle dropped as the cord slammed forward.

Joe whanged his bolt into the roadway in an explosion of sparks.

The dragon snorted. It started to—

For Pete's sake, it was arching its short neck, then

its back. Its monstrous, clawed forelegs were off the ground—

The sight should've been as ridiculous as that of *Fantasia*'s crocodiles doing *The Dance of the Hours* . . . but this close to the creature, it was more like watching an ICBM rising from its silo in preparation to launch.

The dragon was quivering in a tetanic arch, making little whimpering sounds. Its belly plates were red like the scutes of its back and sides, but there were fine lines of yellow skin where the plates met.

There was a hole where the lower jaw joined the first plate covering the underside of the neck. The hole didn't look large, but blood was bubbling furiously out of it.

Joe's quarrel had ricocheted into what might very well be the only vulnerable point in the dragon's armor.

The dragon rose onto the claws of its hind feet. Its tail was stiff. The beast's armor squealed under the strain to which convulsing muscles were subjecting it.

Mary and Delendor sat up, staring at the monster that towered above them. Their legs were splayed, and they supported their torsos on their hands.

"Wow!" said the prince. Joe, fifty feet back in the brush, couldn't come up with anything more suitable for the occasion.

Kiki hopped onto Joe's shoulder. He made what were almost purring sounds as he stroked Joe's hair.

The dragon completed its arc and toppled backwards. It hit the ground with a crash.

Its limbs and tail continued to pummel the ground for hours, like the aftershocks of an earthquake.

Though there were eight yoke of oxen hitched to the sledge, they wheezed and blew with the effort of dragging the dragon's head, upside down, into the palace courtyard. The beast's tongue lolled out to drag the flagstones, striking sparks from them.

Prince Delendor sat astride the stump of the beast's neck. He waved his swordhilt and beamed as he received the boisterous cheers of the crowd.

"Must be the whole city down there," Groag said glumly as he watched from one window of Ezekiel's laboratory.

"Must be the whole *country*," Glam corrected in a similar tone. " 'Cept us."

"*Lookit* that!" said Groag.

"Then get out of the way and I will," snapped the magician, tapping Groag on the shoulder and making little shooing motions with his hand. The big prince stepped aside, shaking his head.

The wreckage was gone from the laboratory, but neither the middle window nor the broken glassware had been replaced. A tinge of brimstone from the rocket still clung to the air.

The scene in the courtyard did nothing to improve Ezekiel's humor. King Morhaven was kneeling to Delendor, though the youth quickly dismounted as from a horse and stood Morhaven erect again.

The cheering rattled the laboratory's remaining windows.

"He'll make Delendor co-ruler as a result of this, you know," Ezekiel said. "And heir."

He turned and glared savagely at the two royal brothers. "You *know* that, don't you?"

Glam twisted the tow of his boot against the floor, as though trying to grind something deep into the stone. "Well," he said, "you know. . . . You know, if the little prick killed the dragon, I dunno what else the ole man could do. Lookit the *teeth* on that sucker."

"Don't be a bigger fool than god made you!" Ezekiel

snarled. "Delendor didn't have anything to do with killing the dragon. It was that magician of his! That *damned* magician."

He made a cryptic sign. A swarm of twinkling demons whisked out of their own plane. Their tiny hands compressed globes of air into a pair of shimmering lenses.

Ezekiel stared through the alignment, then stepped back. "There," he said to the brothers. "Look at that."

Glam looked through the tubeless telescope, despite an obvious reluctance to put his eye close to the miniature demons who formed it. The lenses were focused on the dragon's neck. The wound there was marked with a flag of blood.

"Well," said Glam as his brother shouldered him aside, "that's where he stabbed the sucker, right?"

"Idiot!" Ezekiel said. "The wound's *square*, from a crossbow bolt. And who do you see carrying a crossbow?"

"Oh-h-h," said the brothers together.

Behind the sledge, almost lost in the crowd that mobbed Delendor, was the prince's magician—carrying a heavy arbalest. A servant girl clung to him, squeezed by the people cheering their master.

"I don' get it," Groag said. "Lots a guys shot it with crossbows before, din't they? I heard that, anyhow."

"Of course they did, oaf!" said Ezekiel. "This was obviously an enchanted arbalest which struck the one vulnerable part of the dragon's armor—even though a spot on the underside of the beast's throat *couldn't* be hit by a crossbow bolt."

He swung the telescope slightly by tapping the manicured nail of his index finger against the objective lens. Tiny demons popped and crackled at the contact.

Groag glared at the crossbow. "Don' look so special ta me," he said.

"I don' get it," Glam said. "If he got a crossbow ta kill the dragon, then what was all that stuff with the powder and fire t'other morning? Some kinda joke, was it?"

The magician grimaced. "I'm not sure," he admitted, glancing around his laboratory and remembering how it had looked *before* a rocket sizzled through the center window. "But I think. . . ."

Ezekiel had been shrinking down into his velvet robes. Now he shook himself and rose again to his full height.

"I think," the magician resumed, "that Joe Johnson has been brought here from a very great distance by a—7th Plane inhabitant. He initially attempted to use the magic of his own region here, but the correspondences differed. Rather than work them out, he found it easier to adapt *our* magic to the task."

"You promised us," said Glam in a dangerous voice, "that there wouldn't be no problem with Delendor. An' now you say there is."

"I can take care of your brother easily enough," said Ezekiel in a carefully neutral tone. "But only after Joe Johnson is out of the way. Do you understand?"

Glam guffawed in a voice that rattled the window even against the cheering voices below. "You bet we do!" he said. "Cold iron's proof agin magic, right?"

"Ah, belt up," said his brother, staring through the telescope again. "You charge in like a bull in a boo-dwa, you just screw things up. *I'll* handle this one."

As he spoke, Groag marked carefully the servant to whom Joe Johnson gave his enchanted crossbow.

"And *you* said you weren't a magician!" Delendor crowed.

"Del, careful!" Estoril warned, but the prince had already jumped into a heel-clicking curvette too energetic for Joe's small room.

The feather in Delendor's peaked cap flattened against the ceiling. Kiki bounded from the prince's shoulder and caromed off the four walls before cringing against Joe's ankles.

Joe wrapped the quilt around him tighter. Servants had built up the fire next to which he huddled in his armchair. Despite that and the quilt, he still felt cold enough that the monkey's warm body was surprisingly pleasant.

He wondered where Mary had gone—and whether she'd be back tonight as usual.

He sneezed again.

"Bless you!" said Delendor, slightly more subdued. He sat down again on the cedar chest beside Estoril. "You know," he bubbled to the princess, "I just swung, *swish!*"

"I believe I heard that, yes," Estoril said dryly. Joe thought she winked at him, but he was blowing his nose and couldn't be sure.

Did Lancelot catch colds while carrying out deeds of derring-do? More to the point, did Lancelot's faithful servant catch colds?

"I didn't even know that I'd killed it until I saw it topple over backward!" Delendor continued, oblivious to everything but his own—false—memory. "Joe here's magic guided my thrust straight to the monster's throat! Except. . . ."

Delendor's handsome brow furrowed. "You know, I thought I'd *cut* at the dragon instead of thrusting." He brightened again. "Just shows how memory can play tricks on you, doesn't it?"

Joe sneezed.

Maybe now that the dragon was dead, he'd be able

to go back home . . . though somehow, after the primary colors of life in Hamisch, even the Senator and his shenanigans seemed gray.

"But here, I've been doing all the talking," Delendor said, showing that he had *some* awareness of the world beyond him. "Essie, what was it you came back from Glenheim to tell us?"

Estoril looked at her hands, laid neatly in a chevron on the lap of her lace-fronted dress. "To tell the truth," she began, "I'm not sure. . . ."

"You know," the prince resumed, as though Estoril had finished her thought instead of merely her words, "when Joe arrived here, I really wanted him to find my enchanted princess."

Delendor fumbled within his puff-fronted tunic. "But now that you're back, Essie, I—well, I don't think about it very much."

He opened the oval locket and handed it to Estoril. From the flash of lamplight as the object passed, Joe knew it was still a mirror so far as he was concerned. He roused himself to ask, "Princess, what do *you* see in it?"

Estoril smiled. "My face," she said. "But the locket is very old—and it belonged to Del's mother."

She returned the locket to Delendor. "The Princess Blumarine was a very good woman," she said carefully. "But from what Katya told me, she was very—"

A sort of smile, wry but good-humored, flicked Estoril's mouth. "Powerful would be the wrong word, I think. The Princess Blumarine was very learned. I'm sure that the mirror shows her son whatever he says it does."

Delendor gave her a look of prim horror. "Essie!" he said. "Of *course* I wouldn't lie to you!"

Estoril glanced at the windows. They were again

gray traceries of leading that barely illuminated the room. "Master Joe," the princess said, "would you like us to summon lamps?"

"Huh?" said Joe, aroused from his doze. "Oh, no—I mean . . . after you leave, that is, I think I'll just sit here and hope my sinuses decide to drain."

The problem wasn't just the cold breeze—and being out in it all day while the trophy was dragged to the palace. The shock of everything he'd been through today and the past three days had weakened Joe, leaving him prey to a bug.

"Well," said Estoril as she stood up, "we were just leaving."

"We . . .?" said Delendor, though he hopped to his feet also.

"Are leaving," Estoril repeated. "And we're going to send some hot soup up to Joe."

"Oh, I'm not really—" Joe began.

"Which he will drink *all* of," the princess continued in a tone with as much flexibility as the dragon's armor.

Estoril opened the door and pointed Delendor into the hall; but then she paused. "Master Joe," she said softly, "the kingdom owes its safety to you. And I owe you Delendor's life—"

"Yes, yes," the prince broke in over Estoril's shoulder. "We owe it all to you, Joe."

"I wouldn't want you to think," Estoril continued as though there had been no interruption, "that *we* are unaware of precisely what you've accomplished. Or that we're ungrateful for your tact."

"It wasn't—" Joe said, but there was no way he could explain just what it *was* since he didn't have a clue himself. He started to get up.

"No, stay right there," Estoril ordered in her head nurse/mother persona.

"Kiki?" called Delendor. "*Kiki?*"

The monkey peeked out from between Joe's feet. Kiki had wrapped himself in a corner of the quilt also. After a moment, and with obvious reluctance, the little creature sprang across the cold floor and back on his master's shoulder.

"Remember to drink your soup," Estoril called as she pulled the door closed behind her.

Joe relaxed again. He missed the warmth of Kiki, though. Estoril was quite a lady. Smart and tough, but not cold for all that. She could've made the best ruler of anybody Joe had met yet in Hamisch, but it was obvious that wouldn't happen while there were sons around.

For that matter, Estoril probably couldn't get elected President, either, so long as there was some male boob with a fluent smile and the right connections to run against her.

Delendor wasn't a bad kid, and in a few years he wouldn't be a kid. He'd proved he had guts enough when he charged the dragon—like a damned fool! Maybe with his sister behind to do the thinking for the next while, Delendor could turn out to be a useful king.

Joe wasn't sure whether he was awake or dreaming. The coals in the fireplace were a mass of white ash, but they continued to give off heat.

If he got up and looked through the window behind him, would he really see the head of a dragon in the courtyard? Would he even see a courtyard?

But the warmth was good, and Joe really didn't want to move. Whatever reality was would keep. . . .

Something that sounded like a dropped garbage can came banging its way down the hall. The dragon's claws had sounded like that on the roadway—if there was a dragon, if there was a road. The claws hadn't echoed, but they'd been louder because the beast was so—

Joe's door burst open under the stroke of an armored hand. The latch flew across the room, bar in one direction and bracket in the other. A figure in full armor stood in the doorway with a drawn sword.

"You're in league with sundry devils, magician," the figure boomed in Glam's voice—muffled by coming through the pointed faceplate of a pig's-head basinet. "But your time's come now!"

Joe's skin flushed as though he were coming out of a faint. He jumped to his feet, slinging aside the quilt—

And fell on his face in front of Glam.

A pane of the window behind Joe blasted into the room like storm-blown ice. There was a *blang!* many times louder than the sound of Glam knocking the door open. Joe twisted, trying unsuccessfully to get his feet back under him in the worst nightmare he'd had since—

Since jumping from that demon-wracked Hell into Delendor's carriage, a detached, analytical part of his mind told him.

Glam toppled over on his pointed faceplate. Amazing how much noise a suit of plate armor makes when you drop it to a stone floor. . . .

Delendor, Estoril, and a crowd of servants burst into the room— led by Mary with a lantern and a terrified expression.

"Stop right where you are, Glam!" Delendor shouted. The youth's right hand kept dipping to his empty scabbard. Lack of a sword hadn't kept him from charging Glam as blithely as he had the dragon in the morning.

"Oh, Master Joe," Mary said, kneeling on the stones as Joe managed to rise into a squat. "I saw Glam coming down the hall, so I ran to get help."

"You're all right, then?" Delendor said in amazement. He finally took in the fact that the awkward sprawl on the floor was Glam, not Joe; and that Glam wasn't moving.

Which surprised the hell out of Joe, too, now that he had time to think about it.

"You lot," Estoril ordered, gesturing to a pair of the huskier servants. "Stand the brute up again."

The princess had come running also; and it couldn't have been because she thought Glam in a rage would spare a woman. "Joe, what happened?"

"I'm damned if I know," Joe muttered. "Except that—"

He looked accusingly toward the prince's shoulder. Kiki cowered behind Delendor's head, then peeked over his master's feathered cap.

"—except that I know your little pet tied my shoelaces, Delendor," Joe concluded.

"Then you should thank him, Joe," said Estoril in a voice carefully purged of all emotion. "Because he seems to have saved your life."

She pointed. The fins of a heavy quarrel stood out slightly from the square hole in the center of Glam's breastplate. Crossbows here might not be able to penetrate dragons easily, but they sure punched through steel armor a treat.

Joe looked over his shoulder at the pane missing from the casement. The bolt that blew it out could've been fired from any of a dozen rooms across the courtyard, he supposed; but Joe wasn't in any real doubt as to whose hand had been on the trigger.

Not a bad time to fall on his face.

Delendor swept his hat off and bowed to Joe. The faces of all those who'd come to rescue Joe were suffused with awe.

"Through *iron*," the prince said, speaking for all of them. "What an amazingly powerful magician!"

* * *

"I did *not* tell you to kill the foreign magician, Groag," said Ezekiel. He pitched his voice in a compromise between being threatening and keeping anybody in the hall from overhearing.

"And I most particularly didn't tell you—you, a layman!—to attempt using a magician's own weapons against him!"

"B-b-but—" Groag said. His hands clenched into fists the size of deer hams. The tears squeezing from his eyes could have been either from grief for his brother or from rage.

Or from fear. In which case *both* the men in Ezekiel's laboratory were afraid of Joe Johnson.

"Although the thought of using the foreigner's magic against him wasn't a bad one," Ezekiel added mildly, now that he was sure Groag wasn't going to pull him apart with his bare hands.

The magician's workbench had been partly refurbished into a production line. In a large glass vat, minuscule demons swam through a dark sludge. The demons' blue wings and scales sparkled as the creatures rose to the surface in waves, then submerged for another pass, thoroughly mixing the constituents of the thick mass.

Another work-gang of demons lifted tiny shovelsful of the sludge and spread it on a copper plate pierced with thousands of identical holes. Still more demons hovered and blew their hot breath on the bottom of the plate, keeping it just warm to the touch.

Groag stared at the operation for a moment. "Whazat?" he demanded.

"That," said Ezekiel, "was what you would have done if you'd had any sense."

"You din't tell—"

"You didn't ask!" the magician snapped.

He cleared his throat. "It was obvious to me," Ezekiel resumed in the dry, supercilious voice of a haughty lecturer, "that Joe Johnson's flame magic required some amendments to work here. I consulted my sources to learn the secret of those changes. Thus—"

Ezekiel gestured. "The ingredients were correct, though the proportions had to be modified slightly. Most important, they have to be mixed wet so that each *kernel* of powder retains the proper proportion of each ingredient."

Groag leaned to get a better look at the flowing sludge. His nose almost touched the surface. The wave of mixers broke upward just then; one of the demons yanked a hair out of Groag's nostril before resubmerging.

"Ouch!"

"After the mixing is complete," Ezekiel continued with a satisfied smirk, "the material is spread here—" he indicated the plate "—and dried at low heat. When that process is almost complete, my minions will form the material into kernels by extruding it through the holes in the plate."

Groag, covering his nose with his left hand, furrowed his brow and stared at the production line while a thought slowly formed. At last he said, "So what?"

The magician sighed. "Yes," he said, "I rather thought that might be the next question. Well, my boy, I'll show you 'what.'"

He gestured. A squad of demons whisked together the grains of gunpowder which had already been forced through the plate and carried them to a glass bottle of a size to hold a lady's perfume. When the demons were done, there was just enough room left for Ezekiel to insert the stopper firmly into the bottle's neck.

"When this batch is complete," the magician said as he picked up the bottle and walked to one of the undamaged windows, "there will be enough of the material to fill the brass container on the end of the bench."

He slid the casement up in its frame, then set the bottle on the ledge. A cold breeze rushed into the laboratory, making the oil lamps gutter. A glittering demon began to curvette above the bottle like a blowfly over a corpse.

"If you were to take that large container into Joe Johnson's room tomorrow evening while everyone is at dinner," Ezekiel continued as he stepped back, "you could conceal it under the chair in which he sits. And when Joe Johnson returns to his room—"

Ezekiel gestured. The demon shot straight down and reached a tiny arm through the bottle. When Ezekiel snapped his fingers, there was a spark from the demon's hand and the gunpowder detonated with a tremendous crash.

Groag bellowed in fear. Even the magician stepped backward, startled by the vehemence of what he'd achieved. His hand brushed his fine, gray beard and came away sparkling with slivers of glass.

Ezekiel cleared his throat. His ears rang.

He thought his own voice sounded thin as he concluded, "— *that* might happen to our foreign friend!"

The lock of Joe Johnson's door hadn't been repaired, so Groag didn't need a key to make a surreptitious entry into the magician's room.

Nobody would remark on Groag's absence at dinner. They'd just assume he was still sulking about the way the ole man fawned on Delendor. They'd 've been right any other time, too.

They'd see how long that poof Delendor lasted,

once his tame magician was splattered all across the walls!

There was a small lamp burning in the room. It provided the only light, now, because Joe Johnson had tacked curtains over his windows. Was the magician afraid of another quarrel flying through the glass?

Groag shuddered even to think of aiming an arbalest at the cunning bastard. He'd been lucky his stupid brother came in the door just then. Otherwise Joe Johnson would probably 've turned the bolt around and it'd 've been Groag with wooden fins growing out of his chest!

The brass container, its top screwed down tight on the magic powder, was heavy. Its surface was slick, and it kept turning in Groag's hands as though it wanted to slip away from him.

What if Ezekiel's magic *hadn't* been strong enough to counteract the power of the stranger?

Groag looked at the armchair pulled close to the fireplace. Its seat and legs were bare, nothing whatever to cover the shining container.

The comforter in which Joe Johnson wrapped himself was neatly folded on the bed. If Groag moved the quilt, that would be as much a giveaway as the obvious presence of the container itself.

Which left one sure hiding place. Groag stepped to the fireplace and used the poker to scrape a long trench in the pile of charcoal and hot, white ash. He set the magic container into the trench and carefully covered it again.

The mound was higher than it had been, but there was nothing to draw the eye in the few moments between Joe Johnson entering the room and his sitting down directly in front of the fireplace. . . .

Groag straightened, looking pleased. There was a whisper of sound behind him. He turned like a great cat and met the wide, frightened eyes of the little maid who'd just opened the door.

By god, it was the bitch he and Glam had been chasing the other day!

"What are you doing here?" the maid demanded in a squeaky soprano.

"Nothing *you'll* live to tell about!" Groag bellowed. He didn't bother to draw a sword. Instead, he leaped forward with the poker upraised.

There was a flash as red as the fires of Armageddon.

The blast was equally impressive, but Groag didn't live to hear it.

Mary lay on her back, across the hall from where white haze seethed from Joe's doorway.

Joe had left the banquet before the serious drinking began, so he reached the bomb site as quickly as any of the servants. Wind through the window openings drew orange flickers from the fire within; the stench of burning feathers mingled with the brimstone odor of gunpowder.

Joe knelt, cradling Mary's fragile body in his arms. She was unconscious but breathing normally.

Thank god!

Dozens of servants came running from both directions, many of them carrying firebuckets. Joe grabbed a sturdy-looking female, pointed to Mary, and said, "Watch her! I'll be right back!"

He snatched a lamp from a wall bracket and plunged into his room. His feet slipped.

On Groag.

King Morhaven's eldest son had taken most of the blast. The shockwave blew Mary through the open door; Groag had been driven into the stone doorjamb instead.

Joe couldn't be sure whether Groag's clothes had

been blown off his body, or whether the body had simply leaked through the fabric after impact with the wall. He could be identified by the ornate hilt of his sword.

Confirmation came from the smoldering black beard hairs which clung to the bloodstained wall.

"Joe! Joe!" Delendor shouted as the young prince led a crowd up the stairway from the banquet hall. "Are you all right?"

Servants were tossing buckets of water on the flames, but that was pointless: there was nothing left in the room to save, and the wooden roof beams weren't yet in danger.

Joe grabbed a handful of burning bedding and flung it through one of the window openings. The mass drifted down into the courtyard. Blazing bits of cloth and feathers dribbled away like a slow-motion firework.

Others took over the job, hurling out even the shattered remnants of the bed frame and cedar chest. Nobody seemed to be too concerned about Groag.

Joe wasn't concerned either. He stepped out into the hall again, just as the thundering squadron of nobles from the banquet hall reached the scene.

Most of the nobles. Master Ezekiel wasn't among them.

"Is it . . .?" King Morhaven called. "Is it . . .?"

The king knew as well as anybody else did who was likely to be at the bottom of the current problem.

Joe opened his mouth to answer as bluntly as rage made him wish—but you couldn't blame the father for the sons, and anyway, there'd been enough outbursts of one sort and another this night.

"You'd better look for yourself," he said, and he handed Morhaven the lamp. The king, Delendor, and

Estoril forced their way into the room through the mob of frantic servants.

"I'll take over now," Joe said as he squatted beside Mary again. A firebucket had been set nearby. He dipped his handkerchief in the water and began to sponge powder blackening and speckles of Groag from the maid's face.

The king came out of Joe's room. He'd aged a decade in a few seconds. Delendor and the princess walked to either side of Morhaven, looking worried and poised to catch him if he collapsed. Even Kiki seemed upset.

Morhaven straightened. "Very well," he said. "Events have forced me to the choice I'd already made. People of Hamisch, my successor shall be my son Delen—"

Estoril put one slim, white hand over King Morhaven's mouth. "Father," she said in the shocked silence, "I wasn't sure that I'd ever repeat what Katya told me before she died. I think now that I have to."

"Katya?" Delendor repeated with a puzzled expression.

"Your mother Blumarine's nurse!" the princess snapped. "Don't you remember?"

Which of course Delendor hadn't, but he was used enough to the situation to nod wisely. His monkey aped his motions.

Estoril lowered her hand and looked Morhaven in the eye. "Father," she said. "Your Majesty. Princess Blumarine was secretly married to Sir Delendor. And her son Delendor—isn't your son, Your Majesty."

"Well I'll be!" said Delendor. If there was any emotion besides amazement in his tone, Joe didn't hear it. "Well I'll *be*. Then you're not my sister, Essie?"

"No," Estoril said, "but you *have* a real older

sister." She took the locket from around Delendor's neck and snapped it open. "There," she continued. "That's your sister."

"Why," said Delendor. "Why . . . why look, Joe, she isn't a rabbit any more!"

He held the locket down to Joe. Instead of a mirror, it held a miniature painting on ivory of a young woman with lustrous blonde hair. She was absolutely beautiful.

"*And*," Delendor added, rising with new excitement in his voice, "that means there's no reason *we* can't be married. Essie, will you be my queen?"

"I think," said Estoril dryly, "that the proper question is, 'Del, will you be my consort?' But I think the answer is yes, either way."

She smiled. There was nothing dry about the affection in her eyes.

The woman in Joe's lap stirred. He looked down, his mouth already forming the words, "Oh, thank god you're all right, Mary—"

She wasn't Mary.

She was the woman in the locket painting.

"Good lord!" Joe blurted. "Who are you?"

The blond woman smiled. If there was a sight more beautiful than her face, it was her face with a smile wrapping it. "I'm Mary, Joe," she said.

Mary tried to sit. She was still dizzy from the explosion; Joe's arm helped her. "You've told my brother, then?" she asked/said to Estoril.

Even Estoril looked surprised. "Yes, and you're . . . ?"

"I'm your sister, Del," Mary said, "though for your sake and hers, mother kept it a secret. When the dragon appeared, I wanted to help you—but Katya put a spell on me to hide my likeness to you and prevent me from telling you the truth. She'd promised Blumarine . . . but I came to be near you anyway."

"And I broke the spell," Estoril amplified to Delendor's puzzled expression, "by telling you who your real father was."

Delendor blinked. Then his face cleared and he beamed happily. "Well, anyway," he said, "everything's settled now."

"No," said Joe in a voice that would have chilled him if it hadn't come from his own mouth. "There's one thing yet to be settled. Between me and Ezekiel."

He squeezed Mary's hand as he released her, but the woman didn't occupy a major part of his mind just at the moment.

Joe stood and picked up Groag's sword. The shagreen scabbard had been blown away, and several of the jewels had been knocked out of the hilt, but the weapon was still serviceable.

It would serve.

With the sword in his hand, Joe began jogging down the hall. He was moving at a pace he was sure he could keep up until he reached Ezekiel's laboratory across the building.

Or wherever else the magician ran, this side of Hell.

Joe heard a crash of metal and breaking glass as he neared the last corner between him and the laboratory. When he rounded it, he saw the door of the laboratory open, a satchel dropped on the hallway, still spilling paraphernalia—

And a stairwell door still swinging closed.

Ezekiel had run from the banquet hall to his laboratory to pack the cream of his belongings. When he heard retribution coming, he'd abandoned even those valuables in his haste to escape.

Which he wasn't about to do.

"Hold it right there, Ezekiel!" Joe bellowed as he slammed down the stairs behind the fleeing magician.

The long sword in Joe's hand sang and sparked crazily as its point scraped the stairwell. Ezekiel's black robe trailed back around the stone helix, almost close enough to touch, but the unencumbered magician was able to maintain his distance ahead of his pursuer, past the first landing, the second—

Ezekiel banged through the door to the ground floor.

"Stop him!" Joe called to the servant there at the door by the pantry.

The fellow might have tried, but Ezekiel snapped his fingers. The servant froze with his mouth gaping like that of a surfaced carp. He blinked a moment later, but the magician was already past.

Ezekiel wasn't—*puff*—casting spells at Joe—*puff*— because he was sure—*puff*—that Joe was a greater magician than he was.

Ezekiel ran outside. Joe slipped and had to grab the jamb to keep from falling. A four-horse carriage waited in the courtyard.

The driver was a smirking Mongolian.

Ezekiel recognized the 7th Plane inhabitant also. "I'll be back to defeat you yet, Joe Johnson!" the magician screamed over his shoulder. He grabbed the latch and threw open the carriage door.

A clawed, hairy paw closed on Ezekiel's neck and drew him the rest of the way into the conveyance.

Joe stood panting, still clinging to the doorjamb as the coach drew away. It was accelerating faster than horses should have been able to move it.

Something flew out of a side window just as the vehicle disappeared into the arched gateway. It looked like a hand, but Joe didn't feel any need for certainty on the point.

Someone touched Joe's shoulder. He turned to see Mary, the new Mary, with a wistful smile on her face.

"It's over," Joe said to her, all he could manage while he tried to catch his breath.

"Mother—mother's friends, I suppose—brought you here to save my brother," Mary said. An attempt to make her smile a cheerful one failed miserably. "I suppose you'll go home to your own plane now?"

Joe grunted something that was meant to be laughter.

"I think that was my ride," he said, pointing his thumb in the direction the coach had disappeared. "Believe me, *I'm* not getting in if it decides to come back again."

Mary wet her full, red lips nervously. "Are you disappointed?" she asked in a whisper.

"Do you remember what the king said upstairs?" Joe asked carefully. "About events making him do what he'd already decided he wanted to?"

Joe dropped the sword so that he could use both his arms to hug Mary.

He had a lot to learn about this world, but some things were just the same as they were back home.

From the author of
The Deed of Paksenarrion

ELIZABETH MOON

SURRENDER
N O N E
THE LEGACY OF GIRD

**Coming in June, from
BAEN BOOKS**

The Battle of Norwalk...

"You got to take care of yer own scythe, Tam!" Gird yanked the blade loose and just stopped himself from throwing it on the ground. They couldn't afford to lose a single scrap of edged steel. But every single time he had to check the bindings himself—it was enough to infuriate the Lady of Peace herself. Tam's jaw set stubbornly; the others stared, half-afraid and half-fascinated. Gird took a long breath and let it out. "This time get it tight," he said, handing Tam the blade. He could feel the tension drain away as he went down the line, looking at the other scythes. Most were in reasonable shape, though he wondered if they really would hold against horses or armor.

Fifteen men and three women. Eleven scythes, one pruning hook, two sickles, three shepherds' crooks, two simple staves. Everyone had a knife, and all but one of them were sharp. Before they began the actual drill, he looked around the skyline. Nothing but a flock of sheep to the north, whose shepherd waved from the rise. Safe.

"All right. Line up." They had done this before, taught by Per who had learned from Aris, who had learned from Gird the year before in Blackbone Hill. They moved too slowly, but they did end up in straight lines, three rows of six. Tam was still trying to jam the end of his blade into the notch of the pole, tamping it against the ground. Maybe he'd learn, before he died.

"Carry." They stared at him, then half the group remembered that that was a command, and wobbled their weapons, clearly unsure where the "carry" position was. *Don't rush it*, Gird reminded himself, remembering the defections after his last temper tantrum. *They have to learn from where they are, not from where they should be.* "Carry..." he reminded them. "On your left shoulder—this one—because you have to be able to carry your weapon a long way, and without hitting anyone behind or beside you, or catching on theirs." He reached out and took a scythe from someone—Battin, the name was—in the front rank, and showed them. "Like this."

By the time they were all able to follow the basic commands at a halt, the sun was nearly overhead. Gird looked around again. The northern flock was out of sight over the rise, but another moved now across the slope to the west, and its shepherd waved elaborately. Good. Two more bartons coming to drill. Even so, even with the shepherd's signals, he would take the usual precautions.

"Weapons into the sheepfold," he said. "Another barton's coming in." Much more quickly than before, they obeyed, laying the scythes out of sight behind the low walls of the pens. Two of the women began to cut thistles with their sickles, gathering them into their aprons. The men with shepherds' crooks leaned on the low-roofed lambing hut and began talking sheepbreeding. The others hid in the lambing hut itself. **Gird sat** on one of the walls, and caught his breath.

"Sir? Gird?" That was Per, the nominal yeoman marshal of this barton.

"Just Gird, Per. You've got a good group here." It would be a good group after a year of enough to eat and heavy training, but it would do no good to say that.

"They're...I'm sorry about Tam's scythe. I—there's so much I don't know..."

"Don't worry. You can't do it all; that's why I tell them they have to maintain their own weapons. You've done a lot: eighteen, and fifteen scythes."

"Three women," muttered Per. Gird shot him a glance.

"You believe the lords' sayings about women, Per?"

"Well, no, but—"

"Our women have suffered with us all these years. We never kept them safe; they've borne the lords' children, and lost them if they had one touch of magic: you know that. Now they ask to learn fighting with us: if our pain has earned that right for us, theirs has earned it for them."

"But they're not as strong—"

Gird bit back another sharp remark, and said instead, "Per, we don't ask anyone to be strongest, or stronger...just strong enough."

"Whatever you say."

"No. Whatever you finally see is right—dammit, Per, that's what this is about. Not just my way—not just Gird instead of your lord or the king, but a fair way for everyone. You, me, our women, our children. Fair for everyone."

"Fair for the lords?"

Gird snorted, caught off guard. "Well—maybe not for them. They had their chance." He pushed himself off the wall. The incoming bartons had joined somewhere along the way, and were marching some thirty strong, all in step and clearly proud of themselves. He could not tell, at this distance, exactly what weapons they carried, but at least some of them were scythes. Per's foot began to tap the beat as the formation came nearer. Gird let himself think what they could do with some decent armor, some real weapons. They were marching like soldiers, at least, and impressing the less-experienced group he'd been working with. He called those in the lambing shed out to watch as the yeoman marshal of Hightop brought the formation to a halt. They had a short rest, then all three bartons began drilling together. Almost fifty, Gird reckoned them up, a half-cohort as the lords would call it. For the first time, Gird could *see* them facing real troops, the lords' militia, with a chance to win. He marched them westward, away from the sheepfolds, got them reversed, reversed again, and then tried to convince them that when the column turned, it turned in only one place. Those behind were not to cut the corner, but march to the corner, and turn. Again, and another tangle. He sorted it out, and got them moving again.

It was then that a shepherd's piercing whistle broke through the noise of their marching. Gird looked around, already knowing what it had to be. There, to the east, a mounted patrol out of Lord Kerrisan's holding; already they'd been spotted. He saw the flash of sunlight on a raised blade. His mind froze, refusing to work for a moment. Someone else saw them, and moaned. He turned to see his proud half-cohort collapsing, some already turning to run, others with weapons loose in their hands. The sun seemed brighter; he could see every detail, from the sweat on their faces to the dust on their eyelashes.

"We have to get away," said Per in a shaky voice. He heard the murmur of agreement, a grumble of dissent.

"We'll never make it," breathed someone else, and a heavy voice demanded "Who *told* them we were out here?" "It's a random patrol," Gird answered, without really thinking about it. "A tensquad, no spears—if they'd known we were here they'd have sent more, and more weapons. Archers, lancers." He glanced at the horsemen, now forming a line abreast. One of them had a horn, and blew a signal. Two of the horsemen peeled off, rode at an easy canter to either side. "They're circling, to pen us..."

"But what can we do?" asked someone at the back of the clump that had once been a fighting formation.

I ask for a sign, and I get this, Gird sent silently to the blazing sun. *Lord of justice, where are you now?* A gust of wind sent a swirl of dust up his nose, and he sneezed. "I'll tell you what we can do," he said, turning on his ragged troops the ferocity that had no other outlet. "We can quit standing here like firewood waiting the axe, and LINE UP! NOW!" A few had never shifted; a few moved back, others forward. Two at the back bolted. "NO!" To his surprise, his voice halted them; they looked back. "Run and you're dead. We're all dead.

By the gods, this is what we've been training *for*. Now
get in your places, and pick up your weapons, and *listen*
to me." The others moved, after nervous glances at the
slowly moving horsemen, back into their places. Gird
grinned at them. "And get those weapons READY!" Far
too slowly, the scythes and sickles and crooks came
forward. At once Gird could see what was wrong, besides not having anything but a knife of his own. They
could face only one way, and he knew, knew without
even trying it, that they'd never reverse in formation,
with weapons ready. There had to be a way—what
could work? In his mind, he saw his mother's pin-
cushion, pins sticking out all ways...but then how could
they move? There was no time; the horsemen were
closing, still at a walk, but he knew they would break to
a trot or canter any moment. They must be a little
puzzled by a mass of peasants who weren't trying to
run, weren't screaming in fear.

"We have to kill them all," Gird said, as calmly as if he
knew they could do it. "When they're close enough to
fight, they can recognize you. The only way you can be
safe back on your farms, is if you kill them all. That's
what all this drill is for, and now you're going to use it."
All those eyes stared right at his, blue and gray and
brown. He felt as if someone were draining all the
strength from his body...they were pulling it out of him,
demanding it. "You can do it," he said, not pleading but
firmly, reminding them. Never mind that this wasn't
the best place for a small group of half-trained peasants
to fight a mounted troop. Make do, make it work
anyway. Miss this chance and you'll not have another.

I'll be safely dead, he thought wryly.

Almost automatically, the formation had chosen the side facing the horsemen as the front. Gird walked quickly along it, nodding, and then, talking as he worked, shifted those on the flank and rear to face out. "If they come from two directions, we have to be ready. You turn like this—yes— facing out, and you behind him—yes, you—you put your crook here."

"But do we hit the horse or the man?" asked someone behind him.

"The horse," said Gird. "If you hurt the horse, either it'll run or the man will fall off. Now think—you want to open a big hole..."

He heard the hoofbeats louder now, and faster. Sure enough, they were trotting towards him, eight horsemen with their swords out and shining in the sun. The horses looked huge, and their hooves pounded the dry ground. The two sent around the peasant formation had stopped: clearly they were intended to prevent runaways. The horsemen yelled, a shrill wavering cry, and Gird yelled back, instinctively. His motley troop yelled, too, a sound half-bellow and half-scream of fear. Two of the horses shied, to be yanked back into line by their riders. The peasants yelled again, louder; the riders spurred to a full charge. Belatedly, the other two riders charged the back side of the formation.

He was still thinking *I hope this works* when the riders crashed into the block of peasants. The horses' weight and speed drove them into the formation, but five of them died before they cleared the other side. Gird himself slammed his cudgel into one horse's head, leaping aside to let it stagger past into the sickle of the woman behind him. The rider missed his swing at Gird, but got the woman's arm; someone buried a scythe in his back before he could swing again. Two riders were dragged from their mounts and stabbed; another took a scythe in the belly before sliding sideways off his horse, screaming. Gird saw one of the women with a simple pole poke one rider off-balance; someone else caught his sword-arm and stabbed him as he fell.

It was over in minutes. Ten horsemen lay dead or dying on the ground; seven horses were dead, two crippled, and one, spooked, galloped away to the west. Gird looked around, amazed. The woman who had lost an arm sat propped against a dead horse, holding the stump and trying not to cry. Eight were dead; two others badly hurt. But...but peasants on foot, with no weapons but the tools of their work, had defeated armed men on horseback. Not an equal fight...but a real one.

He knew he should say something to them, but he couldn't think of anything fitting. He looked around the horizon, and saw only the sentinel shepherd, waving that no danger neared. Per came up to him, bleeding from a gash on his scalp, bruised, amazed to be alive. They all were. Per nodded at the woman who'd lost an arm, and said "Gird—I see now."

"Do you?" He felt a thousand years older as his fury drained away. It had to be better to die this way, fighting in the open, than rotting in dungeons or worked to hunger and sickness, but those silent bodies had been people a few minutes before. That woman had had two hands. He nodded at Per, and walked over to crouch beside her. Someone else had already torn a strip of cloth from her skirt to tie around the stump. "You...?"

She had gone pale, now, the gray-green pallor before fainting or death, but she managed a shaky smile, and moved her other hand, still gripping the sickle. "I...killed the horse."

"You did."

"I...fought...they...died..."

"Yes."

"All?"

"All."

"Good." With that she crumpled, and before they had finished sorting out the dead and wounded, she had died.

"Noooo!" That scream came from one of the other women, who fell sobbing on the dead one's body. Then she whirled to face Gird, her face distorted. "You let her die! You, you killed her, and this is what happens." She waved her arms to encompass the whole bloody scene. "You said fight to live, but she's dead, and Jori and Tam and Pilan..." Her voice broke into wild sobbing. Gird could think of nothing to say: she was right, after all. The woman had died, and seven others, and the two worst wounded would probably die, even if their lord didn't notice their wounds and kill them for that. The ten horsemen had probably had lovers or wives, maybe children...the weight of that guilt lay on his shoulders. But another voice, thick with pain, spoke out.

"Nay, Mirag! Rahi's dead, but she died happy, know-ing she'd fought well. Not in a cage in the castle, like young Siela, when she tried to refuse that visiting duke, and not hanging from a hook on the wall, screaming for hours, like Varin. Gird promised us a chance, not safety."

"You say that, with that hole in you, with your heart's blood hot on your side? What will Eris say, tonight, when she has no one beside her; what will your children say?"

The man coughed, and wiped blood from his mouth. "Eris knows I'm here, and she knows why. If she weren't heavy for bearing, she'd be here herself, and the little ones too. This is best, Mirag. Rahi's satisfied, and I'm satisfied, and if you keep whining along like that, I'll say out what I think should happen to you!"

The woman paled, and her mouth shut with a snap. The man looked at Gird.

"She's not bad, Marig—Rahi's her sister."

"I'm sorry." It was all he could say. Marig shrugged, an abrupt jerk of her shoulder; the man beckoned with a finger and Gird went to him.

"D'you know much of healer's arts?" Gird shook his head. "Might should learn, then. If I'd been able, I'd've put a tighter band on Rahi's arm. You'll need that craft, Gird."

"You'll get well, and be our healer," said Gird, but the man shook his head. "Nay...this is a killing wound, but slower than some. Blood'll choke me, inside. But you'd best get all away, before more trouble comes."

A flick of memory, of his old sergeant's words long ago, came to Gird. "We won't leave wounded here, to be taken and questioned."

The man grinned tightly. "I hoped you'd think so. Make it quick, then."

"Is there anyone you'd...?"

"You'll do. You made it work." Gird grimaced; he had to have someone else agree, or it would feel like simple murder. He called Per over, and Aris, the yeoman marshal of Hightop. The wounded man was still conscious enough to give his assent again, and Aris, slightly more experienced than Per, saw at once why it must be done.

But neither would do it. So Gird took his well-worn dagger, and knelt by the man's side, and wondered how he'd feel if he were lying there, bleeding inside and choking, and how he could be quickest. Worst would be weakness, another pain that did not kill. So he put the whole strength of his arm into it, slicing almost through the man's neck.

The other badly injured man was unconscious, having been hit in the head, and then trampled under a horse. He quit breathing, with a last gasping snort, just as Gird reached him. Then it was only the hard, bloody work of dragging the corpses together onto a pile of brushwood and thistles, stacking what weapons they could use to one side. The group from Per's barton left first, to enter their village as best they might without attracting attention. They dared not carry any of the spare weapons, and Gird cautioned them not to take personal belongings from their friends' bodies.

"They'll know someone was here," he said, "to start the fire. But if you're carrying a tool or trinket someone recognizes, they'll know you, too, were part of it. This way it can seem that everyone from this village died, and it might spare you trouble." Not really, he knew: there was going to be trouble for everyone...but there had always been.   They seemed calm enough, even Marig. She had quit sobbing, at least, and she laid the locket she'd taken from her sister's neck back on her without being told twice. "Can't we even take Tam's scythe?" one man asked. "We don't have that many." His own crook had shattered. Gird shook his head again.

"With so few scythes, everyone will know that Tam's is with you. It'll be taken, but not to your village." He nodded to Per, who started them off, in trickles of two or three, moving indirectly.

Aris had the other two bartons ready to move out; each one carried his or her own weapon, and some of them carried a second, taken from the fallen. Gird dithered over the swords. For one of them to be found carrying a soldier's sword meant instant death–but to lose all those blades... In the end he let them decide, and ten volunteers belted swords they could not use around their peasant jerkins.

"Are you sure you need to burn the bodies?" Aris asked. Gird said nothing; he'd never imagined doing anything else...it was in all the tales. "We'll need a good start of them," Amis went on, when Gird didn't answer. "They'll have horses near enough...we don't know but what the smoke could be seen a long way, and the horses might come anyhow, and find us on the way. I don't know...I don't know if I could lead another fight today."

"You could if you had to," said Gird, plunged once more into how different it was in stories and reality. But Amis made sense, and he looked at the stacked bodies. The smoke would draw attention; someone would come, and that someone would likely be mounted, and ready for trouble. No smoke, and another patrol would go looking for the first....might not find them right away...but to let the dead lie out unprotected? He squinted up, and saw the first dark wings sailing far up. That alone would draw attention.

"All right," he said, finally. "No fire." *Lady, bless these dead...these brave and helpless...* Aris nodded, clearly relieved, and set off with his bartons. Gird angled away from them, his own new sword heavy at his side. *Did I do the right thing?* he asked himself. *Am I doing the right thing now?*

He looked back from a farther ridge, some hours later, and saw a column of dark wings. The woman's face came to him, that face so composed, even as she died, and the thought of dark beaks tearing her face, gouging out her eyes—he stopped abruptly, and threw up on the short grass, retching again and again, and scrubbing the dried blood on his hands. Nor could that be the end of it: he had started something, back there, that no crow could pick clean, and no fox bury the bones of...he had started something, like a boy rolling a rock down a hillside, and the end would be terrible.

FRED SABERHAGEN

THE WHITE BULL

Once upon a time, King Minos of Crete angered the Sea God, Poseidon. And Poseidon in revenge, sent a monster to plague him. And that monster was— But everybody knows the story of the Minotaur, right? Wrong—not the true story! Here's an exciting new look at an ancient Greek myth—a look through a uniquely science fictional lens.

"Fred Saberhagen is one of the best writers in the business."—Lester Del Rey

The brilliant craftsman, Daedalus, and his young son, Icarus, haven't been at King Minos' glittering court very long when the realm is disturbed by strange visitors from the sea: a menacing man of bronze and an eerie, white-furred creature, half man, half bull. Little do the Cretans know that this minotaur, this White Bull, is no supernatural being sent by an angry Poseidon. Instead, he's actually an extraterrestrial, come to Earth with a thankless job: administer to the stubborn Greeks the principles of a liberal, high-tech education. But the Greeks aren't the best of students. Daedalus finds himself in the middle of things, trying to keep the peace between King Minos, hot-blooded Prince Theseus of Athens, and the White Bull. But the Minotaur himself must learn that it's not wise to meddle in the affairs of primitive peoples. After all, they just might take offense . . .

December 1988 • 69794-3 • $3.95

To order THE WHITE BULL, please enclose $3.95. Mail this form to: Baen Books, 260 Fifth Avenue, New York, N.Y. 10001.)

Name_____

Address_____

City_____ State_____ Zip_____

Paksenarrion, a simple sheepfarmer's daughter, yearns for a life of adventure and glory, such as the heroes in songs and story. At age seventeen she runs away from home to join a mercenary company, and begins her epic life . . .

ELIZABETH MOON

THE DEED OF PAKSENARRION

"This is the first work of high heroic fantasy I've seen, that has taken the work of Tolkien, assimilated it totally and deeply and absolutely, and produced something altogether new and yet incontestably based on the master. . . . This is the real thing. Worldbuilding in the grand tradition, background thought out to the last detail, by someone who knows absolutely whereof she speaks. . . . Her military knowledge is impressive, her picture of life in a mercenary company most convincing."—**Judith Tarr**

About the author: Elizabeth Moon joined the U.S. Marine Corps in 1968 and completed both Officers Candidate School and Basic School, reaching the rank of 1st Lieutenant during active duty. Her background in military training and discipline imbue The Deed of Paksenarrion with a gritty realism that is all too rare in most current fantasy.